Georgina studied creative writing and film at university and has since pursued a career in videogames journalism, covering some of the most popular games in the world. Her psychological thrillers are inspired by her surroundings, from the congested London streets to the raw English countryside. She can be found playing games, writing stories, and reading anything from fantasy to crime fiction.

 twitter.com/glees_author

Also by Georgina Lees

The Girl Upstairs

After the Party

THE LOST WIFE

GEORGINA LEES

One More Chapter
a division of HarperCollins*Publishers*
1 London Bridge Street
London SE1 9GF
www.harpercollins.co.uk
HarperCollins*Publishers*
Macken House, 39/40 Mayor Street Upper,
Dublin 1, D01 C9W8

This paperback edition 2023
First published in Great Britain in ebook format
by HarperCollins*Publishers* 2023
Copyright © Georgina Lees 2023
Georgina Lees asserts the moral right to be identified
as the author of this work

A catalogue record of this book is available from the British Library

ISBN: 978-0-00-861404-1

Printed and bound in the UK using 100% Renewable Electricity
by CPI Group (UK) Ltd

Chapter One

present

The roads are darker than I thought they'd be. I'm used to the city, to the lit A-roads and motorways, the lights from late-night takeaways and cocktail bars. I've never had to drive that much before now.

I'm gripping the steering wheel down a small country lane, my knuckles white, a soft sheen washing over them. I risk glancing down and see small flecks of crimson on the backs of my hands, flashing in and out as lone cars pass me. I want to cry, for my tears to fall and wash the blood away, but I haven't cried in years, why start now? My forearm throbs and feels damp and hot. The fuel light comes on, a low red light suddenly threatening me from behind the steering wheel. Only fifty miles left in the tank.

There's a murmuring in the back of the car, an almost inaudible snore, but I can feel the warmth of his small body.

I catch the small tuft of dark brown hair in the rear-view mirror as we drive through the night.

I can't see the moon and I feel disappointed, like it has somehow failed in guiding me to safety. There is nowhere safe for us to go, not now. Checking the dashboard, it's nearly midnight. That wouldn't be late in Bristol, but here the remote houses are tucked away behind small verges, fast asleep.

My street would be teeming with students, heading to and from parties and sticky nightclubs. Laughing about something mundane, so carefree and blissful. The moon would shine for them. It would stay out all night just to make them happy.

I reach a fork in the road and take a sharp left. This lane is narrower than before and I think I'm nearly there. I reach down to check my phone and he stirs in the back of the car. Please don't wake up, not until we get there, not until you're safe.

We're still ten minutes away, but it's taken us most of the evening to get here and I didn't stop driving, no matter how much I needed a drink of water, a fresh coffee to keep me awake, or even just to pee; all those normal functions aren't necessary. All I need to do right now is survive. My lips are dry and chapped and I lick them mercilessly, but it only makes it worse. I roll down the window and let the frosty night settle on my chest and blanket my clammy face. It was dark when we left, it'll be dark when we arrive, and dark when we wake up.

These are the darkest days of winter. I remember that

old Italian fable, the days of the blackbird. How a snowy-white bird on the last three days of winter curled up in the ashes and soot of a chimney to find respite from the harsh, bitter temperatures, to emerge as a blackbird, covered in the soot and embers of a forgotten fire.

I hope to be forgotten, to curl up in the cottage we're headed to and wait out the darkest days of winter. It's January. Why would anyone get married in January? I stroke the bloodstained wedding veil sitting on the car seat next to me. This is not how this was supposed to end. It was a happy day, the sun was high, and the trees were dripping with crisp blossom, like they'd been dipped in white paint. It was magical. It was everything I thought it would be. Until it wasn't.

When we turn into an even narrower path, my small car rising and falling with the potholes, I know we're here. I risk looking at the back seat. He's still asleep. I'll wake him when we get there.

There's a wooden plaque obscured slightly behind trailing ivy and rock debris. I check the directions on my phone, which I've propped up on the dashboard.

The sign says 'Bramble Cottage' and I read in the booking description that you can pick blackberries at the bottom of the garden to make blackberry crumble, or brambles if you want a tipple in the hot tub or curled up in the garden room listening to the rain patter or on the sun-soaked veranda in summer. I reach over and stroke the veil; we were supposed to make brambles and cook a warming meal of lamb shank and mustard mash after a long walk across the fields. Maybe we would have had an ale at one of the pubs on the way. I'd slip into the swimming costume and silky robe and dangle my legs off the kitchen counter, waiting for you to come over. I'd take a sultry sip of the bramble. Then we'd forget about dinner. We'd forget about everything.

I can't think like that now, though, things are different. I reach a hand back and stroke his cheek. He is the only thing that matters now.

Bramble Cottage has its own private driveway with a thick, black iron gate. The cottage sits in complete darkness, its outline just visible in the night. It's set back from a stone-lined country road that leads to the quaint little town of Bakewell.

The Peak District has fond memories for us. I remember going up the cable cars at The Heights of Abraham, how I'd draped my legs over yours on the way up, and we'd bought a cup of tea at the top and wandered around the caves and marvelled at the view.

I climb out of the car, pulling my phone from the wire. There's a keylock with a code I need to enter by the gate that should release a fob and keys, according to the check-in instructions. I find it underneath a dangling piece of ivy and work the code until the latch releases. I stab at the fob and the gate gently creaks open, swatting at fallen branches and skimming the pebbled driveway as it does.

I hurry back to the car, shielding myself from a sudden icy gale of wind. When I close the door, his small body stirs in the back, and there's a soft gurgle and light smack of lips.

'Mum?' a small voice whispers.

'We're here,' I reply, edging the car onto the driveway. My car beams cast a light over an impressive circular fountain with a pale stone statue of a woman cupping something in her outstretched hand. I drive slowly around it towards the small rose bushes outside the front of the house. An outside light comes on and illuminates the cottage, its etched grey brick now visible in the harsh glow. The bushes rustle restlessly, like they've been disturbed from a deep slumber.

'Josh?'

He murmurs, pulling the blanket over his head to shield himself from the light.

'We need to go in.'

He doesn't reply.

'I'm going to go in first, okay? Make sure everything is all right.' I get out of the car, locking it behind me in case he tries to get out and follow me. I need to make sure it's safe.

I clutch the door keys and approach the large, grand oak door, twisting the key in the black metal lock. A large lion doorknocker stares at me as sweat licks the bottom of my back. I release the door, pushing against the weight of it until it buckles open.

I'm swallowed by the darkness as the outside light turns off. I feel around for a switch and find a small velvet rope, yanking the soft tassels dangling at the end. The hallway lights up, a yellow hue cascades off a high chandelier onto the dark wooden floorboards. It's more than a cottage, it's spectacular. It looks better than the pictures; the beams frame each wall like they're works of art, and a long thin pillar runs the length of the hallway as if it's begging you to run after it and see what you'll find.

The house is cold. I know they weren't expecting anyone until tomorrow morning and promised to have the log fire going when we arrived. I told the owner, Tracey, we wanted privacy this week, complete solitude from the outside world, and she'd sent back a winky face and said she understood, it's our honeymoon after all.

It was supposed to be, I think wistfully as I move through the house, running my fingers along the rough oak sideboard and past the fresh vase of lilies. There's a door on the left and when I push it open and flick on the light, I gaze around the empty lounge, a fireplace sitting between two suede green sofas, the floorboards covered in a thick-piled cream rug. I move through to the kitchen, but I know all these rooms so well. I've studied them, hopeful and excited about being here with you. On our honeymoon.

The kitchen is the largest room in the house. It stretches across the width of the cottage, with terracotta tiles and deep red walls with light pine counters and a beautiful marble unit in the centre. Next to it, there's a banquet table. I smile, thinking how it would have been just me and you sitting down at it, playing a game of chess, with a bottle of red wine, jazz playing softly in the background. You would hum, of course, but it never bothered me. I bite my lip, trying to stifle a memory I'll never have.

I notice the kitchen counter has a wicker basket sitting on top and propped next to it is a small card saying

'Congratulations' in silver glitter, two crowns sitting above the text. Inside it reads, 'Have a lovely honeymoon, if there's anything you need, you know where I am. Tracey'. I throw the card onto the counter and peer into the hamper, moving strands of straw out of the way to see two bottles of red wine, a box of truffles, and some cheese and crackers. How thoughtful. Tracey owns Bramble Cottage; it's her only holiday home and it's been in her family for generations. I haven't had much contact with her, but I know she's proud of the house, that she's optimistic and eager to please. I've seen her profile picture on Airbnb. She has round, rosy cheeks and bright eyes, and she's standing in front of the cottage, the fountain in the background and a dog at her feet.

I quickly check the fridge, wincing as I reach forward, the pain in my forearm shooting up my wrist, my thumb twitching as I grasp the handle. There's only a pint of milk, some butter, and eggs. Searching through the rest of the cupboards I find a loaf of bread, tea and coffee, granola, and some different herbs and spices. We would have gone to Chatsworth farm shop and done a big food shop for the week. We would have gotten pickles and smoked salmon for the cheese, and meaty pies for nights we felt too lazy to cook.

This won't be enough food, but how long do we have? The cottage has been rented for a week, but I don't think we'll get that far. I search my pockets hoping to find the answer, but I know I don't have enough money on me. I don't have my passport. I don't have a plan. I search a cupboard behind the dining table and find books, board games, and a first-aid kit. I lay the contents of the first-aid kit across the dining table, but it's only a few plasters, a heat pack, and some cold and flu sachets. I swipe at the items and watch them slide across the table. This won't do.

We'll stay here for as long as we can and then we'll get on the road again; we'll find a way. I must protect him from what's coming. I walk back through the cottage towards the car, but there's a soft trill in the hallway as I pass. I notice a small red dial phone on a table under the stairs. I hesitate. Should I pick it up? They'll hear my voice. They'll come for us. I look around. The lights are on, the curtains are open, and the house is now alive. Has someone seen us?

I march around the house, shutting blinds and closing curtains, turning off the lights at the front of the house. I leap up the stairs, ignoring the closed doors, but going straight for the master bedroom. When I open the door, a beautiful four-poster bed looks back, red petals adorning the sumptuous white cotton sheets. There's a lamp on next to the bed and I throw myself at it, suddenly the rage and panic of the day almost too much. It clatters to the floor and I cry out in pain. My arm pressing into my woollen jumper, I can feel loose threads caught in the wound.

The ringing stops, and all I can hear is the low, quick rhythm of my heart and the pulse in my aching arm. This time, my phone vibrates in my coat pocket and I pull it out reluctantly. It's an unknown number. I didn't think it would be this easy to find me. I thought I'd have more time.

'Hello,' I answer.

'Lea? It's Tracey.'

'Oh.'

'Are you at the house?'

'Yes, we've just arrived.'

'I saw the lights on and I wanted to make sure it was you. I wasn't expecting you until tomorrow.'

The lights on? Is she watching? I think about him lying in the back of the car. She sounds concerned. 'Yes, we decided to come tonight, if that's okay?'

'Of course it is. Have you found everything okay?'

'Yes, thank you.' I don't want to speak to her anymore. I don't want her to ask questions I can't answer.

'Was it a lovely day?'

'Yes, it was, really lovely.' I hesitate. 'And thank you for the hamper.'

'You're welcome, and if you need anything during your stay, I'm in the cottage next door. You probably didn't see it on your way in, but you'll see it in the daylight. It's behind a wooden gate on the right of the path as you come in.'

'Thanks, Tracey.'

'Have a lovely stay,' she says, a slight uncertainty in her voice.

'We're just tired, busy day.'

'Of course, hope you settle in okay.'

'Goodnight,' I say, hanging up.

I open the door nearest the master bedroom; it's the one in the pictures. A sky-blue room with a white wooden bunkbed and shaggy cream carpet. He'll sleep in here, nearest to me.

I retreat to the car, the security light coming on again, blinding me as I swing open the passenger side to get my bag.

'Where are we?' a small voice says.

'I need you to stay in the car for a little longer, sweetie, I'm just making sure everything is okay.'

He mumbles something. I can see his two dark brown eyes glowing in the light, the rest of his face and body obscured by a fluffy grey blanket.

'I won't be long.'

'I need to wee,' he says.

We stopped on the side of the road once we got off the motorway. 'Can you hold it for just a little longer? I'm sorry, sweetie, I just need to—'

'I want to go home,' he says, quietly.

I lean forward and he stares at me in the streaks of light. 'We will, but please hang on for me, can you do that?'

He doesn't say anything, he just disappears under the fluffy blanket and all I can hear is muffled whines. I sit for a moment in the passenger seat, something digging into my thigh, I reach for it and pull free the blood-stained veil, threading it between my fingers. We didn't have time; we left so quickly that all I had was a change of clothes and my handbag. I didn't know the day would pan out like this, that I'd be sitting here on the driveway at Bramble Cottage without you.

Out of everything I should feel, I'm disappointed. All the hope I've carried around that things would get better, that we'd come here together and all the lies and secrets would be put behind us, none of it is real.

I glance out the front window at the dark lane ahead, the cottage illuminating the pebbled driveway. The statue in the fountain contorted and worn in the soft glow.

I'm pulling at the veil, pressing my thumbnail into the small hole at the top. I start to tear it, claw at it, my face hot with anger.

Life will never be the same again. I will never be the same again.

All because I never really knew you.

I never really knew my husband.

Chapter Two

one year earlier

It's already dark when I leave work, but I don't mind. I like walking home when the streetlights come on and the after-work crowd and student bars come alive with the sound of laughter and music. I've never noticed the shift after the Christmas break, when everyone's supposed to be on a health kick and doing dry January.

I'd have liked to stay out with friends from work for a drink … a glass of red, I think, as I do my best to avoid dips in the cobbled street. I pause on the side of the road, slipping off my green stilettos, and pull on grey trainers. It's about a half-hour walk back from the office near central Bristol to our townhouse in Redland. I wanted to go home tonight, because it's the anniversary of when Harry and I first met. I picked out something nice to wear and he's booked my favourite seafood restaurant along Whiteladies Road. Maybe I'll order champagne and we'll have oysters.

The walk back to Redland is steep and, despite the cold weather, I can feel the damp clinging to my dress at the bottom of my back as I wade through the busy crowd along Queens Road. I walk past the bakery that sells delicious vegan doughnuts and the small café that serves pasta where Harry and I went on our first date. I would have liked to go back there tonight, but Harry insisted that we'd have a lavish meal somewhere special. I told him it was special, and he'd winked and said, 'You know what I mean.'

It wasn't obvious when I met Harry that he had a lot of money. He had already started his own investment firm, but you wouldn't have guessed it. He didn't wear tight-fitting suits or have a tie strapped around his neck, but instead he wore chinos and chunky sweaters. He never flaunted the money he had, but I've seen, over the years, that he's become comfortable with it. Not only that, but he says we deserve it.

We never had much money growing up. It was mostly just me and Mum when I was younger, and then it was always us after Dad died, in our small house in Bedminster. We'd go for lemonade ice lollies and walks along the canal; she was a photographer and she'd take pictures as we went. Sometimes I'd pose in front of them, other times she'd catch me off guard.

She worked as a receptionist during the day, but she had a connection with one of the local galleries and that's how I was able to get experience when I was at school. I knew I wanted to go into PR for events. I loved the way Mum worked the room, always so cool and collected, flowing in and out of crowds. There was an elegance to her that I never inherited.

Instead, I got Dad's bolshiness, his no-fuss-or-frills direct approach. It could be construed as being cold, standoffish, Harry had once told me in jest. I couldn't help but check myself when I was at his work functions or speaking to a client, just in case I came across the wrong way. I always felt slightly bitter that I couldn't pull it off in the way Dad seemed to, but I chalked that up to being a woman. My dad was respected and revered for being outspoken, but my accomplishments are somehow down to my cutting attitude; I've been described as headstrong on more than one occasion.

By the time I'm at Chandos Road, students are pouring into the streets bundled in layers, and the odd dog walker heads towards Clifton Downs. I slip past our local pub, The Shakespeare, and turn up our road, the one with a small park in the middle where students lounge in the summer and someone occasionally reads a book on one of the worn wooden benches. Our house stands out from the others; instead of contemporary stone with pale yellow etchings, it has a fresh coat of ivory paint, a glossy red door, and black-framed windows.

Harry's car is already on the driveway when I walk up and I as I'm unlocking the door, our son lets out a high-pitched squeal.

'Hello?' I call.

'We're in here!' Harry replies and before I know it he's appeared red-faced in the hallway. 'I won.'

'Won what?' I ask, bemused.

'He didn't win.' I hear giggling from the lounge.

'I bet him I could balance a ball on my head for longer,' Harry says, stroking the bristles along his jawline. His hair is starting to turn grey, dark dappled by silver streaks, only visible in certain light. He's ten years older than me. My friends and family were a bit concerned about the age gap. They thought he'd be ready to settle down while I had my twenties ahead of me.

'Is that right?' I say.

'Come and see, Mummy,' Harry says, gesturing to me.

A little body appears in the hallway, only a blur before he's thrown his arms around my legs and laid his head on my stomach.

'Hello, Mummy,' he whispers. He claws away, the bottom of my dress bunched in his small fist.

'Josh, how are you, my little treasure? Did you have a good day at school?'

He nods into the folds of my skirt, and when I look down I realise his hands are covered in sticky juice and orange remnants congeal on the beige fabric.

'You're home early?' I say to Harry as I stroke the top of Josh's head, his soft hair tickling my fingertips.

'Of course,' he says, puffing out his chest and smiling a wide all-encompassing smile. 'It's our anniversary.' He checks his watch and crouches down to Josh. 'I'm taking Mummy for a special meal to celebrate.'

Josh pivots away from me, letting go of my skirt as I try to smooth out the creases and wipe away the orange stains.

'Can I come?' Josh asks, walking into Harry's outstretched arms.

'I wish you could, bud, but me and your mum need a little time together, just us, and then we'll be back by nine for your bedtime and Mum will read you a story in bed.'

'*The Teddy Bears' Picnic.*'

'Or *The Lion, the Witch and the Wardrobe*?' I ask.

Harry looks up at me. 'I'm not sure he's ready for that yet.'

I chew the side of my mouth and see Harry's disappointment. I know he wishes I was better with Josh sometimes, more patient and understanding, but I worry that Josh isn't growing up quickly enough, that he's too demanding and reliant on us both. He is four years old now, but he's very clingy.

Maybe it's because I was independent at that age, able to dress myself, play on my own, flick through picture books. My mum was always present when she could be, but my dad worked a lot and I had to learn quickly. Maybe I resent Josh for the ease of his childhood, for the fact that I'm not like my mum, who would paint pictures with me on Sunday, always calm and considered in her approach to things. I'm like my dad, absent and unapologetic.

I see Harry gazing at me, waiting for an answer, but I just move past him. Josh skims my dress with his hand as I go, and I stop, bending down as he walks slowly over to me. He throws his arms round my neck and I hold him tight. I love him so much, but it's hard for me sometimes, that's all.

'Love you, Josh.' I look at Harry. He's so grateful, so pleased when I react this way. I'd do anything for Josh, he knows that. When Josh was sick with suspected meningitis and we had to take him to hospital, I was beside myself, I wouldn't leave his side for weeks. When Josh came home from nursery once, crying because another child had stolen his fruit pack, I marched into the nursery and blew up at one of the carers. I said sorry afterwards, of course.

Josh does that to me, though: he makes me resentful, anxious, and angry. I hold him tighter, wishing that he made me happier.

When I release him, he wanders off into the lounge, content and satisfied. Harry cups my chin and lifts me from the floor, kissing me gently. 'Why don't you go and get ready? The reservation is for 7pm.'

I smile, my teeth lightly touching his lips. 'Give me half an hour,' I say, kicking off my trainers and running up the stairs.

I sit on the edge of the bed, picking at the dried juice stain on my dress. I don't know how long I'm sitting like that until I hear Harry.

'Lea,' he calls from the bottom of the stairs. 'You ready?'

'Coming,' I reply, grabbing my makeup and the evening dress hanging on the wardrobe door. I close the bathroom as I hear him coming.

'Are you still in the bathroom?'

'I'm nearly ready, just a minute.'

'Okay,' he says, quietly. 'Your mum's just arrived. She's going to cook Josh pasta. I've just got to take a call.'

'Great,' I say, pulling on the new dress and painting my lips pale pink. I coat my lashes in mascara and a smoky eyeshadow to complement my steely blue eyes. I release my honey-blonde hair from its bun and let it sit in loose curls on my shoulders, framing my square jaw.

When I come downstairs, Josh is sitting between Mum's legs in the living room. She has one hand on his head and the other clutching a cup of steaming coffee.

She beams when she sees me, making an O shape with her lips as she cocks her head. 'Don't you look beautiful.'

Josh doesn't look up; he's making small *choo choo* sounds as he drags a plastic train across the carpet. I spot Harry through the lounge, standing in the conservatory with his jacket already on. He's frowning, one hand outstretched and waving frantically. He looks frustrated, his jaw clenched, the strain of the call turning into concern, as his eyebrows arch and his eyes widen as he lets the phone fall from his cheek.

I couldn't hear what he was saying, but when he slides the door open and shut, he's deep in thought as he swipes my jacket from the back of the dining room chair.

'We don't want to be late,' he says.

'Doesn't she look beautiful?' my mum says to Harry, frowning slightly.

'Yes, of course you do, Lea, I'm sorry.' He leans forward and kisses me on the cheek, but his lips feel dry and rigid.

'Is everything okay?' I ask.

'Fine.' He tries to muster a smile and I can feel Mum's eyes dart from me to Harry and back again.

'Work?' I press.

He shrugs me off, raising a hand to Mum and forcing a grin at Josh, who finally looks up from his toy. 'We'll be back soon,' he says, grabbing his keys and pressing lightly on the bottom of my back to lead me away.

The restaurant is close enough to walk, but Harry insists we drive in the cold weather to save my bare legs from freezing. He's silent on the drive there, only the noise of the indicator and the slight rumble of the tyres over dips in the road. He never answered my question. I don't want to press him. It's our anniversary after all.

I look over at him, his face flashing in and out of darkness as we pass streetlights. He's thinking about something. I wonder what. It's a face I've seen a few times, serious and pensive, like he's assessing something, but the quiet is disconcerting. I wish he wouldn't be like this, not tonight.

I met Harry during university when I was finishing my degree in PR and Communications. He was hanging out with friends outside a jazz pub just off Kings Street, wearing a navy baseball cap, a relaxed T-shirt, and dark jeans. He looked so ordinary that I didn't notice him looking at me for an hour before he came over. It was sunny that day, a late Spring heat where the wind has a freshness to it, licking the warmth of the sun from our faces.

He had some line, I don't remember what it was, but he ended up buying me and my friends a round of drinks, retreating to his bench with his mates until I came over and said my glass was empty if he wanted another. He told me about his job, and we spoke about our love for American Football and ramen.

Harry and I moved slowly after that, until we didn't.

When we first started dating, we'd see each other every week or so for dinner or coffee. It was casual, and I even thought a few times we'd just end up being friends. But there was tension building without us realising it. It burst at the seams when I went to his apartment overlooking the wharf. He made lasagne and tiramisu. I lingered in the doorway when he was seeing me out and he leaned in and kissed me on the cheek. I smelt his citrusy aftershave and then I kissed him, tasting red wine on his soft lips. I stayed that night and every night after that.

I look over at him, so lost in thought. A year after that night at his apartment, we had Josh. It wasn't planned, and that's the first time I saw the look on his face, that serious expression. It quickly faded into elation, and he brushed away whatever it was—doubt, maybe—into a little compartment in his mind that I could never get at, not even five years later.

When we arrive at the restaurant, he opens that box and locks away whatever was bothering him, clasping my knee and smiling at me.

'Reservation for Harry Lewis,' he says, cupping my back as we're shown to our table, our usual table by the window so we can watch people flit past, the noise of the lively street so comforting to me. I thought I'd be living life very differently at twenty-six, at a busy pub with friends or going on cheap holidays in the sun. Instead I'm sitting with Harry in an expensive seafood restaurant, ordering champagne to toast, and going home to our son. I wonder if it's the life I would have chosen.

Harry orders a bottle of red after we've finished our champagne, his eyes glinting in the warm light. I love him a frightful amount, but my eyes wander out to the street where a group of women, must be early twenties, throw back their heads with laughter as they head into the pub opposite. I just wonder sometimes.

'I remember when I first saw you,' Harry says, when the waiter walks away with our empty plates. 'I thought you were so beautiful. I didn't think you'd ever be interested in me.' He smiles bashfully, exposing deep dimples.

'I hadn't found out about your terrible taste in films. If only I'd known,' I reply, taking a sip of wine. 'And that you support the New York Giants, what a disaster.'

'It would have saved you years of disappointment.'

'It would.'

'How about I get the bill and we take a walk?'

'A walk? It's freezing.'

'Humour me.'

I shrug. 'Where?'

'I want to show you something?' He smiles playfully.

'In this dress?'

'In that dress.'

Harry pays at the bar and we leave the restaurant full of wine and oysters and chilli prawns. They let us take the rest of the bottle of wine home with us and Harry kisses me in the car, saying we'll have it in bed when Josh is asleep.

He drives away from Whiteladies Road and turns left onto Clifton Downs, driving through the now pitch-black fields down the small road that leads to the view of the Avon Gorge.

'I thought it was lit at night.'

I laugh. 'Doesn't look like it.'

He drives the rest of the way anyway and we get out the car and stumble through the darkness to the view of the River Avon, the Clifton Suspension Bridge lit up in the distance. I hug my coat in and release an icy breath.

'This isn't as romantic as I thought it'd be,' Harry says, his outline slightly visible in the midnight-blue sky. 'I remember when we came for a walk here the day we found out about Josh, but I knew as soon as I met you that you'd change my life for ever.' He takes my hand in his and pulls me in until his lips are so close, they skim my forehead as he speaks. 'I'm sorry it took me so long to ask, but will you marry me, Lea?'

The words float away and almost freeze as they escape into the cold night, suspended between us. I inch forward, so this time my lips brush against the bottom of his chin.

'Of course I will.'

Chapter Three

present

I pull Josh from the back of the car, trying to encourage him to put his arms around me, but they just fall to the side, catching my forearm. I wince and cry out and he goes limp, his head lolling back, arms splayed out, his eyes wide and unblinking.

'You're in shock,' I whisper. 'But I promise it will be okay.' I try to wrap the blanket around him, using my knee to prop him up, my palms and fingers stretched trying to grasp his small frame. 'I just need you to eat something and have a little water and then I'll put you right to bed, how does that sound?'

No response. I carry him through the open door, wondering if Tracey is watching us from the bottom of the lane. I hope she won't call anymore. I take Josh into the lounge and prop him upright on one of the sofas. He looks so small, his feet barely reaching the end of the cushion. He looks up at me and seems to shrivel into the plumped-up cushions scattered across the sofa. I place his teddy bear, actually a small cream rabbit, on his knee and cover him with the blanket.

'I know it's cold in here, but I've just turned the heating on and it'll get toasty soon, but we'll wrap you up in bed and by the morning everything will look much better.' His arm twitches beneath the blanket as he grabs the rabbit and pulls it into the crook of his chin. 'Mr Rabbit makes things better, doesn't he?' He stares up at me. 'I'll get us some food and water, okay?'

I disappear into the kitchen, but I can feel his eyes following me as I go. I take a moment to myself as I fill up a glass of water; they didn't have any plastic cups and I don't have anything of his with me, only the rabbit and blanket, and he's clinging to those with all his might.

I hope this hasn't traumatised him, so that he'll grow up and blame me, or, worse, that what happened has damaged his core and he'll never recover. I can't have that.

The early morning wind whistles through the house and I can hear the fireplace growl and sigh as it whips through it. Then a low moan; I think he's crying, but he's saying something. I creep closer up the hallway holding the glass of water and realise he's speaking to the rabbit.

'I want to go home too,' he says.

When I enter the room, he's holding the rabbit up to his face.

'Where's Daddy?' He doesn't understand. How could he? 'I want Daddy.'

I want him too, I think as I lean forward, holding the glass up to his mouth. 'Please take a small sip, just a little one.'

He complies, still gazing at me with big round eyes. He looks so much like you, Harry, I don't know why I didn't see that before. Maybe now he's older, he's losing the shine and texture to his hair. Now it's thicker, matted. I reach forward and stroke the top of his head as he sips quietly. There's something dried and clumped together at the back. I take a closer look, running my fingers along the strands. It's blood. I pull away, rubbing my thumb and my finger together, smearing the dried blood across my skin.

'We should run you a nice hot bath before bed.' I raise the glass and hand him a small plate of cheese, crackers, and grapes. 'Once you've eaten this.' He takes the plate from me and nibbles on the side of a cracker, salty remnants sticking to his pale cheeks. 'Everything will sort itself out and then we'll go back to Bristol and you can go back to school and see your friends, won't you like that?' He nods as he picks up a slice of cheese, pressing it between his fingers. 'I'm just going to the bathroom. I won't be long.'

I walk through the grand cottage, not wanting to be around Josh right now. I want to be alone, or with you. I lock myself in the ensuite bathroom in the master bedroom and look in the mirror for the first time since we left Bristol. There are deep lines underneath my eyes and my cheeks are mottled red and purple. My hair is falling out of the scruffy bun I put it in and blonde strands cover one of my bloodshot eyes.

I bend my neck away from the mirror, letting my head fall and my shoulders rise.

Closing my eyes, all I can see is the blood fly across the white bedspread. Then Josh's panic.

After that, we ran. What else could we do?

Josh is starting to whimper. I can make out his small cries through the thin floorboards. How can I comfort him? What do I say? Maybe I'll take him for a walk tomorrow, we'll go along the cycle route, and I'll buy him a hot chocolate with extra cream, and he'll slowly forget what he saw.

I grasp the sink. We shouldn't have come here, we'll be found too easily, but where else could we go? I need to come up with a new plan, try and find somewhere safer. We don't have long, three days at a push before they track us down and... I can't bear the thought of what they'll do to Josh. I must protect him. I have to try. I twist away from the mirror and start running Josh a bath. I find fresh towels and bathrobes behind the bathroom door; there are plush slippers, a pair underneath each robe.

I imagine you rising from the bath, slipping wet feet into the slippers and joining me downstairs with a glass of red wine and our own plate of cheese and crackers.

When I return to Josh, he's prodding a grape around the plate. He looks up at me with a pleading look that I want to wipe away and erase from memory. It's worse than the panic. It's the aftermath.

'I've run you a bath.'

He wriggles away from me as I lean over to take the plate from his small hands, putting it to one side and scooping him up into my arms. He protests before going limp again. It reminds me of when you and I took our cat, Lily, to the vet's and she'd squirm in my arms the entire way and then go floppy as we carried her through the door, unable to fight it anymore. Josh looks at me like a cat, two wide eyes, completely silent, but seemingly understanding everything that is happening. Everything that is about to happen.

Can I leave him in the bathroom? Should I? I lay out a fluffy towel across the bathroom tiles and pry bunny and the grey blanket from his strong grip.

'We don't want them getting wet, do we?' He shakes his head sullenly, reluctantly releasing them and watching as I prop them up on the side next to the sink. I dig my hand into the deep pockets of my long navy cardigan and retrieve two small truffles, one wrapped in gold foil and the other in red, from the chocolate box in the hamper. I place both in bunny's lap. 'One for you and one for bunny when you get out of your bath.'

He smiles at this. 'I'm going to be just outside in the bedroom and I'll keep the door slightly ajar, so if you need me, I won't be far.' I'm still unsure whether I should leave him but I need to look at the wound on my arm and see what state it's in, although the pain is starting to subside from the tablets I took on the way here. It's overtaken by a new, more alarming feeling: it's numb to the touch and my hand is turning an icy blue.

I wait until I hear a gentle splash of water and lay out the first-aid kit on the bed. I ease down onto the end of the bed, watching the open bathroom door. The water laps the side of the tub, almost masking small sobs. I want to comfort him, I do, but what can I say? I need to repair myself before I can try to repair him.

I'm still wearing my duffel coat, my woolly gloves sticking out of the pockets. I pull it off slowly, my chest tensing under the dull pain. I splay my hands, preparing myself for the intensity of what will come next. I start to tug on my jumper, but it's stuck; it clings to my forearm desperately and the pain splinters up my hand. I grab one of the gloves and shove it into my mouth, biting down on the loose fibres that catch my lips.

I try to wriggle free of the jumper, letting it fall from my cold shoulders to my elbows. I peel the sleeve back slowly, clenching my jaw, stray bits of wool disappearing between my teeth.

I risk looking down and the sight of it winds me. I clutch my throat with my free hand and do my best not to scream, not to be sick. The cut is short but deep, and I think I see bone between layers of pale pink, shiny flesh and white slices of jelly. It oozes slightly, bits of grey wool caught in the deep wound.

I need help, but I can't go anywhere, because they'll ask questions at a hospital, questions I can't answer. Then they'll find me, and I won't be able to protect him.

I could try and sort it out myself, not with this first-aid kit, but I have money left, enough to get some better supplies. I could watch a video on how to do it. I just need to sterilise the wound, clean it up, and use a needle and thread to sew it back together again. It'll be as good as new. As right as rain. Then we'll move on to somewhere else, I just need to think where.

I dab at the cut with a sponge from under the kitchen sink and warm soap, just around the edges where the blood has dried and crusted along my arm. I cut up one of the pillowcases into thin strips of fabric and start winding them around my arm. This will have to do for now, until I can get what I need tomorrow. I tie a tight knot to seal it in and slowly pull the jumper back on again. I can't let him see the state my arm is in, he'll worry, and I need to keep him calm, to make him believe this is all under control.

I don't remember in the panic of everything how I got the cut. I shut my eyes and hear the gentle clang of metal echoing at my feet on marbled tiles. It's all a tangled blur, an undecipherable puzzle, and there are pieces missing, gaping, unexplained holes spreading like a disease in my mind until it just goes blank, like an old film cassette when the reel catches and spews back like a violent tongue.

There were words, angry words, but all I could do was press my hands to Josh's ears and stroke his head and tell him it would be okay, that I would get him to safety. I lifted him into my arms as he clung to the bed, dragging bunny and the blanket with him. I ran. I haven't stopped running.

There's a gurgling coming from the open door, the

sound of slippery feet squeaking against the wet tub, and then he appears wrapped in a towel in the doorway. He rubs his eye with one hand and squints at the bright overhead light.

'I can't reach Baker.'

He starts to sob, snot congealing down his already wet face.

'I can't reach him,' he repeats slowly, between gasps of breath.

'I'll get him for you.'

He waits for me in the doorway, watching as I retrieve Baker, the blanket, and the two little truffles. I hold Baker next to my face and make it dance in the steamed-up bathroom. Its matted fur is slightly damp. I feel silly but all I want is for him to smile, to see his face light up like none of this ever happened.

'Shall we put you to bed?'

He nods as I hand him Baker and grab one of the bathrobes to wrap him in. It'll have to do for tonight. I walk him down the corridor to the next bedroom, the one with the white wooden bunkbeds. Any other day, he would have loved this, would have clasped his hands together and looked up at me and you with wide eyes and a perfect smile.

Instead he walks towards the bed and sits down quietly, his emotionless expression fading into sleep. I pull the covers over him and he almost disappears underneath them. The sheets are blue with little silver stars on them.

'Do you want to see real stars tonight?' I whisper. 'I

could leave the curtains open so you can see them, if that makes you feel better?' But he is already asleep, dozing softly underneath the full duvet. I bend down to pull the grey blanket further over him and catch a smell on it, not Josh's, but yours, Harry. It's that peppery, orange smell, slightly floral like the lilies you used to buy me when we first started dating.

I lean back onto my heels and watch Josh sleep, the small rise and fall of his chest as he brings his small hand up to his mouth and squeezes Baker.

'How did we get here, eh?' I say to the rabbit. Its beady eyes stare back. 'We must look after Josh, it's our job, and being a mother is the most important job in the world.'

I turn off the bedroom light, but leave the hall one on, just in case he wakes up and he's scared and needs me. I leave Josh asleep and wander downstairs, deciding to open the bottle of red wine and pour a large glass, swiping the rest of the crackers from the kitchen counter.

I collect my bag from beside the main door and curl up on one of the sofas in the lounge. I gnaw on a cracker and wash it down with a large glug of wine. I cup my sore arm and feel the wine numb it slightly, the adrenaline and exhaustion of the day starting to vine their way through my swollen limbs and puffy face.

I pour the contents of my brown leather shoulder bag onto the coffee table between my legs and watch them spill across the surface, making an unsatisfying clatter. I take note of my only remaining possessions. A hairbrush, a few half-finished packets of mints, a compact mirror and foundation, a couple of painkillers, which I wash down quickly with the wine, my car keys, my phone and charger, and my purse. None of it's useful, none of it helps right now.

The purse is one of those small coin purses with a few cards, my driving licence, and change. I tip it upside down and watch as the cards slap the counter, and a few coins bounce around before settling. There are only a couple of ten-pound notes left in the purse, wedged inside the zipped pocket I have £23 altogether, maybe a few quid more if I search the car.

I can't use my card, as they'll trace it and find me, and I don't have any petrol left after the journey here. I wonder if I could get money from Tracey, make up some excuse about my card not working and you having to go to the bank in town to sort it. She said if we needed anything then to let her know…

I glance at the ceiling. We do need something: we need to leave. To get further away, as far away as possible. I look down at the money again; this will have to do for now. I can wash our clothes tonight and tumble dry them. There are already toothbrushes and toiletries lining the bathroom counter, plenty of soap and fresh towels. This is enough for tomorrow, to buy some food and supplies for my arm. If we can just get through tomorrow, then we'll take it from there.

I turned off all the data settings on my phone. It must be untraceable, right? I haven't used it since we left… I try remembering what I've read in books or seen in films. They can trace it—there is a way, isn't there?—and I can't let them find me. I've seen what they've done before, what they'll do to me, and, worse, what they'll do to Josh. I turn my phone off; it's not worth the risk.

I switch on the TV, flicking through the channels to see if the news is on, but nothing. Just reruns of *Columbo* and *Only Fools and Horses*. I smile, remembering you and me watching *Only Fools and Horses* in the flat before the house, before the rest of it. I loved that flat; it's where my happiest memories are, us cooking side by side in the kitchen and settling down at our small dining table. 'He who dares,' I'd say to you, and you'd wink at me, this devilish wink which revealed your deep dimples and that small scar on your chin you got from when you were little and slipped on a rocky coast in Greece.

It's hard to remember those days and then all the years that followed, all the times you made me laugh and how well I thought I knew you, Harry. It masks the pain you caused me, wins above anything. But your secret ruined everything, and it'll continue to hunt me and haunt me for the rest of my life.

I wish, instead of watching sitcoms over dinner together, I had asked you some hard questions. I wish I had communicated with you more when I was feeling like something was wrong, because something *was* wrong. I wish we were still in that flat and I could erase everything after it. I'd tell you I loved you and ask you to be honest with me, say that I could help, that I could be the person you needed me to be.

You always underestimated me and I always

overestimated you. Maybe that was our problem. But you and I had many problems, and they were bigger than us.

I run my fingers off the table and take another sip of wine.

You beat me at that game before. The husband I never knew.

But I have to win this time.

For Josh.

I have to be the woman you never thought I could be, or you dared not think of me as.

I stroke the stem of the wine glass.

'He who dares, Harry, he who dares.'

Chapter Four

eleven months earlier

The ring rubs my cheek as I wake up, glinting in the sliver of light filtering in between the blinds in our bedroom. It's a sapphire. To match my eyes, he said, on the drive home. An empty bottle of red wine sits next to Harry as he sleeps with his back facing me. I slip my arms around his waist and wait for him to stir, kissing his neck softly and pressing my naked chest into him.

'Good morning,' I whisper.

He doesn't respond, instead he rotates and meets my lips, his hands working their way down my body.

The door bursts open and Josh lets out a high-pitched scream of glee. Giggling, he throws himself at the end of the bed, but can't quite make it, just bounces off, but it doesn't stop him trying again and again and again.

'Enough,' I say, pulling the covers up to my neck. 'Wait outside, Josh, I'll be out in a minute.'

He ignores me, his relentless giggling turning into a threatening cry, his cheeks starting to puff out in frustration.

'Josh, I won't tell you again, wait outside.'

'No,' he cries, ramming himself at the bed this time and then crying out in pain as he falls backwards onto the hard floorboards.

Harry throws back the covers, scooping his jogging bottoms from the floor, he pulls them on quickly and goes around the bed to Josh. 'You all right, buddy?' Josh stops crying instantly and throws his arms around Harry.

'You mustn't let him do that,' I say.

'We'll talk about this later,' Harry says sternly, turning to Josh and brightening his tone, 'but we need to go get this little man showered, dressed, and with a bowl of rice pops, because today's a big day!'

'What's today?' Josh says, delighted with the attention.

Harry glances at me. 'You'll see.'

He leaves, closing the door behind him. I sit naked in bed, my morning ruined. I twist the ring around my finger.

I haven't thought about it for the last month, but I wanted to ask Harry something this morning. Why now? He said he never wanted to get married, and I was okay with that. I bite my lip. I said I was okay with that, but I didn't mean it, did I?

I remember a fight we had a few months ago when we were at a wine bar with his work friends and their wives. I was propped up against the bar chatting to Felicity, his firm partner Oscar's wife. What had she said? That the Harry before I came along wasn't the same Harry. I hadn't known whether to be offended, but she'd laughed and touched my hand lightly, whispering, 'When he met you, he finally relaxed, like he was looking for something and the fact he couldn't find it tortured him to no end, but with you, he's finally himself.'

'I feel the same.'

'I know times have changed since I was your age, but can I ask?' she said. 'Why are you not married?'

'Oh, Harry doesn't believe in marriage, says it's a dated tradition, so I guess times have changed.'

'Do you?' she said.

'Do I what?'

'Want to get married, of course?' She pursed her bronze lips and flicked back her red hair.

'Yes,' I said, so easily.

'Well, I wouldn't listen to the bullshit he's spinning then, if that's what you want.'

'He's committed to me,' I say convincingly. 'We have Josh.'

'I never questioned his commitment, I just know from experience that resentment eats away at you if you're not careful, and it'll break you and Harry. Never keep anything from each other, that's my advice.'

I left the wine bar that night heady on wine as we walked the damp, dark streets and it wasn't until we reached the top of the Christmas Steps that the exhaustion and weight of the evening finally came out, but it was Harry who said it first.

'What's bothering you, Lea? I know you don't like going out with my work, but it's important that we do, for appearance.'

'It's not that.'

'I saw you speaking to Felicity, and you weren't the same all evening after that. What did she say to you?'

'Nothing.'

'She clearly said something that's upset you, and it must be bad because I know you don't care about a word that comes out of that woman's mouth.'

'I'm playing the part, aren't I?'

'The part?'

'Yes, the devoted wife. Oh no, wait, I'm not your wife.'

'Lea—'

'I just want to go home.' I stalked past him, picking up my long maxi dress from the small puddles forming as rain spat in the hazy late evening. 'My mum will be waiting.'

'Is this about your security?' he said, tailing after me.

'No.'

'Because you know what's mine is yours, and I said you didn't have to work, that I'd look after you, that I'd always look after you, no matter what, for ever. Isn't that enough?'

I turned to him, his face illuminated by the orange glow of a streetlamp, his green eyes dancing in the canopy of fairy lights.

'Why don't you want to marry me?' I said.

He didn't reply then, so I turned and walked away

silently into the night and that time he didn't follow me. The sapphire ring sits neatly on my finger as I stretch out my hand and marvel at it. We didn't speak about that conversation the next day or in the months that followed, but maybe this is his reply. I wonder what changed his mind?

Harry appears in the doorway and catches me cocking my head at the ring. He smiles and bends down, throwing a pillow gently towards me, so I'll catch it.

'Josh is eating breakfast and then I'm going to take him to swim club, so you can get showered and ready, have a nice relaxing morning to yourself.' His smile fades. 'I'm sorry our morning was cut short, but there will be plenty of other mornings, for the rest of our lives.' He winks.

'I don't think we should let him in here, or let him get his way all the time; it makes him spoilt,' I say.

'He's just a kid, Lea. He's excited about seeing us in the morning, kept asking when you were getting up and if you wanted to play Mario Karts with him.'

'Not this morning.'

'No, that's what I said, but come on, let's not let it ruin our day. I've organised lunch with your mum to celebrate properly.'

I brighten at the thought of seeing her. 'We'll have to talk about dates,' I say, throwing back the sheets. 'I never wanted a long engagement, but summer would be nice, don't you think?'

He doesn't reply.

'Harry?'

'Yes?'

'Summer?'

He nods, but his eyes are glazed over like he's staring straight through me. 'We'll see,' he says, finally.

We go to a little café along Gloucester Road for lunch. It doubles as a laundrette and people sit at small wooden tables and along benches waiting for their washing whilst sipping coffee and picking at cake or reading a book. The other half of the café is full of people sharing big sundaes or large plates of pancakes and French toast with cinnamon and banana.

I haven't been here before, but Harry's spoken of it; he says he sometimes has business lunches here, but, looking around the café, it doesn't strike me as the sort of place he'd bring investors to. It's full of couples, families, and groups of students with laptops and large fruit smoothies.

We take a table in the corner. My mum pulls out a chair for Josh and helps him into it and he kicks out in elation as she gets out some colouring pencils and paper.

My mum speaks to Josh like she's always spoken to me, like an adult. It's how I speak to Josh, too, and so I dislike when Harry calls him silly names like 'buddy' and 'little man'. He's a person, and should learn to behave like one. Josh starts to fuss, but Mum pushes the paper nearer to him and turns her head away, ignoring him. Josh cottons on to this and quietens down. Picking up a green pencil he starts to scribble, making roaring sounds. I think he's drawing a dinosaur, but I can't be sure.

'What are we having, Josh? Shall we split a stack of berry pancakes?' Harry says.

Josh nods, his small tongue sticking out of his little mouth as he concentrates on his drawing.

'Congratulations again, you two.' Mum beams at me.

She glances down at my hand..

'Just beautiful, matches your eyes,' she says, a rueful smile just visible at the corners of her lips.

'It was very romantic,' I state, squeezing Harry's thigh.

'It wasn't.' He laughs. 'It was pitch-black and we stumbled around in the dark and I completely messed up what I wanted to say.'

'What did you want to say?' Mum asks, directly. 'You told me you were going to keep it simple.' I look over at her, bending my neck slightly. 'Don't look so confused, Lea. Don't you think Harry asked for my blessing before he asked you?' She throws her head back, rolling her eyes.

I smile, turning to Harry. 'Yes, Harry,' I say, leaning forward on the table. 'What did you want to say?'

'Why do you keep looking at Mummy's hand?' Josh says, still scribbling. He hasn't noticed the ring all month, but kids don't notice things like that unless someone points it out, until it's getting more attention than them.

'Well,' I say, splaying my hand out on the table so he can see the ring. 'Mummy and Daddy are getting married.'

'What does that mean?' he asks.

'That we will be husband and wife,' Harry says, rubbing the top of his head.

'So? You'll be together?' he says, holding the pencil in the air at the ready. He looks up.

'We are together,' I say.

'Then what will change?'

Harry laughs, then puts a hand to his throat, trying to suppress it. He glances at me before taking a pencil from the table and joining Josh by doodling in the corner of the paper.

'Nothing will change,' I say, because I know that's what Harry's thinking. It will change nothing. I suddenly feel spiteful, like Harry asked me for all the wrong reasons. Does he really want to marry me or just make me happy? I wonder if I care anymore. They are one and the same, aren't they? I imagine a conversation between him and his work colleagues on Monday, them saying how I finally got him to ask, like it was all me, trapping him. He'll say how he finally caved and gave in to shut me up. I swallow the thought. Not Harry, he loves me; he just wants me to be happy, to be secure. He organised this lunch with Mum and he couldn't wait to speak about our engagement. I have it all wrong.

I lean over and kiss Harry on the cheek and he flashes me a look of concern. I can feel Mum looking between the two of us, trying to work out what we're thinking, trying to decipher the sudden awkwardness.

'It's what people who love each other do,' Mum says, giving me a reassuring nod. Josh shrugs, but lights up when the stack of pancakes arrives. 'Do you have any idea of a date yet?'

'No,' Harry says, quickly, 'but we should enjoy this part, right, Lea? We could plan an engagement party, that could be fun?'

'Oh yes, how lovely,' Mum agrees. 'You could host it at that little café where you had your first date?'

Harry smiles impatiently. 'No, I don't think that's quite right. How about the wine and cheese bar on the hill by the Downs? Just intimate enough, and we can invite close friends and family. How about you both put together a guest list and we'll arrange something soon,' he says.

'That sounds nice, doesn't it, Lea?' Mum asks. She knows I'd prefer the little café where Harry and I had our first date. She knows I'd like to push all the tables to the side and line them with a simple buffet and mimosas. She knows that it's Harry who wants the wine and cheese bar, that his friends would turn their nose up at that little pasta place and say something about the decor being crappy and the wine having a screwtop.

'I could ask work if they'll let me rent out a space in the gallery? I'm sure they would.'

Harry considers this, then nods dutifully. 'Of course, anything you want.' He pauses. 'The gallery would be the perfect space actually. We could ask my friend Jose to do the canapes and a mate at work knows a great DJ. They did our Christmas party. Remember, Lea, you said how much you loved the music. You danced all night.'

I blush slightly. Sometimes when my old life and Harry's

world collide, I feel like I owe Mum an explanation, worried that she won't recognise me in the perfect portrait Harry paints of us.

We never had much money growing up, as Dad died when I was eight and didn't leave us with much. Although I studied in London, I couldn't wait to retreat back to Bristol from a city I struggled to understand and, worse, didn't understand me. Mum was there at Bristol Temple Meads, once I'd finally handed in my dissertation, to greet me and celebrate. She always said London was like a room with many locked doors and you needed the right key to enter each one. None of my keys would fit in any of the locks, but in the folds of Bristol I felt truly at home.

We had lunch and a glass of red in a little pub by the marina and later we went back to our poky terraced house in Bedminster and drank tea and watched an 80s action movie. I never wanted much from life back then; I just wanted it to be me and Mum and her art. I wanted to work in the Bristol galleries and get a toasted cheese sandwich from the deli at lunch and drink coffee and read a book looking out at the harbour.

Now, I have everything. I have the events job in the gallery that is sometimes lined with Mum's photographs. I have a fiancé and a son. I read books and take pictures of the harbour at lunch and go for after-work drinks with friends, either sticky ciders in the sun or a warming ale somewhere cosy. I have money, a beautiful house in Redland, and I go to wine and cheese bars and drink bottles of champagne without a second thought.

It's a far cry from my old life, and although there's a part of me that relishes it, when I'm around Mum I can't help but feel exposed and materialistic. She's looking at me with that sweet all-encompassing smile, but I can't help but look away. Because the worst thing about all of this is, would I want a simple buffet in the café where Harry and I met? Or would I feel slightly embarrassed in front of work friends, in front of Harry's friends? Do I want the sophisticated drinks in the wine and cheese bar and to get the best pinot noir and Gavi out for our guests, with cheeseboards and biscotti? Maybe I don't know myself anymore.

On the walk back home, Harry and Josh run ahead and Mum links arms with me. We stroll along the grey roads, lined with bare trees and grand stone houses.

'So how are you doing?' she says, once Harry and Josh are just far enough ahead.

'Me? Fine.'

'And Josh? How have things been with him?'

'Also fine.'

'He's a lot like his dad, isn't he?'

I consider this. 'No, I don't think so.'

Mum laughs. 'He has your stubbornness and spirit, that's for sure, but'—she pauses, pulling me in tighter—'he has Harry's silence. I can see it sometimes … how Josh disappears into himself, like he's internalising something, figuring out how he wants to present it to us, but he just lets it run away.'

'Is Harry like that?'

'Yes,' she says, without hesitation.

I think about the silent car journey, how there have been other times like that over the years and I'd never asked or pushed Harry. Maybe that's my fault. I never questioned anything.

'When he asked me if he could marry you, he said the wedding wouldn't be for some time, but I said you'd want to get married soon. He said proposing was enough for now.' She slows down. 'I shouldn't be saying any of this— you know I love Harry—but it was the same look I see in Josh, the averted eyes, him shutting the door on a conversation with the briefest of looks.'

'You think he's hiding something?'

She shakes her head then shrugs. 'I've photographed a lot of people over the years, and I don't mean to sound like I know Harry better than you do, of course, but you pick up on people's mannerisms, their little gestures and idiosyncrasies. I just know that he wasn't being hundred per cent forthcoming about something.'

'I don't think so. He just works a lot, he gets tired. That's all.'

She rubs my hand gently. 'I know, I'm sorry, I just want you to be happy. *That's* all.'

'I am happy.'

'I know. I shouldn't pry.' She pauses. 'How is his job?'

'I don't ask him about it, to be honest. Josh and I are his escape. He's under a lot of pressure and I want home—I want us—to be his happy place. For him to feel like the long hours are all worth it. But I think he enjoys it for the most part.'

'Well, I'd love to help you plan an engagement party. I know you plan events for a living, but if there's any way I can help…'

'I'd like that.'

She squeezes my hand and we pick up the pace to catch up to Josh and Harry. Josh is holding Harry's hand, swinging his arm, but Harry pays him no notice, he's looking at his phone with that same perplexed look. We walk home in silence.

Chapter Five

present

When I wake up, it's still dark outside. I used to enjoy the light flooding into the bedroom in the morning, the white blinds fluttering in the breeze, and waking up next to you, Harry, running my fingers along the curves of your back.

Now I'm alone, lying on the landing, on a makeshift bed of a spare duvet and blankets I'd grabbed from the cupboard. I'm guarding Josh, because I can't bear the thought of him waking up in the night in a strange place and me not being there. I watched the small crack in his door, but there was nothing but silence the whole night.

I tiptoe downstairs and see that it's 5.45am on the oven clock. I can't risk switching on my phone, but I turn on the TV to try and catch the news. I hope I won't see anything, and I have more time. I wrap myself in a blanket and eat a truffle with a cup of black coffee. The news flashes on and off by the time I'm finished. Nothing.

It should be a good thing, I should be relieved, but my shoulders rise slowly as the newsreader's voice drifts off and I'm left alone again. Alone except for Josh. I pull the blanket further across my shoulders, forcing a sigh, to try and ease the pain in my chest. I taste my stale breath; sour chocolate and bitter coffee linger on my lips. My armpits feel clammy and a musty sweat sticks to my collarbone and neck. I haven't showered since we left, scared of getting my arm wet, terrified of what else I might find beneath my clothes. More blood, but not mine? My hair is pinned back into a tight bun, but there's some dried and hard-flecked against the wisps of hair lining my forehead.

I pad back upstairs, quickly checking in on Josh, but he's still asleep, curled up with Baker and blissfully unaware.

I close the bathroom door and slowly peel off my clothes, taking extra care around the makeshift bandages on my swollen arm. I notice blood and a clear liquid seeping through the fabric, but I'll have to address it later when I'm able to get supplies. Turning on the shower, I let the room fill up with a fresh, crisp steam, a dry lavender scent masking the stench of sweat and dried blood.

I should be stepping into this shower with you, the rose petals from the bed stuck to our naked bodies as you kiss me gently, then harder… I don't risk looking in the mirror and I'm careful to keep my arm extended away from the water. I glance down. The water runs a dull, burnt red and I wince.

'It's over,' I say under the mask of the shower, the shallow beat of the water drowning my perilous thoughts. I stare at my bare feet until the water runs clear and it's safe to remove myself, to step away like yesterday never happened and life can resume. It's cleansing and for the first time I force a slight smile and consider the possibility that Josh and I could make it out of this unscathed. My arm itches as if reminding me: not completely.

All we need to do today is to make it to a shop and back without being seen, nice and simple. I load our clothes into the wash and set it for a fast spin and a quick tumble dry. I don't have enough to pay for new clothes, but they'll be clean at least. I'll give him some granola for breakfast and scrambled eggs and bread for lunch. If we can make it that far, then it's progress. I know I'm trying to find a plan amongst the wreckage, but we'll emerge the other side and there'll be nothing but blue skies and sunshine.

I dry myself and put on the other bath robe, letting my damp hair rest on my shoulders. I enjoy the fresh chill, the iciness from the tips of my hair brushing the back of my spine. I've been so hot, so unbelievably exhausted, and that tired heat had invaded my body and hadn't relented, until now.

I peek in on Josh, expecting him to still be asleep. His chest rising and falling. His mouth slightly parted, tickling the fur of the rabbit's ear.

I push open the door, a smile planted on my face in case he's waiting for me. But my smile quickly fades.

The bed is empty. The covers thrown back and in an untidy clump on the edge.

There is no Josh, no Baker.

I scream his name, but the house says nothing in reply.

I run along the corridor and throw myself down the stairs, crying desperately into the empty house.

Please be okay.

The phone is off the hook, the handle dangling next to the small table. I think I hear a voice on the other end and I rush forward to put it back.

'Josh?' I plead.

I hear a scrabbling, like nails clawing at glass. I run down the hallway and see Josh by the back door. He's sobbing and pawing at the glass, frantically trying to release the handle. Baker in one hand, his other hand outstretched. He's whimpering like a puppy.

'Josh,' I whisper, approaching him slowly.

He releases his hand and falls to the floor, sobbing into Baker. 'I just want to go home.'

'We can't go home, I've told you this. We have to stay here, just for now, but I'm going to fix things, I promise you.'

'You can't fix it.'

'I can.'

'How?' he cries, louder.

'Listen to me, Josh, who did you call?'

'I … didn't, I was trying to call Daddy, but I didn't know how.'

'You can't call Daddy, I told you. It's dangerous,' I say,

pulling his small body into me. He rests his head against the collar of the bathrobe and releases a small, sharp sigh.

'There was this woman and she told me to stay calm…'

'What woman?' I say, pulling him away to see his face, but he bends his neck, shrugging. 'What woman?' I repeat, shaking him a little.

'On the phone,' he whispers.

'Who did you speak to?' I say, louder, the urgency rising in my strained voice.

'I didn't…' He starts to cry again, then lets out a painful wail, a shriek that I fear anyone could hear. But there's no one for miles, is there?

No one. Except Tracey.

'I'm sorry,' I say, easing my grasp on him. 'We just have to be really careful.' He doesn't stop, each cry sounding more agonising than the last. I need him to be quiet so I can think. 'We have to be careful because otherwise the bad people will find us.' He tightens his grasp on Baker. 'The people I'm trying to protect you from, and if we're too loud, too careless, they'll find us.' He stops crying and stays completely still. He turns an icy white, blue veins snaking up his face. 'There's a good boy, nice and quiet.' He sniffs, edging away from me. 'I'll get you some granola, would you like that?' He doesn't respond, but he walks slowly over to the dining table and pulls himself up onto one of the chairs.

I pull a bowl out of the cupboard when a dull ring reverberates down the hallway. The front door. I drop the bowl and it shatters at my feet, but Josh doesn't even react;

he's so quiet and composed, he's numb. Who was he speaking to? Have they come for us already? I ignore it, but my car is on the driveway; maybe I should have parked it in the garage, tried to hide it around the corner under the trees and bushes. It goes off again, this time twice, and the ring is sharper, like whoever's pressing it is putting all their weight into it, and then there's a rap, a hard, deliberate knock on the door.

'Lea?' a voice echoes down the hallway.

'Are they here?' Josh whispers.

I shake my head. They can't be.

'Lea?' Louder now, but I recognise that voice, the way she pronounces it, accentuating the 'a' in a higher pitch.

It's Tracey.

She knows I'm here. We've spoken.

What do I do? What do I say? She'll see my shadow through the frosted glass.

I remain completely still.

She knocks again.

'Is everything all right?' she calls.

Was it her on the phone? I turn to Josh and whisper, 'Is that the woman you heard?'

He doesn't move, doesn't even blink, he's completely frozen.

I have to answer the door. There's no avoiding it, otherwise she could call the police.

'*Coming*,' I call, as I wrap the robe tighter around my body, pushing back my damp hair.

I swing open the door to see Tracey has a hand held up

to knock again. Her bushy red hair is in a messy top bun and she's wearing an oversized khaki-green raincoat, her freckled face etched with concern.

'Lea,' she says. 'I'm so sorry to disturb you. I'm Tracey.' The worry seems to dissolve from her features and her brown eyes soften.

'I was just in the shower,' I say, clutching my wet hair.

'Of course, I just … I think I spoke to your son? The phone in the hallway connects directly to my house. It's on speed dial.'

'Yes, I found him playing with that this morning. I'm sorry he bothered you.'

'Oh, it's no bother,' she says, waving a hand. 'I just wanted to make sure everything was all right. He sounded a little confused, something about his daddy I didn't quite catch, but he seemed a bit upset.'

'Oh, no, he's fine, happily eating his breakfast.'

'Well, that's good.' She hands over a Tupperware box lined with tin foil. 'I made muffins this morning, double chocolate chip, like there's any other type.' She laughs.

I take the box from her and smile. 'That's so lovely, thank you. Josh will be chuffed.'

'Congratulations, again, by the way. Have you settled in okay? Is there anything else you need?' she says, taking a step back.

'We're great, thank you!'

She catches something behind me and grins, waving. 'Hey there,' she says, beaming up the hallway.

I turn around and Josh is standing in the kitchen

doorway still wrapped in the grey blanket and clutching Baker. He ignores Tracey, racing back into the kitchen.

'He's shy,' I say, relieved.

'Oh, that's okay. I have a grandbaby just like him.' I smile, pushing the door slightly, but she continues. 'All my kids moved out and my husband died a few years ago.'

'I'm so sorry,' I say.

She shrugs. 'Life, 'tis all. We used to live here, in this big ol' house with our four kids, but it was too big for me. Still, I didn't want to sell it, I couldn't bear to part with all those memories for ever. There's a little guest house, just a small studio I live in with my dog, Bully, at the top of the lane, and I turned it into my home so I could rent this out to guests. Now it's full of life again.' She smiles at me. 'Of new love.'

I nod. 'It *is* really beautiful. We had a great first night and I think we're going out exploring today and to the shops, to get a few bits and bobs.'

'Well, the nearest shop is just down the road to your left, next village on. There's a great pub that way as well, The Crispin, and for something special there's some fine dining places in Bakewell. I could jot some down for you? Pop them by later?'

'No, that's fine.'

She nods. 'Well, have a lovely time, and my best to Harry as well. I'm sure I'll see you three out and about.'

'Yes, I'm sure.'

She waves and says goodbye as I close the door, still clutching the Tupperware box. You aren't here, but she can't know that. I walk over to the phone and yank it out of the wall, pulling it from the coffee table and throwing it into a cupboard under the stairs. I sit opposite Josh at the dining table and open the Tupperware box, pushing a chocolate muffin towards him.

'Was it the bad people?' Josh says, picking a white chocolate chip off the top.

I shake my head. 'Not yet.'

Chapter Six

ten months earlier

The door to Harry's office is locked. It isn't usually locked. At least, I don't think it is. Have I ever gone in there when he's not here? *No*. I'm not that type of person. I trust him, implicitly. I'm sitting with my back to the office door knowing he'll be home from work soon and he'll ask what's for dinner and I'll shrug and he'll roll up his sleeves and cook us something delicious.

I decide to text my best friend, Megan, to see if she has plans tonight. She messages back almost ten minutes later saying, 'Pub?' I smile. I haven't seen her since the weekend Harry and I got engaged. She'd taken me for lunch and I was still in that heady place where it was all 'let's see the ring' from everyone at work and coos from friends. But the congratulation texts have slowly started to peter out, the novelty of the engagement wearing off.

I've started to plan the engagement party. Because of Harry's work commitments, I arranged it for a few months' time at one of the galleries. Work gave me a hefty discount considering they're closing it for a private function, but they were elated for me, even helping me ring round caterers and order in mini personalised cupcakes and Harry's favourite champagne.

But the more I plan and the more excited I get about every aspect of our wedding, the more Harry seems to take a step sideways, and now I can't reach out my hand for his anymore. He's too far away. I haven't spoken to Mum about it since the lunch we had. I don't want her to worry, or maybe I don't want her to be right.

Harry is hiding something. He hasn't been himself lately and he retreats to his office late at night for whispered phone calls that he tells me are about work, clients in other countries that are on different time zones, but I don't believe him. He's always had those types of calls in front of me, smooth talking, winking at me as he hustles, squeezing my foot as we lounge across the sofa once we've put Josh to bed.

I miss those evenings, but since we got engaged he just sits in his office and I drink wine on the sofa or read a book alone in bed. Shouldn't this be the time of our lives? Shouldn't we be having lots of sex and going for late-night dinners and taking wine to bed like we did a month ago? Why did that only last a month? Did it all become too intense for him, too real…?

I tried backing off, giving him the breathing room that

maybe he needs. I pushed the engagement party back and held off going to wedding venues that I desperately wanted to see. Mum said she'd come with me if I wanted, but this was all wrong. When we'd celebrated with work, the wives had all welcomed me to the club, making dated jokes about marriage that I swallowed and then sicked up to Harry later. Not us, I said, not *us*.

The front door opens, and I pull myself off my spot on the landing as Josh tears through the house screaming about carrot cake. He's never happy to see me, and maybe that's what's worst about this whole thing. The more Harry detaches, the more Josh does too. He feeds off Harry's emotions. As I stand at the top of the stairs looking down, Josh catches my eye, but then ignores me completely.

'What's this about carrot cake?' I call to Harry.

'It was someone's birthday at work, so I brought some back with me, want a slice?'

'No, I'm going out.'

'Oh?' he says. 'Where?'

'I'm meeting Megan for drinks.'

'Well, that's nice, I've got some work to do anyway.'

He disappears down the hallway after Josh and I hear him whisper that I'm going out, to which Josh spits back, '*Why?* We were going to do papier-mâché tonight. She *promised*.'

I never promised anything, I think, twisting my engagement ring until it's nearly off my finger.

And, anyway, promises can always be broken.

I'm waiting in the pub for Megan, the pub across the street from the seafood restaurant that I watched a group of friends pile into just a few months ago. I haven't been out for drinks with Megan for a while. Being in events is difficult as it means working evenings and weekends a lot of the time. I don't mind though. I like having something that's mine.

It was hard to get work when I came out of university and got pregnant shortly afterwards, but the galleries knew me through Mum and it was a foot in the door, in a way. I've worked hard though, despite Harry asking, then pleading, that I give up my job and focus on Josh—on us. He thought I didn't want to work, that I felt obligated, like I had something to prove, but that couldn't be further from the truth. I told him that would never happen, no matter how many children we had. I needed my job more than any of it.

That had turned into a sour argument that had lasted weeks, maybe months.

Maybe it had never really ended.

Megan walks through the door wearing a leather biker jacket and tight skinny jeans, her dark fringe and smart bob combed neatly to shape her small features.

'Lea, well, as I live and breathe,' she says, throwing her rucksack onto the bench seat. She shimmies along, her rosy cheeks illuminated by the soft glow of the candle on the table.

'I ordered us a bottle of red,' I say, filling up her glass.

She rubs her hands together. 'Goodie, I've had a bit of a day.'

'Oh?'

She wiggles her head from side to side and jigs her shoulders up and down in a little dance. 'I got a promotion today. Creative Director, baby.'

'That's amazing! Well, here's to that,' I say, raising my glass.

'And you? Still all loved up in Lea Land?'

'Yes, yes… I've been planning the engagement party next month,' I say, biting my lip.

'Yes, yes, you're fooling no one. What's up?' she says, slouching back onto the bench and pursing her lips. She knows me so well, of course she knows I'm lying. We became fast friends in our first year of high school and although there's a small group of us from school that still hang out from time to time, Megan is the only friend I couldn't bear to lose.

'I don't know,' I whisper.

'Is it Harry? Or Josh?'

I shrug.

'Or both? I told you, Lea, you don't have to be this fucking perfect woman who pleases everyone and smiles at everything and doesn't have fucked-up thoughts like the rest of us. Honestly, who would want to be friends with someone like that?'

'I'm not like that.'

'I know you're not, but if you start being a little more

honest with yourself, and admitting that your feelings are completely normal and don't make you a bad person, then you might, I don't know, accept it? Be able to actually do something about it, instead of suppressing it? Because it'll all come out one day, and it'll be really ugly when it does.'

'I know, it's just, it's been hard with Josh, and I see you doing things like getting promotions and travelling and living this amazing life and I feel...'

'Trapped?' she says.

I nod.

'You seemed so excited about the wedding, what happened?'

'I think Harry is hiding something from me.'

'Oh, what makes you think that?'

'He's been in his office a lot, on long phone calls, and sometimes he says he has to work on the weekends and disappears for hours.' I take a sip of wine. 'He doesn't seem that excited about the wedding.'

'You don't have a date yet?'

I shake my head.

'Have you asked him?'

'Kind of.'

'So you haven't?'

'Well, not exactly. I've given him the space he seems to need.'

'You can't be annoyed at him if you aren't speaking to him. That makes no sense,' she says, finishing a glass of wine and pouring another. 'Maybe he's just busy at work.

Have you asked him outright, "Let's set a date for the wedding. How does August 5th sound?"'

'No.'

'Maybe you should.' She cocks her head. 'Is this really about the wedding?'

'Yes. No... I don't know.'

'I think you need to have it out with Harry, ask him if something is going on and tell him how you're feeling. You know he didn't want to get married before, but he clearly changed his mind and maybe that still troubles you slightly,' she says.

'That I think that he doesn't really want to get married?'

'Exactly.'

'And what if he doesn't? What if he says proposing was a huge mistake and that's why he's been acting strangely?'

'Then you address that *if* he says it, but there could be some really simple explanation. You know you always overthink everything,' she says, topping up my wine. 'Now, how about you cut yourself some slack, realise that being a young mum is hard and you're doing a great job, and it's okay to want to go out with your friends and get a little shit-faced from time to time without it making you the worst parent alive.'

I smile. 'I needed this.'

'Of course you did, you're human. Now, back to me. It's not all about you, Lea.' She winks. 'I'll order another bottle and a pizza to share.'

She wanders towards the bar and I'm left alone with my thoughts.

My smile soon fades, because she's right, I do have to talk to Harry. But what if I don't like what he has to say? What if Harry is hiding something from me, and it's worse than I could have ever imagined?

When I get home Josh is asleep and Harry is in his office. The house is so quiet. On any other day I would have loved the chance to curl up on the sofa and watch what I want on TV or read a book in the snug in the kitchen overlooking our small courtyard garden strung with fairy lights. But the peace is unsettling, like there's a small rumbling in the background threatening to erupt at any time. The silence is worse than the noise.

I plonk down on the sofa in the darkness and pull a blanket over my legs. Maybe I'll sleep down here tonight. Would Harry even notice I'm gone? The wine has misted my thoughts and my eyes feel heavy, my limbs succumbing to the weight of sleep.

'Lea?' I open my eyes to see Harry standing in the lounge doorway clutching his phone. 'I didn't hear you come in. I was just about to call.'

'Were you?' I say sleepily, wiping my mouth with the back of my hand.

'I've just got to make a quick phone call,' he says, starting to close the lounge door.

'No,' I cry.

He flicks on the light and now I can see his features; he's

68

confused, but there's something else: irritation. He softens as he walks over, kissing me gently on my forehead.

'I know things have been difficult recently,' he says, easing my legs over and sitting next to me. He places a hand on my calf and grips it gently.

'This is supposed to be the happiest time of our lives. We've just got engaged and it's like we're strangers to one another. I never see you anymore; you're always working, always holed away in your office.'

'I know,' he admits.

'Why?' He won't look at me. He looks ashamed. 'Is something going on?'

He shakes his head. 'Nothing to do with you, Lea, nothing you've done wrong. I'm just so sorry.' He leans into his hands. I hadn't realised how tired he looks now. Ever since we got engaged, something has been weighing on him and his usually healthy skin is pallid and taut, his lips thin and dry, his eyes lost and unhappy.

'What is it?' I whisper.

He hesitates before saying, 'Nothing you need to worry about.'

'You're my fiancé, my partner, of course I worry, and it's affecting us, so you need to tell me.'

'I can't.'

'Is it to do with the company?'

He shrugs.

'Is the firm in trouble?'

'I need something from you, Lea,' he says, this time looking at me. His expression intensifies, and he leans forward, clutching my hands between his. 'I need you to be patient.'

How could he say that? I *have* been patient. I waited for him to propose, I never pushed him. The last two months have been torturous, but I've tiptoed around him, given him the space and time he needs. Patient? I've always been patient, and now I'm done with it.

'No, you need to tell me exactly what's wrong and we need to work through this together, otherwise'—I pause—'how can we ever have a successful marriage if we don't communicate?'

'Do you trust me, Lea?'

'What kind of a question is that? Of course I do.'

'Then I need you to trust me now. I'm sorry I haven't been around more and I know things have been difficult, but believe me when I tell you, it's nothing to do with us. Or you.'

'So it *is* the firm?' He screws up his face and presses the palms of his hands into his eyes. 'Maybe we should hold off getting married then, if we're in trouble.'

'No,' he says, releasing his hands, his brown eyes anguished. 'We're absolutely fine financially, and you'll have the wedding of your dreams.'

I nod slowly. The wine has dried my lips and my temple's pulsing. All I want to do is go to sleep.

'Will you come up to bed with me?'

He smiles, taking my hand in his. 'Of course. I love you, Lea.'

Chapter Seven

present

Josh and I split one of the double chocolate chip muffins and for the first time in 24 hours, I start to feel more like myself. Josh has brightened up too. We're both dressed in clean clothes, warm from the tumble dryer.

I want to leave him at home whilst I go to the shops to get some food and medicine, but I don't feel comfortable knowing Tracey could knock at any moment. I could lock Josh in one of the rooms, but that seems cruel and I don't want to upset him.

He's asked about you a few times this morning and I don't know what to tell him.

I could lie, but the truth seems easier and less painful, in a way.

Your father isn't who he said he is.

Maybe I'll take Josh for a walk and hot chocolate this afternoon. Clear the cobwebs, as Mum would say. I'll tell Josh what happened and he'll have to learn to accept it and together we'll move forward. We have each other, after all.

I decide to take Josh with me and leave him in the car. I'll only be a few minutes, just in and out, quick as anything. We drive to the shop in silence, along the stone verges and rolling misty hills. There aren't many cars on the road, but it's icy and cold, everyone's holed up indoors with a roaring fire and a cup of tea. I smack my lips.

'I'll cook us something nice for dinner. How about pasta?'

Josh doesn't reply.

I glance at him in the rear-view mirror, but he's busy gazing at the blackened fields and brown-tipped grass. The narrow road leads to a village, so small that I think we've missed the turning, but I see the red post office and a green pharmacy sign next to it and feel relieved that there are so few people around.

When you and I came it was summer. We sat in those fields and I stretched my legs over you and you swept a hand up and down my calf as we sipped bottles of cold ale and nibbled slices of sweet lemon cake.

Now it's beginning to drizzle and that summer is lost underneath a sheet of icy rain and slops of trodden mud. I turn to Josh, who is wide-eyed and almost excited at being here. I smile, the pain in my chest easing slightly as he looks at me in anticipation.

'Where are we?' he asks, clutching Baker and showing him the view out of the window.

I've pulled up in a small layby just a few houses away from the shop. Close enough for me to get in quickly, far away enough for no one to watch me.

'I need you to stay in the car, with Baker, is that okay?'

'Why? I want to come.'

'I'm going to get us pasta, remember, spaghetti carbonara and gingernut biscuits like you wanted, but you can't come.' He doesn't say anything, maybe he understands why. 'I'm going to lock the door, but if anyone tries to get in or speak to you, what are you going to do?' He isn't listening, he's staring longingly out of the window. 'Josh, what are you going to do?'

'Lean forward and press on the steering wheel,' he mumbles.

'Yes, but you aren't going to talk to anyone, are you, in case it's the bad people?'

His face darkens and I think he might cry. He sucks in his lips and lets out a big sigh.

'I'll take that as a yes, shall I?'

He nods.

I close the door, hoping the tinted windows will mask Josh's face, but he's pressed against the glass, holding Baker next to him, both their faces tickled by the condensation.

The streets are bare, the only noise a sharp exhale of wind that rattles the shutters lining the stone terraced cottages. I zip up my coat and wrap my scarf twice around my neck so it covers my lips and lines the tip of my nose. I pull my woolly hat until it sticks to all parts of my scalp, rubbing the tops of my ears.

There's only one other person in the shop, an elderly woman who shuffles down the aisle to the right with a walking trolley, loading it with a loaf of bread she's carefully selected from the shelf. She pays no attention to me as I slowly walk around the shop, picking up the biscuits and ingredients for pasta. I can't find everything I need, but it'll have to do. There's a pharmacy through a wide opening in the wall and I can hear the low chatter of the people working there.

The cashier in the post office is a young woman with striking red hair. She's chewing gum and doesn't look up from her phone as I place my things on the counter. For that, I'm grateful. I ask for a bag and she lays a thin plastic blue one on the counter without muttering a word. When I turn, the elderly lady is waiting; she's looking up at me expectantly and smiles, her wrinkles pushed aside by a toothy grin.

'It's cold out there. You look like a snowman,' she says, emptying her trolley. I nod, avoiding her gaze. 'It's supposed to snow today, did you know? We're going to get a lot of it.'

'Snow,' I say, almost to myself, as I manoeuvre towards the pharmacy. It's brighter in here and warmer, and I can feel sweat building at the base of my neck under the layers of my scarf. The fluorescent lights are blinding, and a headache threatens my eyes as I strain to see below my hat.

Two women are talking at the far end of the pharmacy,

their faces obscured behind a tall row of boxes. I move around the shop quickly, trying to find bandage strips and saline solution. I need more painkillers too, but they're protected under the watchful eyes of the pharmacists, and can I risk it? Will they ask me what they're for? Now I'm worried about the snow, what that means for us.

'Can I help you?'

I freeze, my back turned to the counter. 'No,' I whisper. 'I'm fine.'

I can still feel her eyes on me, burning into my back. I turn, placing the items in front of her, but I don't meet her gaze. She looks young, judging by her manicured fingers and smooth hands.

'Is this everything?' she asks, picking up the items to scan them.

'And some co-codamol, please.'

'Can I ask what it's for?' She's holding the saline solution.

I instinctively stroke my arm. I need these supplies. I shake my head, my eyes moving to meet hers. I lean forward.

I could take them. I could run.

Would they follow?

Would they find me?

My thoughts are broken by the sound of a loud car horn. *Josh*.

I dart for the door, the woman calling after me. She doesn't hear the urgency, she doesn't know. I throw open the door, and a small bell dings above me as it slams shut. I can see down the road, but the car is where I left it, closed. I race towards it; I can't see him through the tinted windows.

'Josh!'

I throw both hands at the back window, screaming his name. For a moment, I can't see him. I yank open the driver's door and see Baker propped up next to wisps of dark hair.

'Josh,' I breathe. He appears, his eyes glistening, his cheeks red and sore like he's clawed at them with both hands. 'What happened?'

'The bad people,' he whispers. 'They came.'

'Who?'

He starts to cry and pulls the blanket back over his head. 'I just want Daddy.'

'Is he all right?' a voice says behind me.

I jump, startled, hitting the back of my head on the roof of the car. When I turn, the pharmacist that served me is standing there. She's young, with soft features and creamy blonde hair.

'He's okay, just a bit upset, that's all. I need to get him home.'

She's clutching the items to her chest along with my blue grocery bag and she holds them out to me. 'You forgot your things,' she says. I look down, taking the saline solution and bandages from her, but there's also a small box of co-codamol.

'Thank you,' I say breathlessly, 'I need to pay you.'

'That's okay,' She hesitates. 'Will you be okay?' She's

looking at me strangely, and I don't know what she means, but I nod and she smiles ruefully.

She walks away, leaving me cupping the items. I tip them into the grocery bag and close the car door. I sit there for a moment, wondering why she did that. Then I catch my face in the rear-view mirror. I look haggard; the scarf has slipped down, revealing blue chapped lips, and, worst of all, there are deep purple lines running down the left side of my face, the faint traces of a bruise, tinged green as they twist towards my red nose. I didn't see it in the bathroom mirror. It doesn't hurt, it's barely noticeable, but it's there. Anyone who looks closely, who can read the signs, can see that I've been hit.

I look down at the items resting on top of the bag. The pharmacist was trying to help me.

'Thank you,' I whisper. Josh is still huddled under the blanket. I twist and reach out a hand, trying to pry it away gently. 'No one is here, Josh, just us. Please come out.'

'There was,' he cries. 'They held up their hand like they were going to grab me.' He sniffs, revealing bloodshot eyes. I glance up the street and look at both wind-mirrors. There is no one.

I leave Josh under his blanket. If that makes him feel safe, then that's what he needs. I used to feel safe when you and I were huddled on the sofa, your big arms cradling me as I nuzzled into your chest. It couldn't have been further from the truth, and when that place wasn't safe anymore, I had to adapt. This is me adapting, Harry. I chew the inside of my mouth. I don't get the luxury of missing safety; I have to think about Josh now and what he needs.

'Let's go back to the cottage. We'll have tea and gingernut biscuits.'

He doesn't respond and stays under his blanket until we make the turn into the long driveway up to the cottage. I catch a glimpse of Tracey's small guesthouse between the thick branches and tall fir trees. I can just make out a white door framed by brown stone. It must be lonely there, just her and her dog. I've never liked dogs, never understood how anyone can like the slobber, the smell...

The gate is already open when we arrive and my stomach twists. Maybe we shouldn't have come back here.

I don't see any cars until—

There it is.

The back of a white van jutting out from behind the old shed next to the house.

It wasn't there before. I would have seen it.

I start reversing, panic rising in my throat. Josh whimpers, then cries, sensing my fear.

'Is it the bad people?' he screams.

'*No*,' I cry. It can't be.

My tyre strikes the edge of the metal gate, making a loud crunch that shocks me into slamming the brakes. I look up at the house and see a shadow, a figure, looking between the slit of the curtains down at me. How did they find us so quickly?

I ram the car into first gear and skirt the fountain. My eyes feel heavy. The statue in the middle has—somehow—

changed. It's now dappled white and scratched, a weathered face, a slanted smile oozing damp moss.

I drive away.

I can't feel my arm as I start to lose full control of it and it falls to my side, the pain unbearable.

Josh screams as we accelerate but I don't stop, even though I know we won't get very far.

Chapter Eight

nine months earlier

I'm wearing an emerald-green dress with a plunging neckline. I've painted my lips a deep red and arranged my blonde hair into neat, silky curls on my shoulders. Hand in hand, Harry and I walk along the cobbled sideroad just off the harbour and into the small gallery for our engagement party.

Our friends are waiting inside. We'll pretend it's a surprise even though it isn't and then we'll drink champagne and eat carefully curated canapes and Harry will give a speech about how much he loves me. I tighten my grip on his hand, and he squeezes back, glancing at me through his stormy grey eyes, his stubble brushing slightly against the crisp white shirt and red tie that I bought him especially for this.

When we enter, they're playing our song, 'Detectorists'

by Johnny Flynn. There are fairy lights lining the brick archway, and the white walls are adorned with Mum's photographs. It's beautiful.

The room is full of our friends, who shout, 'Congratulations, Mr and Mrs Lewis' as we round the corner. They're already clutching champagne flutes, some half empty. Mum swoops over to me, handing us both a glass, and kisses me on the cheek.

'Happy engagement,' she whispers, 'you look stunning.'

Harry has already left my side and has wandered over to his work friends and their wives, who have their backs turned to us, standing in a tight, impenetrable circle by one of the vibrant paintings.

Megan rushes over to me, followed by my boss, Carly. Mum grins, leaving me with them.

'It looks amazing in here,' I say, beaming, but my eyes wander back to Harry and his work friends. Felicity leans into him and whispers something, and he glances at me, but he isn't smiling.

'Maybe we should do more private parties. It looks great in here,' Carly says, taking in the room.

'It does,' Megan agrees, nudging me.

I raise my glass in a 'cheers'. 'Thanks so much for letting us have it here, and for putting up my mum's photographs, that means a lot.'

Carly waves her hand and narrows her eyes. 'There are a lot of nice-looking men here,' she says, taking a sip. 'You'll have to introduce me.'

Megan laughs. 'They're all married or not worth the

hassle, believe me,' she says, rolling her eyes. 'But we should go out another time, a girls' night, what do you say, Lea?'

I don't reply. I'm distracted.

'Well, Lea has to do the rounds, doesn't she?' She gently grabs Carly's wrist and leads her away into the crowd.

I spend the evening thanking people for coming, and telling groups gathered around me about plans for the wedding. Harry and I still haven't spoken about it and when I'm talking, it feels like a distant fantasy, something I've made up in my head, a piece of fiction. I realise I'm reciting the same words to everyone, 'We haven't set a date yet, no, but we're hoping for late summer.' 'We want an outdoor wedding in a rural setting, like a barn in Somerset.' 'We're going to have glamping, so everyone can stay afterwards.' I say the words so many times, they mean nothing to me anymore.

I haven't spoken to Harry all evening. I can't see him in the crowd, and it'll be time for his speech soon. He wanted to stand up and say some words about us, about our journey. He wanted to speak about Josh, although we left him with a babysitter tonight as we both agreed we wanted a grown-up party.

I step away from the group and head for the doorway, hoping to get some fresh air before heading back in. I stop in the corridor to look at Mum's photographs; they're ones of me from when I was little. I smile at the picture of me in dungarees and a hat sitting like a grown-up at a table outside a café in Clifton. I'm grinning into the sunshine, but the faces of everyone behind me are miserable.

'Hello, you,' Felicity purrs draping her thin arm over my shoulder. 'Darling pictures.'

'Yes.' I force a smile.

'Didn't I tell you? He was always going to propose. He loves you, and you're so perfect together.'

'Have you seen him?'

'Who?' she says, stepping towards the picture.

'Harry.'

'No.' She turns to me, her cat-like eyes dazzling under the low fairy lights. 'I can go find him?'

I shake my head.

'He told me, you know, that you've been having problems recently.' Her smile fades. 'You shouldn't push him. He proposed, didn't he?'

I catch my reflection in the photograph. I don't even recognise that young girl anymore. I shrug Felicity off, catching a glimpse of her wry smile as I storm away towards the toilets.

I throw open the door, but no one is here. There are only two cubicles and I throw my bag onto the side of the washbasin and lock the door of one, sitting down on top of the lid of the toilet. I want to scream, still feeling Felicity's polished hand resting on my shoulder. Why would Harry do that? Why would he tell her? I think about what she must have whispered to Harry earlier, the severe look he had given me afterwards.

I don't like where my mind is going. I need to find

Harry, to ask him what's going on. I'm angry at him. He should be talking to me about our problems, but he'd insisted, hadn't he? That it wasn't me, us?

The toilet door creaks open. The music floods in and is then stamped out again as the door closes. There's a click of heels across the tiles.

Has Felicity followed me? I don't want to speak to her. I can't.

The footsteps stop outside the cubicle and for a moment there is only silence as I hold my breath, but whoever is on the other side of the door doesn't say a word. I catch burgundy stilettos, just visible beneath the door, pointing straight at me.

Then, just as suddenly as they arrived, they leave, and confusion replaces anger. Felicity should have apologised. I wouldn't have had to say anything back, but I would have listened.

I need to find Harry.

The door swings open again.

'Lea, are you in here?' Mum calls.

'Yes.'

'Are you all right?' She knocks gently on the door.

'Of course,' I say, taking a deep breath.

'A few people are starting to leave and wanted to say their goodbyes.' She pauses. 'I can't find Harry, though.'

I push open the door.

'He isn't here?'

She shrugs. 'He might be outside? I'm not sure.'

I march past her, my heels rubbing slightly as I ignore

people trying to congratulate me or say goodbye. I burst out into damp evening, slipping slightly on the steps as I try to shield myself from the spitting rain.

There are a few smokers, amongst them Megan, who throws back her head laughing, until she sees the concern on my face. Mum has tailed me outside and Megan's face is now so close to mine I smell the red wine on her breath.

'What's up, Lea?'

'It's Harry,' Mum says, 'we can't find him.'

I walk back into the gallery and through the thinning crowd, past waiters holding empty silver trays, and tables full of stained glasses, and tablecloths with patches of spilled drinks and crumbs of food.

Across the room I see Harry's work friends, but I don't see Harry.

'Have you seen Harry?' I ask, approaching them for the first time this evening.

They shake their heads, eyeing each other like they're in trouble. Children who have been caught out and are relying on the rest of the group to keep ranks, to not crack, stick to the plan. I can't see Oscar either, Harry's partner at the firm. Maybe they had to rush into work? Maybe something was wrong?

'Where's Oscar?'

'He didn't come tonight. He couldn't make it because he's away on business.'

Now they look confused, like how could I have not known that? But Felicity was here, I just assumed... I look around. Felicity isn't here anymore. Neither is Harry.

I bite my lip and turn on my heels as Megan and Mum catch up to me.

'We couldn't find him,' they say, breathlessly.

I shake my head, forcing a smile, walking just out of earshot of Harry's friends. 'I've just spoken to Harry; he had to leave, an important work call from Oscar.'

'Tonight?' Mum says, bringing a hand to her face.

But Megan hasn't bought it. She's crossed her arms and she's about to say something, but I stop her.

'He said he'll meet me back at home, so I'm going to head off now. Thanks for a lovely evening, it was magical.'

I hug them goodbye and Megan takes a few steps after me, but stops. She knows I've lied for you, Harry, and I can't offer her the truth right now.

When I'm in a taxi, I call Harry, but he doesn't pick up. I don't expect him to. He's buried in the secret he's clearly been keeping from me.

My head swirls with the question of what it might be.

Harry was in his office when I arrived back in the taxi. He was on the phone speaking in a low hushed voice but went silent for a moment when he heard me stop outside his door. I thought about knocking, but I needed to compose myself. He left our engagement party without saying anything to me. He didn't answer my calls the whole way home. So I went to bed, and I lay there for what felt like hours until the door crept open, and Harry came in smelling of orange peels and bourbon.

He got into bed next to me and it felt so wrong to fall asleep, to end the day like this.

What started off as hopeful clutched hands in the early, wet spring evening has turned into a rank smell of confusion and alcohol.

Two strangers and so much to say.

I wake up earlier than Harry. He doesn't usually drink much but when he does, he must sleep it off and will spend most of the day trying to convince himself he's not hung over.

I climb out of bed, checking my phone and seeing messages from Mum asking if I got home okay and from Megan asking if I want to meet her and her dog Bruno for a walk at the Downs this afternoon. There's also an email, not unusual for a Sunday when you work in events, but it's from Carly, which *is* unusual. She'd call or text me. Though maybe she doesn't want to disturb me today. I glance at Harry. Not the day after my engagement party.

The message is short, clipped, with the subject line 'today'. 'Hi, Lea, please can you come into the office today at 11.30am?'

I respond that I can and ask if everything is okay. What could she want that can't be said over the phone? It must be serious. I hope the gallery wasn't left in too much of a state last night, but the cleaners were due to arrive this morning.

My head pulses and my mouth is dry. I need to get Josh

up soon; I can't risk him coming into our bedroom this morning and seeing Harry like this. Seeing me like this.

I wander down the hallway, looking back at our closed bedroom door and try Harry's office just in case he's left it open. No luck, it's locked. I realise that I never asked him why. The doorbell rings and it's enough to wake Josh, who calls for Harry from his bedroom almost immediately. I push open his door and he's alive with concern.

'Where's Daddy?' he asks.

'He's sleeping in today. I'm going to see who's at the door and then we'll have breakfast together, yes?' He retreats under the blankets and I hear a heavy sigh. 'I'll take that as a yes,' I call, descending the stairs.

I can see Mum through the frosted glass and when I throw open the door, she's wearing a dense frown that makes her look older than she is.

'I messaged you. I was so worried.'

'I'm sorry,' I whisper.

She sighs, leaning back on her heels as she throws her head back. 'Well, I might as well come in for a cup of tea now.'

I open the door to let her through and Josh launches himself down the stairs screaming, 'Granny!'

'Hello,' she says, scooping him into her arms. 'Are you only just getting up?' She glances back at me, knowing the answer as I stand there in my long-sleeved silk pyjamas. 'Why don't we go and get you some breakfast whilst I talk to your mum.'

Josh takes Mum's hand and leads her down the hallway. I follow them as Mum tries to mouth something to me.

'Is Harry awake?' Mum says, giving up with a shrug.

'Daddy's sleeping in,' Josh says petulantly, taking a seat at the kitchen table.

'Oh, well, it was a big evening last night. He must be tired,' Mum states.

I make Josh some toast and jam and put him in front of the TV while Mum makes us coffee. She's waiting for me at the table as I come back in the kitchen, but I don't sit down. I remember what she told me months ago when Harry proposed, how she thought he was hiding something.

'I have to go out. Would you mind watching Josh until Harry gets up?'

'Go out? Where?'

'Work.'

She nods. 'Where did Harry go last night?' I fold my arms. 'Megan didn't seem to think he did have work.'

'Well, Megan's wrong. You know how busy Harry is, and that his partner is currently in America trying to close a big deal for them. Something must have gone wrong.' I throw my arms up. 'I don't know.'

'You haven't spoken to him?'

'No, but it's all fine, I have to go.'

I leave her and go to shower and get ready, unspoken words hanging in the air between us. I can't answer her questions. I take one last look at Harry before I leave. I wonder if Mum will ask Harry herself and if he'll answer her honestly.

He confided in Felicity. He told her we're having problems.

I can't help but feel getting engaged was a huge mistake. But somewhere dangerous and deep within me, at the core of all of this, I think meeting Harry and everything after him was a mistake too, and the thought is like a poison that slowly seeps into every part of me. It makes me want to run away.

———————

Our offices are above the neat row of galleries along the river with a view of the old railway and, in the distance, the SS *Great Britain*. My desk is by the window, not that I spend much time in the office, but when I do, I love to watch the view of the rolling fields leaping towards the glistening water as crowds saunter along the bank and groups climb into the little ferry boat that takes you to and from each side. There's a tall mast next to my window and I can almost smell the rust and metal. Further down, the sun beats on the water and the rain patters on the worn paint of the small wooden boats.

I reach into my bag for my work fob, but struggle to find it. Crouching down on the pavement as people pass me clutching coffee and bags of chips, I search my bag, pushing my hand into all the pockets and then tipping it over to see if it's caught anywhere, but it isn't there. I must have left it at home, but this was the bag I used last night, my black shoulder bag with the large gold buckle.

I press the buzzer, hoping for Carly to appear at the door, all smiles, saying she's just put on a fresh pot of coffee and she needed my help desperately with a project, apologising for not responding to me. But she doesn't appear; instead one of the cleaners arrives, and she isn't smiling.

She hesitates before opening the door.

'Sorry, hi, I work here, but I couldn't find my pass.'

She nods slowly, before widening the door, and I follow her down the narrow hallway. Off it are the event spaces: the small gallery I had my engagement party in and two other spaces to the back which are open to the public today, showing a special exhibit exploring grief and loss, featuring local artists in different styles and mediums. I said to Mum I'd take her one night this week and she was thrilled at the idea, but I know grief has its own meaning for her. She didn't contribute to the exhibit, but if she had, what would the photograph be? My dad? Stoic and unflinching, sitting back in his big leather armchair wearing that cheap striped suit Mum hated? Or my grandparents whom I never knew. What would *I* paint? I push away the thought.

'Is everything all right with the gallery? Hopefully we didn't leave it in too much of a state, just a few messy tables,' I ask, stopping by the door to the small studio.

She frowns, confused, pointing towards the door to the two main galleries. She shakes her head, before disappearing down the hallway and through the door at the end. Maybe that's why Carly called me; maybe there's been an accident and she needs the extra help. The thought settles me a little. At least the cleaner didn't open the door to the studio. I do, though, and peek in. It's spotless, Mum's photographs still hanging along the corridor, washed in the morning sun. Carly's right, this is a lovely space that we should use more often for private events. I smile. That's what she could want to talk about.

I go upstairs to the offices, but Carly's not here yet and I can't resist checking out the exhibit downstairs. Just a peep to see how busy it is. Maybe I'll get a photo for our social media. I descend the stairs and continue down the dark corridor and towards the white door. The cleaners aren't anywhere to be seen anymore; it must have just been a little spill. Sometimes Carly likes someone on call just in case. I feel relieved, happy even, opening the door I expect to see groups of people having lively conversations, discussing the beautiful paintings lining the walls and pointing, a promising optimistic hum in the air despite the subject matter. But there is nothing.

The creak of the door is the only noise echoing through the empty rooms. It shuts behind me. A soft thud that makes me jump slightly. I am alone in the gallery; the front door is sealed shut and the blinds are down. It is closed to the public and it's obvious why.

Thick, blood-red paint has been thrown over every inch of the wall. It's dried and crusted over the frames of the pictures and portraits and paintings.

I take a step forward. Directly ahead, just visible beneath streaks of red, is a picture of a woman shrieking, her mouth wide open, but she doesn't make a sound. Red paint slips from her open mouth like she's spitting venom. She went from being unheard to being angry. The room is covered in anger, not an act of rebellion or boredom, but hatred and spite.

Whoever did this wanted to be seen.

They wanted to be heard.

Chapter Nine

present

Josh cries as we speed away from the house. I don't know where we're going and the searing pain in my arm threatens my grip on the wheel, every shift of the gears is agony. I need Josh to stop crying so I can think straight. I check my rear-view mirror, but there's no one there. Was I imagining it? I bite down on my lip.

'Please stop crying, Josh. How about we go get a nice hot chocolate, would you like that?'

He calms a bit, the cries turning into sharp whimpers as he clutches Baker to his chest, whispering something into its raggedy ear.

I know a place, just off the Monsal Trail that you and I cycled once. We had ham and cheese toasties outside a café while it rained, sitting under cover listening to the gentle beat on the plastic roof. The smell of moist leaves and damp bark lining our nostrils as we drank tea and spoke about our future…

It's now bitterly cold. Fractured ice climbs the windscreen and the tips of my fingers are numb, but I can't turn the heating on, I can't risk running out of fuel and not being able to escape.

I turn into the carpark and there are only a few cars there, not like in the summer months when it would be teeming with families and dogs, kids screaming gleefully as they cycle after their parents into the late afternoon sun, their big golden retriever chasing them. That's what we spoke about, didn't we, Harry? About coming here again as a family. We just never made it that far.

I take Josh's hand and we make a dash for the café, passing an upturned table and chairs. No one is sitting outside today. All those memories appear like a photograph, and I squeeze Josh's hand, wishing he could see what I see, how happy we could have been

There are a few people in the café. I want to avoid them, so I usher Josh outside to a bench seat that faces the trail.

'One hot chocolate coming up,' I say, pulling the scarf tighter around my neck, the hat further down my face. Someone could ask about me in here. The figure in the house. The person who tapped on the car. The people that are coming for us.

I order a hot chocolate, a coffee, and a flapjack for us to share, mentally counting my change as I put it away. We can't afford petrol, we can't run, we can't go back to that house where someone is waiting for us. What can we do?

Josh drinks his hot chocolate in silence, nibbling at the flapjack and feeding little pieces to Baker.

'Why Baker again?' I ask finally.

His legs stop waving and he looks up at me with solemn brown eyes.

'Daddy's favourite book.'

'Of course,' I say, stroking his hair.

How could I forget? *The Hound of the Baskervilles*. Baker Street. I'm Watson, he's Sherlock. I smile.

It starts to snow, a soft pearly flurry, and Josh points at it, and for a moment we're like that photograph I imagined.

'Would you like to go for a walk?' I ask, as he holds Baker up to look at the snow.

'In the snow!' he cries in excitement.

I help him into his coat, doing up the zip to his chin, so his furry hood covers his small features, and take my scarf off, pulling it round him to keep him warm.

'We need a clear head, don't we, Josh? Just to walk it off.' He doesn't respond. He doesn't understand. Maybe we'll just walk, for ever, until somehow this resolves itself. I used to be fond of walking around Bristol, along the harbour and up Brandon Hill to take in the view at the top, and on the weekends we'd go to Leigh Woods with our friends and imagine living there one day in one of the grand gated houses, with a wild garden and fresh potted herbs.

The trail is empty apart from a few dog walkers and Josh coos at the dogs. He would love a golden retriever; maybe we'd call it Mycroft or Lestrade. We still could get one, I think hopefully. The snow has eased so that it tickles our faces and melts on the damp ground. I let Josh wander ahead a little; he has more energy now, and I forgot that children need to run and climb and jump. I wish I was young again.

I grit my teeth as my arm throbs underneath my coat, a burning pulse that pinches at the top of my wrist. Maybe this is it.

Up ahead there's a tunnel shrouded by browning grass, moss seeping between the cracked grey brick. Inside is black apart from a few dull overhead lights. The whistle of the wind chews through openings in the stone, and the mouth of the tunnel gapes like it's screaming, but there is no noise. It reminds me of that painting in the gallery, red paint streaming down her face like she's crying blood.

My heart starts pounding as water cascades off the brickwork like it's waking from a deep slumber and the whole tunnel moves slightly.

We must turn back.

'Josh, let's go.' But I can't hear him. I spin around. I can't see him. In the corner of my eye there's movement in the tunnel. 'Josh,' I scream, but it's over already, the motion so swift, like the flutter of a bird's wing, and my strained voice echoes through the opening.

I grasp the brickwork to support myself, feeling my chest tighten.

'*Josh.*'

Now I'm running, my boots slapping harshly on the dry floor as I flail my arms desperately, trying to feel my way around, to find his arm and pull him in. But there's nothing.

'Please, Josh, where are you?'

I step on something soft and reach down in the darkness to grab it, bringing it up to my face to study it under the low lights. Two black, beady eyes stare back. I run my hand over it, the tattered ears, the furry belly, the warmth and smell of Josh.

I fall to the floor screaming his name, over and over again, until the darkness takes hold.

Chapter Ten

eight months earlier

It's been a month since Carly told me I was fired. Now I float around the house without purpose.

Harry thinks it's a good thing, that I could work on my own art, that I could spend more time with Josh. I don't want to be his stay-at-home wife. I don't know if I want to be his wife at all.

He told me I was grieving for the job, but it wasn't like that at all. It was the injustice of it, my untethered anger wanting to set it right, to clear my name.

Carly had found me that day in the gallery, staring at the red-soaked walls. She didn't look surprised, just ushered me out of the room and up to the offices and told me to sit and wait. And maybe I knew then.

When she came back, she sat across from me, the desk

separating us as she did the best to compose herself, to find a place where she was my boss, not my friend.

'What's happened?' I asked, finally.

'Someone's defaced all the paintings,' she said, like it's news to me.

'Do you know who? Why?'

She squirmed. 'The thing is, Lea, there was only one person who accessed that room in the early hours of the morning.'

Then it all came crashing down, the realisation of why she'd called me in. My missing key.

'You think it was me?'

To my surprise she shook her head, but then wavered. 'I don't think so, but it was your key fob that was used.'

'Someone took it, stole it, they must have.'

She looked concerned. 'Who would do that?'

I shrugged, racking my brain. Then I remember the clip of heels, the hiss of Felicity's voice, the way it curled around Harry's shoulder as she whispered in his ear.

'I've called the police; they'll want to speak to you.'

She looked defeated, exhausted, the night before etched on her usually bright features.

'I'm so sorry, Carly, but it wasn't me.'

'Where did you go last night?'

'Home,' I said, incredulously. How could she even think I was involved?

'You'll have to tell the police that, but I think it's best you take some leave until we can figure this out.'

'Leave? You're firing me?'

'No, I'm asking you to take some leave while we figure this out.'

'But I didn't do this. You know me, Carly, why would I?'

'You were acting strangely last night, and you left suddenly.' She raised her voice then. 'You haven't been yourself for weeks, months. Something inside you has been building up and I blame myself because I never asked you what.' She looks at me directly for the first time. 'Are you okay, Lea?'

I stood up and told her to fuck off. I marched out of the office wishing I had been the person to deface the paintings, my own interpretation of grief. I realise now, as I sit on the sofa sipping tea and wishing Josh and Harry would never come home, that I am grieving. I'm grieving for the life I never had.

The doorbell rings. It's Megan, who's come round with croissants and coffee to give me a pep talk. She'll tell me not to wallow in it, but for the first time in a while I feel better, watching my house of cards come crashing down. I just need to keep going.

'You're being destructive,' Megan says, curling up on the sofa and blowing on her coffee.

'I know,' I agree.

'Well, snap out of it. You've spoken to the police; they know you didn't have anything to do with it.'

'But Carly thought I did. Maybe she still thinks that.'

'Is that why you won't ask for your job back?'

'I don't want it.' I stretch out on the sofa and look out of the window as a group of students pass clutching clear cups full of brightly coloured smoothies and velvety lattes.

'I know that isn't true,' Megan says, opening the bag of croissants. 'Maybe you need something else to focus on? Have you thought about dates for the wedding?'

I shrug. 'Not really.' Harry has been much more attentive since I lost my job. He's come home early every day and says we should plan a holiday soon, maybe in the Peak District. I never did find out why he left, the night of our engagement party. In the shock of losing my job, when I came home afterwards, he was laid out on the sofa with a cold flannel to his head protesting to Mum that he was fine. I told them both what had happened and he was livid, fuming. He got dressed and stormed out and came home two hours later, saying I wasn't in trouble, but did I really want to work at a place like that?

'I do miss it,' I admit to Megan, 'but I can't go back. I have to move forward.' I force a smile. 'There will be other things.'

'Harry's right, you should work on your own art. You've got that little shed at the end of the garden. Turn it into a studio and pour all this energy you have into something good, then hang it in every gallery that isn't Carly's, because fuck her.'

I laugh. 'Maybe.'

She's made me feel better, just slightly. It would be a way to find some light in all this, to be an artist like Mum, to see my paintings alongside hers one day.

She nods defiantly before taking a large bite out of a

croissant, chocolate oozing over her cheek. 'Still not found it?' she asks.

'What?'

'Your fob?' I shake my head. 'And still no idea who could have it?'

I haven't told Megan about my conversation with Felicity, about the fact that Harry confided in her. I haven't said a word about Felicity following me to the bathroom, the only time I left my bag unattended the whole night. I've tried to shake off the thought that she could have done it, always coming back to the why.

I've been backtracking on nights out with Harry's work crowd and dinners with just Felicity and Oscar, and now I see that the way she and Harry were together did bother me, I just didn't let it do so at the time. It wasn't flirtatious. It was worse than that. It was little knowing glances at each other, small moments they shared together while Oscar and I sat there, completely oblivious.

I remember the night we fought about marriage very differently. What had he said? *'I saw you speaking to Felicity, and you weren't the same all evening after that. What did she say to you?'* Was it something else he was worried about her telling me?

'Do you think Harry would cheat on me?' I say, suddenly. Megan stops mid bite; flakes of pastry fall from the corners of her mouth. 'Don't look so surprised that I asked. We both know he's been acting strangely ever since we got engaged. Maybe the other woman isn't happy about it.'

She almost chokes, glancing around the room like she's trying to make some sense of it. 'No,' she says, finally. 'I don't think he would do that, but you clearly do, if you're asking.'

'I just think, for someone to steal my pass from me, at my own engagement party, and then get me fired from my job, isn't that the act of someone who's feeling cheated? Who's feeling like they've finally lost?' I shrug. 'He won't set a date for the wedding, and we've been having problems.'

She nods. 'Is this about where he went that night? You told me he was here when you got home.'

'He never offered an explanation,' I say, 'but I never asked.'

'So, you think he's cheating on you and the woman was at the party and she stole your fob and defaced a whole gallery out of spite?' She laughs. 'That's quite some imagination you have, Lea.'

'Is it?' I say, seriously.

She cocks her head. 'Who do you think it is?' I don't reply. 'Who?' she presses. She's moved closer to me. She's frustrated. She goes to press me again, but I pull away, and it's just a fleeting look but it knocks me off balance. She's worried … about me? About her? About Harry?

'You better go,' I whisper, 'I have things I need to do.'

She looks disappointed in me as she sucks in her lips and collects her things. 'I'll message you later,' she says, and I feel awful, but I'm not thinking straight, I'm not myself. I reach forward and pull her into a hug, whispering that I'm sorry. She hugs me back, stroking the back of my hair like Mum does.

After she leaves, I pad out into the garden in just my socks, making my way along the stone pathway to the little green summerhouse at the back, just visible between a narrow wooden archway and rows of overgrown shrubs.

The door creaks as it swings open. Dust and dry dirt dance along the wooden floorboards and kick up into the air creating a musty scent that fills my lungs. I cough, shielding my face as it settles around me. I could make this work. I could fill this space with colour.

I think about the red paint dripping down the woman's face. I'm done grieving now.

'Lea,' Harry calls across the garden, 'are you back there?'

He meets me halfway along the pathway and we collide awkwardly. He goes to kiss me, but I reach around to hug him, and we fall into a clumsy embrace.

'What are you doing out here?' he asks.

'I was just looking at setting the summerhouse up as a painting studio. It needs a clean,' I say, pulling away and dusting myself down.

'What a wonderful idea. I came home early to see you. I can help?'

I shake my head. 'No, that's okay, I expect you're busy.'

He takes my hand in his and leads me back towards the house. Once we're in the kitchen, I watch seated as he makes us both tea. I'm waiting for him to make an excuse to go upstairs; he came home, but he doesn't have to spend any real time with me. I shake my head. He offered to help me clear the summerhouse. He's here, and he's trying, isn't he?

'Where did you go the night of our engagement party?' I blurt.

He twists mid pour and almost looks confused for a moment; he's trying to remember something that has been playing on my mind every day for a month.

'I came home. I had that call from Oscar and he needed my help with a negotiation. I told you this, didn't I?' I shake my head. 'Well, I must have forgotten, because of what happened the day after.' He places the tea in front of me. 'Has this been bothering you?' I nod. 'Why didn't you say anything?'

'I don't know. Like you say, a lot happened the day afterwards.'

'I never apologised to you, though. I'm so sorry, Lea, I've been awful, I really have, not the husband you deserve.'

'Husband? Not yet.' I laugh, but he winces slightly. 'I've been thinking about that night.'

'Oh, yes?' he asks.

'About something Felicity said to me.'

'Felicity?'

'She said that she knew you and I were having problems,' I say, taking a sip of tea like my words mean nothing at all. They have been caught in my throat for a month, and now they run freely, but I can't look at him as I say it; I don't want to read the answer on his face.

'I told Oscar in confidence, and I never said that exactly,' he says, quietly. When I look up he seems broken, like he's about to cry. His eyes gloss over with a watery sheen and his skin turns a pale grey. 'I told Oscar that—' He pauses, stifling a choke, his complexion turning red as his eyes darken. Then he suddenly looks horrified, glaring at me across the table. 'For all this time,' he says, reaching over and clutching my hand, 'I never said we were having problems.'

'Then what?' I pull my hand away.

'I said that I had a lot on my plate, and it was causing a strain, that's all. Never you, never us, never that we had problems. Lea,' he says, breathlessly, 'I promise you I didn't say that. How awful for her to tell you, and on the night of our engagement party.'

'Not that you were there,' I reply.

He nods rhythmically. 'You're right, I wasn't, but I'm here now, and I'm so glad you told me. I thought something was wrong, but assumed it was the job. I'm sorry,' he says again.

I let him lean over and kiss me. He keeps his face close to mine, his lips inches from me.

'We should set a date for the wedding,' he says then. 'I know you wanted summer, but I've actually been looking into places and I found a beautiful castle in Somerset available in January. It has a grand long hall and stunning views. I think it will be incredibly romantic, don't you? Plenty of time to plan as well, so we don't feel rushed.'

'A castle?'

He kisses me softly. 'A castle,' he whispers.

'In January?'

He smiles. 'In January.'

'Sounds cold.' I smile. 'Okay.'

He kisses me again, but this time it's more forceful, there's an urgency, a need for me. He threads his fingers through my hair and we kiss like we used to when we first met and I'm relieved to find that passion, that fight, that hunger.

There's just one last thing I need to do.

When I arrive at the bar, Felicity is already propped in the corner stroking a wine glass. She smiles awkwardly when she sees me. She knows this won't be pleasant.

I sit down opposite her and she does her best to avoid my gaze as she reaches for the wine menu and pokes at one on the list. 'I think you'll love this one, Lea. It's similar to the pinot you had at my birthday party, don't you remember?' I say nothing. 'Oscar told me about your job. I'm so sorry I didn't reach out. I should be a better friend to you. Let me get you a glass of wine.' I accept, because I'm starting to shake. I've never been good at confrontation, and I have a feeling she is.

Felicity is one of those people who attracts life. She's always at a show, a function, a charity ball. She travels a lot with and without Oscar, has friends all over the world, and brags about the places she's been, the things she's done. She was always quick to lecture me and dress it up as friendly advice when I started dating Harry, but it's the odd comment, the veiled snipe. She used to hide it better at the beginning, but now I see it all: she doesn't like our age difference, but, more than that, she's jealous of it, worried even, that Oscar might do the same.

It was always a joke, like 'when is Oscar going to trade me in for a twenty-one-year-old?' but it quickly became sad. I remember her looking at me one night when we were clearing away in the kitchen after she'd cooked a lovely dinner. She'd had too much wine and it was obvious there was tension between her and Oscar. She said suddenly 'I'll never be beautiful again.'

But I could never not see Felicity's beauty, and maybe there was a point when I thought we could be true friends, but I didn't like how easy she found it to mask herself, to pluck a trifle from the fridge and dress her face in a big grin, strutting out into the dining room like she'd never said a thing.

'I just came here to tell you to stay out of my business,' I say, looking down at my wine.

'Excuse me?' she says, her voice strained, but there's a note of anger. I know she heard me. I wait. 'Your business? Is this about what I said at your engagement party? Because, sweetie, if it is'—she doesn't say 'sweetie' endearingly, she spits it sarcastically, and when I look up, her whole face is scrunched—'I said what I said because you deserve to know.'

'No, you said it to get a rise out of me, and you did, and because Oscar and Harry are business partners and best friends means we have to be civil,' I say, rising from the table. 'We won't speak of it again, but Harry and I are getting married in January and we're happy. You don't know a thing about our relationship, so don't involve yourself and just be happy for us like everyone else.'

I grab my bag and go to leave, but Felicity leans forward and grabs my wrist. Digging her long nails into my skin she hisses, 'You don't know anything about him, you silly child.'

I pull away. 'Whatever you think is going on with us, or going on with you two, it isn't, and you need to let it go.'

'With me and him?' She pushes back her chair and stands to meet my gaze. 'You are a fool.'

She saunters past me and leaves me standing alone in the corner of the bar.

I sit back down and finish my wine, my palms sweating, my lips dry. I order another and stay like that until my head starts to swim and I call a taxi..

But can I go home like this? To my family? Drunk and tired and with only one thing on my mind?

That I know nothing about the man I'm marrying.

Chapter Eleven

present

I fight through the biting cold as the wind snaps like a disturbed animal. I'm at the centre of it, clutching Baker to my chest, trying to shield him from the mutating storm. It was bright, sunny, clear when we left Bristol, but now I've entered another realm. A fantasy. A nightmare.

'Josh,' I cry, but my voice is carried away in the fusillade of snow and dirt, stray branches whipping at my face like I've wronged them.

I see the café up ahead, but there's a shield of white covering it like a dome, and I'm infected, and I need to be kept out. I stagger, trying to focus, and a bush reaches out and scrapes my arm like running fingernails down my skin, the heat and pain almost unbearable.

'*Josh*,' I scream, helplessly.

'Lea?'

Someone is calling me, but it isn't Josh. Have the bad people finally found me? Have they tracked me down? I wouldn't be that hard to find, I haven't made myself invisible to your dishonesty. All the mess you made is about to come crashing down on me.

Do I run? I can't let them have Josh. I can't let them take him from me. You aren't here to protect us. You aren't here to make sure we're safe, so that burden has fallen to me.

'Lea?'

A hand reaches out and threads through mine, pulling me into the warmth of the café, the noise of the wind and snow smothered by the slam of a door.

'Lea?'

I finally look up and Tracey is gripping my shoulders, her hands close to my neck, her eyes staring straight into mine. She sees me fully in the fluorescent overhead light of the café.

'Josh,' I whisper, 'he's out there.'

She smiles reassuringly, but it just makes me want to get further away, the comforting smile of a stranger. 'He's here. Don't worry, Lea, he's safe.'

'Where?' I say, pushing her off me. She releases my shoulders and lets me fight past to where Josh is sitting on a wooden bench facing me, unharmed, huddled in a little blanket clutching a bar of chocolate.

'I found him,' Tracey says behind me. 'He was wandering back towards the café alone and then I saw you coming. You can't see much in the storm; it must have been really scary.'

I bend down next to Josh and place my hands on his knees. 'Are you okay?' I whisper to him.

He nods, taking a bite of the chocolate and chewing it slowly.

'Would you like a glass of milk for him?' the waitress says, joining us.

'That would be lovely, thank you,' I reply, still watching Josh's eyes slowly open and close as we both compose ourselves. 'I thought I'd lost you. I was so worried.'

'I'm here,' he replies, and for a moment he sounds like you. So grown up and mature. But what happened yesterday was sobering, for both of us, and I can see him figuring out the next step, where we go from here.

I'm doing that too, Josh. I should be the one to carry the weight of our situation and get us to safety.

I can feel Tracey lingering behind me.

'Thank you,' I say, pulling the blanket further over Josh.

'We lost each other in one of the tunnels.'

'He seemed so nervous of me; it must have been from our run-in earlier,' she says.

'Run-in?' I ask, taking the glass of milk from the waitress and sitting next to Josh on the wooden bench. I hand him Baker. 'I saved him from the storm.' He reaches out slowly in disbelief and brings Baker to his mouth, pressing his small face into him.

'Yes, I saw Josh in the car earlier. I think you were in the shop. I thought he'd recognise me, but he was so terrified, it really shook him up, and I didn't want to stick around and make it worse.'

'You were the person who tapped on the car?'

She nods. 'I was actually just headed to your place, to let you know about the snow coming, when I saw your car in the carpark. Is Harry not here?'

Josh gasps, slowly looking up at Tracey, and he's about to speak, but I cut him off. 'No, he's back at the cottage.' Josh whines. Tensing under the blanket, he pulls away from me and whispers something inaudible to Baker.

She smiles. 'I was going to pop by anyway and apologise. I thought you were coming tonight, so I'd asked my handyman to do a few bits and bobs around the cottage, but I forgot to call him this morning. I think he let himself in, so he might have startled Harry.'

'Handyman?'

'Just to replace some lightbulbs and look at one of the leaky taps in the bathroom. Nothing to worry about. The property is just old, is all.'

'Of course…' The white van, the figure in the window, the tap on the glass, the bad people are closing in on me, nothing to be afraid of. But that's what you always said when we were wrapped in each other, Harry, that there was nothing to be afraid of, but of course there was, and it was my biggest fear and worst nightmare realised. It was the day I spoke to your lawyer.

'We best get back before the roads close; it's going to be bad and we might get snowed in.'

'We don't have enough food,' I whisper to myself.

'Oh dear, well, I have plenty. I can drop some round for you, to get you through the next few days.'

The darkest days of winter.

We make our way home slowly, the tyres crunching on snow. It sounds like gravel, like the house's driveway in Bristol, and I dream of stepping inside, hearing Josh's giggles as he sits at the breakfast bar while you make lasagne. You beam at me down the hallway, a red wine poised in your hand as I walk towards my family, my life.

When we turn into the narrow country lane, Tracey's already parked up, her red 4x4 tucked away on her small driveway, and she's waving at me through the smoke of snow. She sees a woman who was terrified she'd lost her son, not a woman who is running, who is hiding, who is frightened of what's to come.

The white van isn't on the driveway anymore, but I check the house anyway, just to make sure. It's freezing and I grab blankets from upstairs and pull them around Josh, wrapping him up on the sofa with Baker and a cup of tea and some biscuits I bought earlier. He doesn't seem fazed by what happened earlier, but he is quiet. He is thinking about you, Harry.

I spend a while setting up the fire, trying and failing as bits of kindling don't light and damp logs snuff out the flames. I can feel Josh watching me from where he's perched on the sofa. He's too young to speak his mind, to sort his thoughts into something rational to say to me, so he just stays quiet, silent like his dad.

'I'm sorry,' I say to him, but I don't mean it. I just want him to know that I care, that I didn't want it to turn out this way.

The doorbell goes just as the logs collapse and squash the small flame I'd managed to start. I curse under my breath, but Josh hears me and whispers, 'You shouldn't say words like that.'

'No, you're right, I shouldn't, but I think this calls for it, don't you?' I reply, bitterly. I'm annoyed at him. He wandered off, didn't care that he'd left me alone in the dark. I thought we were in this together.

I know Tracey is at the door and she'll have bags of food and drink and she'll offer to help with the fire, and I'll let her, because it's over. The snow has already covered the car, and I didn't have any petrol anyway. Tracey has seen my face, in full view; she's seen Josh; soon she'll know our secret. The whole world will. What's the point in trying to run from your mistake? I'm your wife, in sickness and in health, that's what I promised.

There's a sense of relief in acceptance, in knowing that I've done all I can, and none of it was my fault—it was all yours—and I hope Josh blames you for the rest of his life when I can't help him anymore.

Tracey bustles through the door holding two full bags, which she insists she's fine to carry through to the kitchen. It throws me off for a moment, that this used to be her house where she lived with her family, and now she's alone in the guest house, just an onlooker on other people's memories in her beautiful cottage. It doesn't seem to faze her. She's happy that the cottage is full of life again. She brushes the snow off her jacket and starts unpacking the bags.

'Just a few bits, some milk, bread, jam.' She pauses. 'I didn't know if you were vegan or vegetarian or what's that other one where you can't eat fish?'

'I'm not, neither is Josh,' I reply.

'And Harry?' she asks.

Harry. 'Well, he isn't feeling too good actually, he's taking a lie down, so, he'll just have some bread and butter later probably, something plain.'

'Ah, bad stomach? I hope that doesn't ruin your holiday.' She laughs ruefully. 'I suppose it's already been ruined, what with this snowstorm and that fright you had with Josh.' She turns to me. 'Is he okay?'

I nod. 'Fine, it hasn't been ruined. We're just going to get cosy by the fire and watch a nice film, I think. Maybe go outside for a snowball fight,' I say, looking hopefully through the patio doors at the lawn covered in a fresh layer of powder-white snow.

'That sounds wonderful. It should clear up in a few days, and we'll be left with slush and ice.' She laughs again, a sharp snort which mimics her disappointment. She wants us to have a nice time, but she doesn't know that we won't. She has no idea what's coming. 'You can get back to enjoying yourself then, take a few trips to the caves, go to some of those cosy pubs I recommended.' She closes the fridge. 'There's a homemade steak and ale pie in there, quite rich, so maybe wait for Harry to feel a bit perkier.'

'Thank you for all of this.'

'Don't mention it, I always have too much food. I have a little storage room at the back of the guesthouse, as I run a little pie stall at a market a few towns over.' She smiles. 'They seem to go down well.' She shrugs. 'I'll let you get back to the little man and your film. I can help with the fire, if you want. I saw it had gone out and it's quite chilly in here, despite the heating. I assume the heating is working okay?'

'It's all fine, thank you, and I don't want to keep you.'

She laughs, and this time it's sincere. 'You're not keeping me. No one but the dog would know I was gone, for days, maybe weeks.' She zips up her coat and I follow her into the lounge where Josh is still sitting silently with Baker. He studies us as Tracey grins at him.

'Hey, Josh, I'm going to get that fire going for you, so you can get toasty and watch a film.'

He doesn't respond, but Tracey isn't looking for a reply. She just wants to help.

I glance out the window up the winding path towards the guesthouse. That 4x4 could cope in the snow. I bet it has a full tank of petrol. No one would know she was gone.

Chapter Twelve

seven months earlier

We've been planning the wedding, and while initially I thought January sounded cold and miserable, Harry took me to see the castle on a dull day and I couldn't imagine getting married anywhere else. It sits on top of a steep hill just south of Bristol, miles of hedgerows leading up to stone walls like crowds flocking to a festival within its high battlements.

Even the shaded gravel pathway leading up to the iron gates is beautiful, lined with oak trees and fields of bluebells. Thick clouds mask the turret and settle on the parapet, dark windows with the ghosts of the past brooding in the heavy morning mist. There was something so eerie about it, and the interior was equally haunting and mesmerising with a musty scent of cold walls and old wood.

Harry squeezed my hand and we agreed on the venue, making plans for each room: the small stone archway we'll stand under when we say our vows, the long table we'll lay a feast along for our guests, and at the top of a small passage, a huge private chamber where I'll get ready with Mum and Megan before the wedding, and where I'll sleep next to my husband for the first time. It's perfect.

Seeing the castle and planning our wedding day together convinced me that Felicity was just being spiteful, and all I had to do was wait a few weeks for her to send a message saying she was sorry. It sounded begrudging, and I knew Oscar and Harry were behind it, but as Harry asked Oscar to be his best man, it was just easier if we both got along. Harry never asked what Felicity and I spoke about, maybe he knew from Oscar, but I had a sense that he admired me for sticking up for our relationship when I thought it was in danger.

I didn't tell him what Felicity said about not knowing him, because jealousy—I know better than anyone—can make you cruel, but I don't know if it makes you bad. It's something I've had to toy with for the last five years, jealous of a life I never got to have, jealous of Josh for being so carefree and at ease with the life he does have. Jealousy can quickly transform into resentment, and then, of course, guilt.

I've been painting recently, and plan to contact some galleries to see if they'd be interested in hosting my collection. I've even commissioned a website so I can start trying to sell them, though I'm not sure if it'll go anywhere.

I have a bunch of contacts from Carly's gallery, and Mum is well connected in that world. I don't know why I didn't think about it sooner, taking the time for myself, and for my family.

I've started picking Josh up from school, hoping we'll bond, hoping he'll get excited when he sees me standing by the front gates with the other parents. I've taken him for ice cream and chips a few times as a treat and it's made me realise how little I know him, and how little he knows me. It feels odd to say you have nothing in common with your child, because do I expect him to paint, drink red wine, and read Stephen King novels with me? I feign enjoying videogames to amuse him, but he's starting to get wise to it. Still, I'm hoping through spending more time together we can find some common ground, or maybe we'll just sit together in silence, content with each other's company.

I'm waiting outside the school gates and the usual crowd starts to mill around. Some of them keeping to themselves, standing away from the entrance, on their phones, others flocking together and catching up on the day. I remain alone with my Kindle, propped against the black-chipped railing, avoiding the smiles of other parents.

'What are you reading?' a voice says. I look up and a man is opposite me, half sat on a low brick wall clutching his phone.

'*Verity*,' I reply.

'I'm Owen, Lucy's dad.'

'No,' I say, smiling, 'the book is called *Verity*.'

'Oh.' He laughs awkwardly, blushing.

'I'm Lea, Josh's mum.'

He nods slowly, raising the phone back up to his chest, but his eyes remain on my Kindle. He smiles, seemingly to himself, and I can't help but think he looks more out of place here than all the other parents. He has a neatly trimmed dark beard and bright blue eyes that sit behind large, wide tortoiseshell glasses. I haven't seen him around here before, maybe because, like me, he seems too young.

'What year is Lucy?'

'She's just started year 3. Josh?'

'He's in reception.'

'I'm sorry,' he says, putting away his phone and holding up his hands. He starts to back away, but he turns and composes himself. 'I know you.'

'Do you?' I ask.

He's flustered; his glasses slip on his nose and he pokes them back up, looking everywhere but at me. He takes a deep breath and then stares directly at me. He goes to speak, but pauses. 'From the gallery,' he sighs at last. 'You work at the gallery.'

'Oh, I used to, yes.'

'Your mum, she's a photographer.'

'She is.'

He nods, considering all this. 'Sorry if this is intrusive, I didn't mean to disturb you.'

'You didn't,' I say, as the school doors open and the shriek of delighted children and the slap of shoes across the playground sound as loudly as the after-school bell.

Owen points towards the gate. 'I better get going. Lucy hates it when I'm not right by the gate when she comes out.'

I laugh. 'Well, she's proud of you then. I'm the pariah parent, ushered to the back so as not to embarrass my five-going-on-fifteen son.'

'It was nice to meet you, Lea.'

'You too,' I call after him as he walks away towards the school gates. I continue reading. Josh is always the last one out as he stays to help tidy up after school. He says he enjoys tidying and it makes me laugh, but now I think about it, he is unusually organised for a child. He likes structure and routine, so much like Harry, and nothing like me.

When he rounds the corner, he's clutching a papier-mâché pineapple and he holds it up to me with a huge grin on his face. 'I finished this today.'

'That's very good,' I say, taking it from him. The leaves are made from frayed bits of paper, and he's coloured in small pieces of paper to look like the skin. It really is impressive for a child, and I wonder if he got my artistic talents after all.

'I wanted to make a carrot for Baker, but the teacher said no and we had to use balloons.'

'I think it's marvellous. Shall we have it for pudding with some yoghurt?'

He giggles, his whole face lighting up in the late afternoon sun. 'No, you can't eat it.' He laughs again, taking the pineapple from me and clutching it like I once held him in my arms.

We walk back to the car and once I've settled him in the car seat, I see Owen hand in hand with his daughter, walking her to the car. He really is quite handsome. He can't be much older than me, and we're kindred spirits in being young parents. *But it's not all that bad, is it, Josh?* I think, glancing back at him, the pineapple resting on his lap, the spikey paper leaves obscuring his face.

'Straight home tonight, I'm afraid. It's my turn to cook.'

'Spaghetti,' he screeches.

'Spaghetti it is.'

Harry won't be home for a while, so I suppose it was a little white lie that we had to come home straightaway, but I wanted a glass of wine and to sprawl out on the sofa with Josh entertained by his console, if just for a few hours. I don't see the harm in that.

'Got to be a little bit selfish, haven't we, Josh?' I say, pouring rosé into the glass as he swings his legs gleefully on one of the bar stools. He's deep into a Lego game; he won't have heard me. I lift him off the chair and he follows me through to the lounge, plonking himself on his small beanbag Harry got him for Christmas.

'I'm going to put some comfy clothes on, okay? Won't be two minutes.'

I head upstairs, checking if Harry's office door is open, like I do every day. It's locked, of course, like I expect it to be. He said he locked it as he didn't want the cleaner to see sensitive materials about the company, and I believe him, some days. Other days, I'm not sure, but I've been too wrapped up in the wedding, too consumed by my paintings and my progress with Josh to care anymore. But I still have to check, just in case.

I swing open the bedroom door and pull my pale pink joggers from the end of the bed, but something catches the corner of my eye. It reflects the early evening sun. It's leaning against the pillow on my side of the bed. It's my ID card from the gallery. I walk towards it slowly, trying to understand what it's doing there. Did it fall this morning, did it wriggle free from wherever it was hiding? My tongue is dry, the rosé bubbling on the edge, my stomach turning with a hollow hunger.

No, it's been placed there. I turn slowly on my heels and walk down the empty hallway. I tread carefully at first, and then with more purpose, suddenly throwing myself down the stairs and out the front door. The soles of my feet sting as I run barefoot across the gravel driveway and onto the street. I don't know what I expect to find, who I expect to find, but someone was in my house, someone did this to me.

I look up and down the road, but it's completely quiet, there's no one there. Even on the green opposite, the trees rustle in the breeze and a few birds beat their wings against overgrown shrubs, but it's empty.

'Mummy?' Josh appears in the doorway, still holding his console. He waves it and rubs his eyes. 'Mummy?' he repeats, concern lacing his small voice.

'I'm coming,' I call, but I can't stop pacing up and down the street. I can't tear myself away from the feeling that someone is there, hiding behind one of the trees or sitting along the road in a parked car, watching me. 'Get back in the house, now,' I shout.

I let it go before. I told the police everything I knew. Carly didn't think I had anything to do with accessing the gallery and defacing the paintings, she said that. But I didn't have an explanation, and it was my key card. Someone had to be blamed. I understand Carly had to fire me for the gallery's sake, otherwise she wouldn't have any clients; they were all furious, looking for the culprit, demanding that someone be held responsible. That was reasonable. But there's no reasoning with this: someone took it, someone framed me.

I turn back towards the house. Someone was in my home.

Chapter Thirteen

present

I wish she would be quiet, but there's not anyone around for miles, she said so. I made Josh wait in the kitchen with a cup of tea and biscuits. I didn't know I was going to do it, but I'm scared. I've had my whole life taken away from me, my husband, my home, my career, everything. I can't have them take Josh too.

It all goes back to the night of the engagement party.

I should have left with you, Harry. I should never have been alone and vulnerable like that.

'Where is the lady?' Josh asks, peering up from his mug, clutching a half-eaten biscuit.

'She had to leave,' I reply.

'She was a nice lady.'

'Yes, she was.'

I hold Tracey's keys in my hands. This is our ticket out

of here, Josh, we're going to escape the bad people and we'll go somewhere they'll never find us.

Josh hasn't asked about you for a few hours. I don't know what he must think, but I'll have to tell him soon. You're not coming.

I shove the keys into my pocket. 'I need to go and shower. Will you be okay here?'

'Yes.'

'You won't try and leave… Remember what's out there.'

'I won't.'

'And you won't go into the lounge, you mustn't,' I say.

He nods, reaching for another biscuit. I leave him in the kitchen, sitting at the dining table, Baker propped on the chair next to him like they're having a tea party. I need to dress my wound before I can do anything; the moisture from the cut has dried and crusted around the sleeve of my jumper, and the damp heat has passed but it's been replaced by a dull ache that reverberates up my shoulder.

Sitting on the side of the bath with the shower on, I slowly peel back my cardigan and gag at the sight of it. Thick yellow liquid seeps from the edges of the rags, sealing them together, and in the centre, a deep red like a bloodshot eye looks up at me.

I almost scream at the smell and pain as I slowly unfurl the bandages, one strand at a time. The cut has expanded; wide scarlet lines wind up my pale skin, and my wrist is almost double its normal size, obscuring the entrance to the wound. I don't have much time. I need these medicines to work, but will they be strong enough?

The steam from the shower irritates the wound further and I can't bear to wash it. I can only dab it lightly with a clean towel, wincing, my teeth grinding with every touch.

'Fuck!' I yell, tossing the towel onto the floor. I carefully apply the solution and reapply bandages. The woman in the pharmacy thought I needed them because I'd been abused. I suppose I have, in a way.

Once I've managed to pull my clothes back on, I decide to leave the cardigan; the sleeve is moist and it's starting to smell rotten and acidic. There will be fresh clothes at Tracey's, maybe even some things for Josh. We can stock up Tracey's car with food and drink, plenty of blankets and warm clothes for wherever we're going. Despite the pain in my arm, I feel somewhat excited about my and Josh's future.

I turn off the shower and go back downstairs, glancing out at the steady fall of snow as I pass bedroom window. It's threatening our plans slightly, but like Tracey said, what comes after snow is a lot worse, ice and road closures, and we can't afford that.

Josh is still sat at the dining table, whispering something to Baker.

'What are you both talking about?' I ask, taking a glass from the cabinet. I do my best to fill it with water, but the skin around my wound has tightened and restricts my movement, the dull ache now a sharp sting.

He ignores me, and instead asks, 'Are you okay?'

'Just my arm, nothing to worry about,' I reply.

I lean on the counter with the bandages around my arm in full view. I don't try and hide them.

'What happened to your arm?' he asks, pointing at it.

'Just a little accident, but I'm feeling a lot better.' I swallow another glass of water with a few tablets, gasping for breath. 'We're going to go on another trip today,' I say.

'To see Daddy?'

'No, not back to Bristol, we're going to go somewhere a lot further, maybe to Scotland.'

'I don't want to go to Scotland,' he says, slamming Baker onto the table. 'I want to go home.' His voice catches, a tired, confused anger creeping into each syllable. He spits slightly at the end, like he's about to scream or cry.

'We can't go home. Home doesn't exist anymore.' It's the firmest I've been with him, but that's only fair, isn't it? I can't continue to speak to him like a child because he needs to be more than that now. 'I need you to be brave,' I say.

'I am brave.'

'The bravest,' I agree. I'm distracted by the snow outside, masking the entire garden like someone has smeared white paint across a canvas. How much time do I have? I can't turn on my phone, they could track me, but … I look up the hallway. I have another phone. I open the kitchen cupboard where I placed Tracey's bag and start rummaging through it, then tip the entire contents onto the kitchen counter out of panic and frustration and excitement. The pain in my arm starts to subside a little and I almost allow myself to feel hopeful.

The bag is full of hand sanitiser, pocket tissues, and

scrunched-up bits of paper. Among the tat is a slim leather purse and a phone.

It's locked—surprising for someone Tracey's age, but I guess you can never really be too careful. The purse contains fifty quid in cash, which I imagine you need more of in the countryside, unlike in Bristol. I put the money back. I could probably use contactless on the cards a few times locally, before Tracey reports what happened, and the police get involved.

'Wait here, Josh, have some more biscuits,' I say, closing the kitchen door. I stand for a moment in the hallway looking down at the lit screen of Tracey's phone. A picture of her in a bright pink top, standing in front of a white rose bush, looks back. At her feet is her German shepherd and on either side four men, about my age, who I can only imagine are her sons.

It's sad that no one would know for days if she was missing, that her sons don't call her every day or stop by to see how she is. I imagine her life is lonely, making pies in silence, with market days or people staying in her old home as her only interaction throughout the week. Maybe she talks to her dog like Josh speaks to Baker.

I don't know what to do about the dog, I'm worried it might attack me, it might sense what I've done to Tracey, and I won't be able to get any of the things I need. You always wanted a dog, something neat and tidy like our lives, a whippet maybe or a Doberman, but I never liked them, and they never liked me. Your parents own a brown Labrador, and I hate the smell and slobber, the way dog owners coo over their pets like children. As I open the door, I don't imagine that Tracey is like that; I think her dog is loyal and obedient, that he sits at her feet while she cooks and she speaks to him softly and he nuzzles into her on the sofa while they watch TV.

'Hello,' I say, closing the door.

Tracey doesn't respond. She can't, I've shoved a cushion cover into her mouth to stop her screaming and upsetting Josh. She's clearly tried to move, but I've tied her hands with some rope I found in the garden shed whilst I was getting wood for the fire. The knife I threatened her with sits on the small teak drinks cabinet behind the sofa, and I hope I won't have to use it again.

'I'm going to remove this,' I say, tugging gently on the cushion cover. 'But I need you to stay quiet, otherwise I will have to use that.' I nod towards the knife. Tracey's thick curls are stuck to her damp forehead as she squirms, tears rolling down her full cheeks. She looks older now, sat on the sofa, her face glistening in the heat of the fire. I want this to be over quickly, but I know if I explained to Tracey why I was here without you, if I asked for her help, if I was honest, she would run.

I pull the cushion cover out of her mouth and her jaw snaps shut and she takes quick breaths, relief flooding her blotchy, tear-stained face.

'Why?' she gasps.

'I can't tell you why,' I reply, crouching in front of her. 'But I don't want to be doing this to you, and, like I said, you'll be fine, completely fine. I just need your car.'

'Bully,' she whispers.

'Is that your dog?'

She nods, biting her lip as snot bubbles around her nostrils and silent tears pour down her face. She doesn't understand.

'You can go back to him soon, I promise.'

'He needs his medicine.' She sniffs. 'He's diabetic.'

'You can give him his medicine, just tell me the password to your phone.' I hold it up to show her, and the picture of her children must be too much as she starts wailing.

'Shh,' I plead. 'I really don't want you to upset Josh, please.'

She doesn't stop. She shakes her head and her whole expression changes. She glares at me, fresh angry tears clinging to the wrinkles around her eyes, and for a moment it's like she's frozen, captured in a photograph that I could see hanging on the gallery walls.

'Lucas,' she spits, vehemently. 'The password is Lucas.'

'Thank you,' I say, rising. I sit on the sofa opposite her and type in the password. 'Is Lucas your son?' I ask.

'Grandson,' she whispers.

I nod. 'I am sorry, Tracey, I didn't mean for this to happen to you.'

'Please tell me why,' she begs.

I stare at her. 'When I leave, you'll call the police, that's why I can't tell you.'

'If you tell me, I could help you. Are you'—she pauses—'running from someone?' I look at her. 'You are,' she says.

'Is it Harry? Did he do something to you?' It's the closest I've ever been to crying, to hear another person ask me that, to hear, despite everything, the compassion in their voice. I nod. 'Oh Lea, I can help you, I know people, and a safe place you can go.'

'There is nowhere safe for me.'

'Yes, there is, they can protect you and Josh. You don't have to do this.' She relaxes. The realisation of why I'm running is a comfort to her; she wants to help me. 'You must feel so desperate, so terribly frightened, I understand now, and I would do the same, I would do anything to protect them.' I look down at the image of Tracey and her children.

'I'm sorry, Tracey,' I say, leaning forward and grabbing the cushion cover.

'No,' she cries, repeatedly, but I force her head back and shove it into her mouth. I leave quickly. I can't bear to see the panic and betrayal in her eyes anymore.

When I go back into the kitchen, Josh has moved to the floor, sitting cross-legged with his back against the kitchen island. He's staring out at the garden, not like a child who wants to play in the snow, but like he's fed up with it, bored almost. He sighs, his small head hitting the counter softly as he throws it back to look up at me.

'It's still snowing,' he says, simply.

The snow causes problems, but I don't believe Tracey when she says the roads will be blocked. I shake my head, lowering myself into one of the dining room chairs. I open the phone again, this time opening a new tab and typing your name. There you are, front page of the BBC website. I throw the phone onto the table and scream, so loudly that Josh scrambles across the tiles and starts to cry.

'I'm sorry,' I say, rushing towards him, but he backs further away until he's huddling in the corner whimpering. I rush back to the phone. It's too soon; we need more time. I look out at the relentless snow. We must leave now.

'The bad people are coming, Josh. We have to go.'

He starts to cry and I don't know how to comfort him. There's only one person who can help us now, one person that I trust, who understands what I've been through. I grab the phone and dial his number. He picks up on the second ring, sounding breathless and confused.

'Owen,' I whisper. 'It's me.'

Chapter Fourteen

six months earlier

Harry convinced me not to go to the police about the ID card, and we've spent the last month arguing about it, until too much time has lapsed, and the doubt has set in. It could have fallen out of my bag. Or, like Harry says, it might have been in his jacket pocket all along; maybe he saw it drop from my bag and he swooped and picked it up and forgot about it. Maybe.

It's raised more questions, though. If my keycard was used to deface the gallery, if it was the reason I was fired, then who used it and why? Harry doesn't think it was targeted at me, but at Carly. He never liked her, called her fake and rolled his eyes whenever he had to attend one of my work events and was stuck in conversation with her. He would say to me, after we'd left, that she was capable of evil. I never asked him what that meant, I just laughed, shrugging it off as an exaggeration. She was just someone who rubbed him up the wrong way, that was all.

Capable of evil. I haven't spoken to Carly since I left, and the police never got to the bottom of it. Harry said over dinner one night, when Josh was in bed, that Carly was jealous of me, that it was plain to see. I'm talented, young, and—worse—threatening to her career. Her boss had been due to come to see the gallery and he took an instant shine to me, calling me extremely bright and gifted when we all went out to lunch that day. I hadn't thought about Carly before that moment, but now… Did she want me gone? It's so extreme, I told Harry, that anyone would go to those lengths, when she could simply fire me. What had Harry said? That it's not that easy to fire anyone anymore, unless they do something *really* bad.

Harry must be used to firing people, or he has people who do that for him. I could ask him about it, but I don't think I want to hear about that side of him, about the things people have done at his company to warrant being fired. *Something really bad.*

Harry showed me the security footage of the day I found the ID card, and he's right, no one came to or went from the house that day. I imagined someone slowly opening the side gate and tiptoeing past me whilst I was painting at the bottom of the garden with my headphones on. Gliding their hand over the kitchen surface, making their way upstairs and leaning over our bed, planting the keycard like a trophy on my pillow. In my head it's always Felicity, her pink manicured nails on my furniture, her perfume settling on Harry's cushion, but that's where it remains, all in my head.

When I arrive at the school to pick Josh up, I settle into my usual spot, smiling politely and saying whispered hellos to the parents waiting by the gate. I flick open my Kindle just as Owen arrives, looking flustered.

He smiles as I wave at him. 'Phew, I thought I was late. I just came from work,' he says, breathlessly.

'Did you run here?' I ask, dryly.

He smiles between panting. 'I don't think I could.'

'Do you work locally?'

He shakes his head. 'No, Lucy's mum and I split a few years back. I work by King Street in tech, all the boring IT stuff, and live in Bedminster. Do you work locally? You left the gallery, right?'

'If painting in my back garden counts as working, then yes, I live in Redland.'

'Oh, you're an artist too, like your mum,' he says, but he doesn't seem surprised. 'What medium?'

'Watercolour mainly, sometimes acrylic.'

'Maybe your paintings will be up in that gallery one day.'

'Maybe.'

'I'd like to work from home, get out of the city and find a cottage somewhere.' He shrugs. 'One day. Are you going to the summer fair? I hate those things, but it's important to Lucy I go.'

'I hate them too, but like you said, it's important to go.'

He shuffles awkwardly on the spot. 'Assume you'll be there with your husband?'

'I'm not married,' I blurt, and he steps closer. Is he interested in me? I can't tell. I used to be able to tell, but when was the last time I went out and met people? When was the last time I flirted?

'Maybe I'll see you there then? We could get a weak coffee and a shitty homemade cupcake with too much icing.'

I smile. I'd like that, but I should tell him about Harry. 'I'd love to, but—'

'Mummy!' I'm interrupted by Josh, who wraps his arms around one of my legs, looking up at Owen suspiciously.

'We better get going,' I say, ruffling Josh's hair.

'Of course, I'll see you around.'

I smile and Josh slips his hand through mine, leading me away towards the car. When we get home, I call Harry, feeling slightly guilty about my conversation with Owen. But maybe it's not the conversation that I feel guilty about, but the feeling I got, not about Owen of course, but the flattery. I used to get a lot of attention from men. I suppose I still do when Megan and I go out, or even when I notice Harry's colleagues staring at me at work functions.

I look in the mirror in the hallway. I'm old beyond my age—that's what Josh has done to me—but I'm beautiful, a strange thing for a woman to admit perhaps, but it's true. I have long slender legs and toned arms, sharp blue eyes, full lips, and glossy blonde hair. I never thought the school gates would be a place to meet people. I smile, thinking about Owen. I don't think he thought it was, either.

Harry doesn't pick up, so I leave a message, asking if he fancies getting takeaway for dinner. Josh squeals, demanding pizza, and I laugh, hoping Harry will smile when he hears this, that he'll come home early, to be with his family.

When it gets to 6pm, I send Harry a message asking what time he'll be home, so I can order the pizza for when he gets here, but he doesn't reply. He must be busy in meetings. It's not unusual for him to work late from time to time.

By 7pm, I order the pizza anyway. It's nearly Josh's bedtime and he starts complaining. Tired and hungry, he keeps asking for Harry, and the more he does, the shorter my text messages to Harry become. *When are you home? Can you respond now? You'll miss Josh before bed.*

When it gets to 9pm, Josh and I have shared a medium pepperoni pizza and a side of garlic bread and played through a level of Minecraft Dungeons. I put him to bed, but he doesn't ask for Harry when I try to kiss him goodnight; instead he turns over and sighs, a disappointed, angry sigh.

I go to call Harry again but start doubting myself. He must have a work thing I've forgotten about, a dinner with clients or an impromptu meeting with his team in the US. Instead, I decide to go to bed. Whatever the reason he's late home, he'll have had drinks, only a few, but enough that he'll be tired and a conversation with him would be pointless.

I must have dozed off reading. When I wake up it's dark outside and the hall light is still on, but Harry's side of the bed is empty.

I check my phone: 4am.

He must have stayed at a hotel in town, but that's rare; he's only ever done that once, years ago. Has he gone away? I check the shared calendar on our phone, which is full of his evening and weekend meetings and events, appointments, and Josh's activities. The calendar is empty for yesterday and today.

I try calling him again, but this time it goes straight to answerphone. I don't leave a message; instead I suppress the panic rising in my stomach and throw back the sheets.

I walk in my pyjamas through the empty house, desperately trying to think logically about where Harry could be, but out of all the possibilities, I keep fixating on one troubling thought: he's not here with me.

When I wake up, Josh is standing over me holding the rabbit Harry got him. I blink into the early morning sun coming through the lounge shutters.

'Why are you sleeping here? Where's Daddy?'

It takes me a moment to get my bearings, but Josh's voice rises with urgency.

'Where's Daddy?' he repeats.

'I don't know,' I snap at him. He starts to cry, loud, angry tears, grasping the rabbit's arm and smacking him against the arm of the sofa. I reach forward to hug him, but he jolts away. 'Daddy's on a business trip, but he's going to bring you back something nice—he told me how sorry he was he couldn't have pizza with us last night, but said we'll go for a nice dinner this weekend instead, maybe that chicken place you like—would you like that?' He nods, the tears subsiding as he climbs onto my lap. I stare out the window, checking my phone, but there are no messages or missed calls from Harry. 'Let's go and get some breakfast,' I say, lifting him off my lap.

Josh runs down the hallway into the kitchen and I follow him slowly. I make him a bowl of cereal and shut the patio door, stepping out into the morning sunshine to call Oscar.

'Lea?' he says. He's already on the move. I can hear the rumble of traffic and the breathlessness of his pace, the distant click of his shoe heels on pavement.

'Do you know where Harry is?'

He hesitates. 'He might already be at the office,' he says slowly.

'He didn't come home last night.'

'Didn't he?' He doesn't sound surprised. He knows something.

'Why didn't he?' I ask.

'Look, Lea, it's not really for me to say, I'm sorry.' He hangs up and I'm left standing in the garden of our house in shock, Josh pawing at the window for my attention, anger replacing any panic, any concern I felt last night and this morning.

I slide open the doors. 'Eat up, Josh, quickly. I'm going to drop you off early.'

'Why?'

'Just do it,' I say, standing over him. I pull the bowl away when he starts to slow down; I don't have the time or patience for him to deliberately irritate me like this.

Once he's dressed, I drop him at school, apologising for being early, but promising Josh would help with setting up the class for the day. Josh seems pleased about this, like he's special, and I can imagine him sitting at one of the tables with a smug smile as other kids walk in.

Is that what Harry will look like when I burst into the office? Will he be sitting at his desk looking smug? Will he— as with the ID card—tell me that he doesn't know what all the fuss is about?

When I arrive at the office block, the receptionist on the ground floor waves at me and calls, 'Good morning, Lea!'

I've seen her before at their summer and Christmas parties, but when I don't stop to talk, when I don't wave back, her face falls.

'He's not in,' she calls, standing up and leaning over the desk to catch my eye. 'If that's why you're here?' she says, more quietly.

I turn and stride back to the tall marble counter and place both forearms on top of it. 'Do you know where he is?' I ask, trying to sound like everything's okay.

She frowns. 'I'm so sorry,' she whispers. She sits back

down, fiddling with papers on her desk like she's trying to find an excuse. She's about my age, but she makes me feel old as I stand over her. I wonder if I make her feel young.

'Where is he?' I repeat. This time my tone is clipped and it makes her more flustered as she picks up an A4 leather diary from under a wodge of papers.

'He's out today, see,' she says, pointing at the date. It just says 'Harry OOO', but nothing else.

'Where?'

'I don't know,' she says, putting the diary back on her desk.

'I'm going up. I need to speak to Oscar,' I say, walking towards the lifts.

'Oh, okay. I can call him, telling him you're coming up? He might be in a meeting.'

'No need,' I say, pressing the elevator button. 'I can wait if he is.'

She disappears behind the desk, and I hear the click of a phone. She's calling Oscar anyway. Of course she is. She's loyal to them both. I wonder if she knows their secrets.

When the lift doors open onto the empty open-plan office, Oscar is already standing there expectantly.

'What's going on?' I say, coolly.

'He isn't here, Lea,' he replies, placing his hands in his pockets. 'I think you should leave. Whatever is going on is between you and Harry.'

'Do you know where he is?' I ask, craning my neck to see Harry's glass office at the back of the room. It's empty. He shakes his head. 'But you know something?'

'Like I said, Lea, I don't want to get involved.'

'He isn't asking you to lie for him, then?'

He smiles at this. 'It isn't what you think.'

'So you do know where he is?'

'You should speak to him when he gets home, but right now I have a business to run and I need you to step out.'

I nod, slowly, then push past him. He goes to stop me, but his hands fall to his side. He doesn't want to cause a scene. The lift doors slide open and a few people step out clutching coffees and laughing. I walk away from the chatter and towards Harry's office. I close the door behind me, but everyone can see through anyway. I wave and smile, and a few people hold up a hand in a half-wave, maybe unsure who I am, and what I'm doing here.

I sit at Harry's desk and imagine him about to start the day. It's characteristically tidy, with a slim silver MacBook on a walnut desk, and a green lamp. There's a tray of paperwork to the right above a drawer. I sift through it, but it just looks like client documents. I glance out of the door self-consciously and notice a few people looking at me. I sit back. What am I doing? I run my hands through my hair, spotting Oscar whispering to another man in a navy suit. He's carrying a briefcase and Oscar ushers him into one of the meeting rooms.

It isn't what you think.

What does that even mean? That I think he's having an affair? I've thought it before, haven't I? Since Harry and I got engaged it's been nothing but secrets and lies, but I'm done with it.

I pull open the drawer and rifle through more thick ledgers and notepads crammed with numbers and meeting notes. Then I pause. Tucked away at the back, in a little plastic pot, is a small brass key.

I glance around the room looking for something it could open but there's nothing.

Could it be for his gym locker? A spare key to the office? It isn't for the car, or the front or garage door.

Oh.

I close my hand around the key.

Could it open his office?

I'm standing in front of the locked office door at home. Harry wasn't in when I arrived back, and he still hasn't answered my calls or messages.

I passed Oscar on my way out of the office, but said nothing. Whatever Harry is involved in, Oscar knows, and he won't tell me despite my worries. A part of me hopes that Harry will arrive home, all apologies, with an explanation that makes me hate that I ever doubted him, but I know that won't happen. Something is wrong.

I slide the key in the lock and twist it. The door gives with a creak, echoing off the walnut floorboards. I haven't been in here for a while, but I remember painting it for Harry when we moved in, a deep forest green. I found beautiful antique furniture, a mahogany desk and dark oak drinks cabinet. I wanted him to have a place he could retreat from the world, to have a moment to himself. I didn't expect it to become somewhere he shut me out, where he locked away his secrets.

It's smaller than I remember and there's a musty smell like the curtains haven't been opened for weeks. I throw them back and dust flies into the stale air. It's like he's been gone for ages.

Like his office at work, the space is sparse, except from a half-finished bottle of whisky and a dirty glass sitting in the middle of his desk. I almost wonder if he's cleared the place out … if he's left us. I walk around the desk and start pulling open drawers and find stacks of papers, seemingly work-related.

The bottom drawer is different. It contains photographs of our family, a few drawings from Josh and some of my own, including a sketch I did of him one night on holiday in the Peak District years ago. This is his personal drawer. I start pulling out anniversary cards that he's kept over the years and certificates and silly awards that Josh won at school.

Maybe he is telling the truth, that his office contains sensitive materials that he must keep locked away, just in case. That he can't share as much with me anymore. What if there is some reasonable explanation to all this and I'm just overthinking everything?

I go to put his things back. I shouldn't have come in here, shouldn't have invaded Harry's privacy. I glance at the sketch of him, the way I've drawn him against the rolling backdrop overlooking the sheer, jagged landscape.

That was the holiday I fell in love with him. I've drawn him in soft pencil, light, uncomplicated strokes to mirror how I felt about him. How would I paint him now? How do I see our relationship? An anger sears me as I grab a pen from the top drawer and run my hand down the length of his face, leaving a thick, black line. I drop the pen to the floor and wriggle away from the picture.

That's how I see you, Harry, two different people.

I stuff the picture between Josh's paintings, hoping Harry will never see it. Or hoping he will, to finally give me the courage to confront the part of him I don't like. What about the parts of me he doesn't like? What about the parts I've never shown him?

I place all the papers in a stack and, as I lower them back into the drawer, I notice a small white card tucked under the edge. I pluck it out and read 'Hopkins Solicitors'. Turning it over, I realise it's a business card. It has a thin blue edge and in black letters at the top it says, 'Travis Hopkins, solicitor' along with contact details and a London address. I place everything back, with the business card on top, and close the drawer slowly.

I rise, looking out of the window at the empty street, feeling like something bad is closing in.

Chapter Fifteen

present

I brace as I open the door, whips of icy wind lashing at me as snow pinches my exposed cheeks. I locked Josh in the master bedroom, I hated doing that, but I'm worried about what's coming. Something worse than the storm outside. I can't leave him alone and vulnerable, whispering to Baker and asking where you are, Harry.

Tracey is still in the lounge; I gave her water and a ham and cheese sandwich from the food she brought over. She made a comment about trusting people and I felt for her in that moment. I too have relied on people who have abused my trust and it all led here, to me doing irreparable damage to a woman just so I may live. I'll never be able to thank her enough, but maybe once all of this is over, I'll try.

As I close the door, I can't help but think we may be the last people to live in this house. That afterwards, when we've left, it'll become some haunted tourist attraction—a place where teenagers slow in their cars and try to spot it through the thick trees at the end of the overgrown lane, suddenly speeding up when they see a figure standing in the empty upstairs bedroom. Josh and I will become ghosts, vanishing into the waves of white snow.

I make my way across the driveway, tightening the collar of my coat as I struggle to see in front of me, but I place a foot at a time, slowly, until my trousers get caught on something, I look down and just visible through the sheet of snow is the fountain, its chipped stone covered in white and the woman in the centre now dripping in blue icicles from where water once touched her features.

I trudge on, fresh snow crunching under my thin leather boots. I don't remember the last time I saw snow this relentless, this vicious in its quest to smother the land, like something biblical, otherworldly, unnatural.

The path blends into the cluster of trees that frame the entrance to the house. The gate is lost behind a screen of ash-white, and when I glance back, the house is but a spectral mirage, so faint that I can see only traces of the outline, like someone started painting it but didn't finish.

The path takes me longer than I thought it would and when I reach Tracey's gate, I can already hear her dog barking furiously behind the front door. To the side of the house is Tracey's red truck, but as I tread closer, flickers of red disappear before my eyes and the thick black raised tyres give in to the hunger of the storm, drowned in a swell of bright white.

'Fuck,' I whisper into the cries of the bitter wind.

I climb into the car anyway, snow cascading from the door as I pry open the driver's side. Starting the engine, I'm hopeful as it roars to life in an instant, grumbling at the anticipation of the journey ahead.

I rub my gloved hands over the steering wheel, whispering to the car, 'We've got a plan, my friend.'

I move the gearstick and ease my foot onto the gas, but it doesn't move. It spits angrily, a spew of muddy, grey snow churns through the wheels and there's a loud, hostile clang and the engine collapses. The windscreen wipers thrash piles of snow, scraping against a layer of ice, then freeze mid-swipe, as if to say to me, *Haven't we tried hard enough?*

I try the engine for a second time and it sputters back to life, moaning at the thought of having to try again. But the snow is just too much right now. We must admit defeat.

Owen said I have time, and he's given me the address of a flat in Liverpool owned by a friend who's currently out of the country. That's where he'll post our passports and send money. I just need to get there.

It was risky to call Owen, stupid even, but a last resort after what I'd seen on the news. He said he'd book a flight for tomorrow evening, but after that, it was over. They'd find me. He's put himself in danger too, but that's what love does, makes you behave irrationally, desperately.

I have until tomorrow night and Liverpool is less than two hours away. There's still time.

My eyelids feel clammy and warm despite the cold. I yank at my collar, trying to release some of the heat around my neck, and take a deep breath to ease my tight chest. The dog is still barking, a deep howling that's turned into a more desperate, painful shriek.

I lied to Tracey. She can't go home just yet, and her dog has become a problem. I think briefly about making the walk back to the house to ask her for instructions on how to give Bully his medicine, but my throat is dry and raspy, my legs feel heavy and my head pounds with every beat of snow against the windshield. I need to lie down for a bit. I haven't slept properly since we've been here. It's only adrenaline and the need to keep Josh safe that are keeping me awake.

But we'll make it. We have a plan now.

I open the car door and head back into the thrashing winds towards Tracey's guesthouse. I place a hand on the flaking wooden door, listening to the dog growl on the other side. He senses danger. I leave the palm of my hand there for a moment longer. 'I'm not danger,' I whisper.

He barks louder as a response, snarling, his paws scrabbling against the other side. I can't go in there; I can't risk him attacking me. I edge around the side of the house; Tracey doesn't have a lock on her side gate. It's propped open with a plant pot, leaving her garden completely exposed. She trusts her neighbours, her community. Her garden is small, but I imagine, beneath the turbulent snow, it's beautiful. Bushes shrug off powdery layers, flashing deep green leaves beneath.

I stumble on what I think is a patio, or decking, a firmness beneath the snow that makes it easier to navigate to the back of the house. Clutching Tracey's keys, I rattle through them, my woolly gloves making it difficult to separate each one.

I try a few keys, then Bully flies into the patio door, barking, teeth bared, hair on end, tail stiff. I realise now why Tracey feels safe. He growls, a low, threatening growl that frightens me. I try smiling and make calming noises, hoping his tail will start wagging and his tongue will loll out and he'll smile at me, but he doesn't. He throws himself at the glass patio door and I almost stumble back and trip.

I need to get in there. Tracey has money, medicine, clean clothes, a suitcase for us to pack everything we need to escape. Owen gave me strict instructions to pack what we needed, and he would book a flight, he didn't tell me where, so I don't know what to pack. We couldn't speak for long, and I worry that they might find him, go through his phone, see the unknown number—Tracey's number—and find me.

I step back into the wisps of snow as the wind starts to settle, the high-pitched whistle falling to a low hum. I follow my footsteps back around the side of the guesthouse, stopping at the gate where a shovel is propped up against the side of the house. I slide the plant pot through the thick snow until it hits the brick edge. I try and force the gate shut, but it catches on piles of snow, so I grab the shovel and thrust it into the path of snow, scooping, the agony of my forearm pressing against my chest. I turn and retch into the flowerbed, a mucous green running over pure white.

I have to keep going; I'm so close now. I throw the

weight of my body into the gate until I'm confident the gap is only big enough for me to slot through. I go to the front of the house and clear snow off the doorbell, pressing it with a gloved finger. Bully howls, nails on floorboards, as he charges towards the front door. He's quick. My footsteps are already starting to fill with more snow. I won't have much time.

I pull a glove from my hand and open the letter box. Bully is so close now, his teeth brushing the other side, the warmth of his spit inches from me. I push the glove into the letter box and Bully's teeth are already clamped down on the fingers, yanking it through the thick bristles. I quickly step away, moving to the side of the house and down the path, through the gap in the gate, until I'm by the patio door again. I look through, but I can't see him. I fight through the keys, trying and failing at a first attempt to make one fit. The second key glides in and I yank open the patio door. Silence. I move quickly. The side gate is only a few metres away. Bully screeches, claws thundering.

I flinch, expecting a jaw to take hold of my calf, sharp teeth to sink into my skin, but I'm through the gate, turning and throwing myself at it until it's shut. Bully comes tearing through the patio door and doesn't stop. His teeth career into the splintered wood and he whines, a deafening squeal, as the weight of him pressing against the gate throws me backwards onto the snowy ground. With both legs I thrash at the gate as snow tickles my face, the wind pulling at my hair, dried sick sticking to the corners of my mouth. The lock is rusty and frozen, but I wiggle it free and lock the gate as Bully gnaws at the planks.

I stagger to my feet, looking around for something, anything to distract him. The glove has been ripped apart and discarded, a flash of red threads by the patio door. I pick up a thick branch, shaking the snow from the bark, and I wave it at him, trying to get his attention.

'Bully, what do I have?' I shout. I throw the stick as far as I can, watching hopefully as it lands among the trees in the distance. He doesn't pay it any attention. I glance towards the front of the house. I could try and lock him out, but I'd need to get through the house to the back door without him knowing. The kitchen is at the back of the house, I saw it through the patio doors, and a small staircase led off it. Everything I need is just out of reach.

I lean against the side of the house, Bully snarling at me as sprinkles of snow land on us both. The wind has disappeared between the trees, and there's only the gentle rustle of leaves.

'It's over,' I whisper. 'Josh and Harry would have liked you. Harry wouldn't have called you Bully though; it would be something like Poirot, or Columbo…' I smile as Bully raises both paws and runs them down the gate. 'No, Josh would have called you Baker.'

I grip my bare hand around the shovel sitting to my right. The snow falls away as I use it to lift myself onto the raised plant bed. My forearm throbs, my throat full of bile and my face numb from the storm, but survival is an instinct. And I'm a survivor.

I raise the shovel into the air, screaming from the pain. With everything I have left, I bring it crashing down.

I sit for a moment in the snow, my legs aching from the cold, a dull pain in the bottom of my back.

I am not a cruel person, but as I sit, my face stained in Bully's blood, I do not know who I am. I let you define me for so long, I never stripped it all back before, to look at myself, the raw truth of who I am. Is this it? I didn't know I was capable of something so feral, so cruel.

But that's what Josh has done to me; he's lit this maternal instinct to keep him safe at all costs. I need to get into that house. I need the medicine and supplies to make it out of here.

I feel like I'm in a tunnel, and at the end there's you and Josh, and no matter what else is in the tunnel, I am blinkered, there's only our family, the light at the end. All the cruel things I've done will be worth it to get to the end, all the ugliness of the inside of that dark, damp tunnel will be rewarded.

I make my way back to the main cottage with two large plastic bags full of clothes, medicine, and a wodge of cash I found in Tracey's bedroom. My arm cries in pain, pins and needles working its way along my collar bone, pulling on a nerve in my neck. My pulse throbs in my throat, and my head feels like it'll explode. I took a handful of tablets at Tracey's to dull the pain, but it's taken on a new form; it feels like I've been injected with a serum and it's making its way through my body.

The snow relents, and the crunch amplifies as a new, icy layer forms, a quiet, piercing frost that feels even worse than the snowy wind.

When I get to the gate, heat surges through me, throwing me off balance, and when I look up, desperate to reach the house, the statue in the fountain turns to face me, shaking the snow from its blank expression, its hollow eyes, its smirk. Hands spout from flat stone and reach towards me.

I scream, dropping the bags, sweat dripping down my face.

I rub my eyes and see the statue is still upright, looking away towards the house, the same blank expression on its pearly grey face. I look down. My gloveless hand is covered in diluted blood.

What is happening to me?

I grab the bags and rush towards the house, not daring to look back at the fountain, but I can feel something touching my neck, just slightly, not the wind, not the snow, not a stray leave from the barren trees—a rough touch, like the fingertips of cold stone.

I throw open the door and collapse, Tracey's belongings spilling over the hallway floor. Josh is crying, wailing from upstairs, and I can hear stifled tears from Tracey. I want the noise to stop.

I hit the hardwood floor and curl up on the hallway rug, my eyes so heavy, my cheeks swollen and my limbs and joints aching mercilessly. Then, I fall asleep, or maybe I die?

Either way all I see is you, Harry.

We're together at our wedding and you're smiling at me and Josh is standing between us, beaming up at us.

We're finally a family.

Chapter Sixteen

five months earlier

I'm waiting for Megan in the pub on the corner of our road. She wanted to come round, but I need to speak freely.

Megan's late, as usual, and I'm nervous, thinking about how I'll explain this. The voicemail I left her that night after finding the lawyer's card was hysterical and I haven't spoken to her since. She called me back, sent me messages, and all I replied was 'It's okay now.' But it isn't.

I'm sitting in the back corner in the quiet section of the bar, sipping a gin and tonic. I didn't get our usual bottle of red, because I know Megan will be angry, a frustrated anger, because I've caused her to worry. I know she won't believe me. She'll roll her eyes and tell me Harry is lying.

Megan bursts through the doors, ordering a drink at the bar before she joins me. She doesn't smile, just twists on the spot as if looking for someone in the empty bar that she knows, her eyes gliding over me like I'm not there.

Her leather boots clip on the tiles as she slides onto the wooden chair in front of me. She takes a long sip of white wine and then leans back, finally looking at me, her features passive and unreadable.

'I'm sorry,' I whisper, 'for worrying you.'

She sighs, her lips relaxing as she replies, 'I always worry about you, Lea. I know you're going to tell me that it was just some silly misunderstanding, but'—she closes her eyes—'it's not about that.'

'Isn't it?'

She shakes her head. 'You've been unhappy for years, and…' she pauses, taking a deep breath, pressing her eyes closed like the next part will sting, '… I don't think getting married will fix that.'

'Oh,' I say, reaching forward and stabbing my straw into the melted ice cubes at the bottom of the glass.

She leans forward. 'You're not happy.'

'No, I am happy,' I say. 'And it *was* a misunderstanding. Harry came home that day and he told me everything.'

'Everything?'

'It's the business. It's in trouble,' I say, 'That's why I asked you to come here, because I didn't want Harry or Josh overhearing anything. To be honest, I shouldn't be telling you at all.'

'The business is in trouble? As in it's going under?'

I shake my head. 'No, there's a disgruntled ex-employee and they're causing trouble for the company.'

She doesn't expect this. 'What kind of trouble?'

'I don't know. I just know that it's bad,' I reply.

'So bad he left without saying a word to you? Not even a quick message to tell you everything was okay?'

'It wasn't like that.'

'No, of course it wasn't,' she says. 'Is that why he needed a lawyer?'

I shrug. 'That's what he said.'

'So, all that shit about his business partner telling you he wasn't getting involved? What did he say to you?'

'That it was between me and Harry,' I say.

'It doesn't sound like it's between you and Harry. It doesn't sound like it has anything to do with you. Well … if he's telling the truth.'

'I believe him. Why would he lie about that? He had to go to London to meet with some lawyers at the last minute and his phone died, so he just stayed in a hotel.'

She nods, unconvinced. The last month has been difficult. When Harry came home that night he was exhausted and frightened; something had shaken him, and he didn't need me to make it worse. He apologised over and over again when I confronted him about what I'd found, and it all seemed plausible, but I couldn't put what Oscar had said out of my mind. It was between me and Harry.

I shouldn't have gone into his office – it was an invasion of his privacy, an abuse of our trust – but he wasn't angry; he was mortified that I'd been forced into doing that.

'I wonder how personal it is with this ex-employee,' Megan says, finishing her drink.

'What do you mean?'

'Well, I wonder if Harry fired them without any grounds, you know, something like that,' she says, collecting her bag. 'If you say everything is okay now, just promise not to worry me like that again.' She rises. 'And think about whether you are really happy, Lea, because this wedding won't solve everything.'

She leaves me with an empty glass sitting alone in a bar thinking about the last month, the conversations with Harry, what Oscar had said when I barged into the office, the lawyer's business card, the night that Harry came home.

I wander back along the tree-lined streets towards home, glancing in at other people's houses, wondering if they have secrets too. Maybe Harry had fired someone and they were upset, but wouldn't that be a company problem, wouldn't Oscar be worried too? Wouldn't he tell me exactly what was going on? Or was it a lie? I open the front door and Harry is standing over the oven. The house smells of paprika and chorizo, and his face is submerged in a cloud of steam.

'You're home!' He grins at me.

I'm home. I walk slowly down the hallway towards him, Megan's voice playing like a soundtrack in my head. *I wonder if Harry fired them without any grounds, you know, something like that.*

'How's Megan?' he asks. 'You haven't seen her for a while. All's good?'

I nod, watching him smile blissfully at the meal he's

preparing, about to have dinner with his family. Josh sits at the dining table with his colouring pencils, the rabbit propped up next to him.

'Dinner's nearly ready.'

Maybe we'll open a bottle of red wine and listen to music. Maybe we'll go to bed after dinner and make love.

Maybe the something like that is nothing at all.

———————

Today is the day of the school fair, but Harry has already said he can't make it. I've seen Owen a few times at the school gates but he never brought up coffee again, never asked me out; he only ever spoke about Lucy and the places he liked to take her, what they were having for dinner that evening, books he read her at night.

He did ask me a few weeks ago how my painting was going, saying he'd love to see what I was working on, but I brushed it off, saying nothing was ready, which it isn't. I did tell him about Harry and he was surprised; there was a flutter of disappointment, but he smiled and shrugged it off. I could tell he still liked talking to me, even if it was for ten minutes every now and then at the school gates. I never saw his ex-wife pick Lucy up, but unless Owen was there that day, I kept my head down in my Kindle.

I'm wearing my favourite white summer maxi dress with dark blue flowers scattered around the hem. I hold Josh's hand as we walk through the school gates and into the crowd of stalls and fairground games set up in the car park.

'There's a cake stand in the field. Miss Winters said there would be,' Josh says. 'We can get one for Baker.'

'That sounds like a plan,' I say, swinging his arm.

He giggles. 'Then we'll get our face painted and find Jack so we can go on the bouncy castle.'

Jack is Josh's best friend at school, and it was a relief that he made friends with a child who has busy parents. There's no small talk at pickup or invite in for coffee and a natter when I go to collect Josh after playdates. I wonder if Jack's parents will be here, but I've never seen them at events like this. I wonder if other parents think the same about me.

I've had more time since I left my job, and although the past few months have had their up and downs, I'm getting married in five months; I'm at a school fair with my beautiful son; and I'm going to go home after this and sip wine and paint on a fresh canvas. For the first time in a long time, I feel content.

My stomach sinks, like an invisible anchor that knots itself around my throat and pulls. I see Owen through the crowd, sitting on a chair next to Lucy getting his face painted. For a second, I feel something I shouldn't.

'Face painting, Mummy,' Josh screams, yanking my hand.

'I thought you wanted cake?'

'Noooo.' He pulls at my arm. 'Cake after.'

He leads me over to the face painting stand. Owen is

laughing. Flecks of pink paint stain his beard, and his daughter squeals with delight as she leans across his thighs.

'It suits you,' I say, before he notices me.

He looks up at me, a pink and blue butterfly drawn across his face, his cheeks two wings, and glitter smeared across his eyebrows.

'Lea—'

'I want to be a rabbit like Baker,' Josh beams, taking the seat as Owen thanks the woman painting his face and gets up.

'That sounds like a better choice,' he says awkwardly, as Lucy grips his hand. She also has a butterfly painted across her small features, milky blonde hair framing the purple outline of its wings.

'Hi Lucy,' I say, holding up my hand in a small wave.

'Hello,' she replies, shyly.

'How are you?' Owen asks.

'I'm good. We're going to get cake after this, if you wanted to join us?'

He smiles, the tail of the butterfly skimming his lips. 'We would love that, wouldn't we, Lucy?'

'Yes,' she says, but she's looking at Josh. 'I like your bunny.'

'Baker,' Josh replies as the woman dabs his face with a sponge. 'His name is Baker.'

Owen smiles at the interaction. 'When Josh has had his face painted, we'll get cake,' he says.

'Chocolate cake?' Lucy asks, politely.

'No, carrot cake, rabbits like carrot,' Josh screams.

'Okay, Josh, we can get both,' I say, looking at Owen, 'and a coffee?'

Owen smiles, the wings of the butterfly folding into his dimples. He glances around. 'Is your partner here? I'd love to meet him.'

'He isn't here today; he has to work,' I say.

He nods slowly. 'Well, his loss is our gain.'

Josh finishes getting his face painted, as I stand chatting to Owen. I can feel him getting closer to me throughout the day. He buys Josh a slice of carrot cake and me a brownie and then we sit on a bench and watch Lucy, Josh, and Jack play on the bouncy castle.

We spoke about his love of film and museums, how he spent too much money on artwork and lived like a university student despite being twenty-eight. I said he seemed young for a dad and he nodded, saying that he and Lucy's mum had never been serious or in love, but they gave it a go for Lucy. They realised that she would be happier if they were happy themselves. So it was an amicable breakup; not a lot of people can say that.

As we drink our coffee, I laugh at the foam smeared on his pink lips, smudging the paint up his face like the Joker. He doesn't try and rub it away, just laughs back, and then goes into detail about the Joker and all the other DC comics, saying he collected too many of them as well.

It's a wonderful afternoon, and as I swallow the last dregs of coffee, I feel sad that our meetings will go back to ten minutes once a week by the school gates.

I haven't thought about my conversation with Megan all

day, until now, when it's time to leave and Owen hovers awkwardly in front of me, not sure whether to hug me or walk away. The time away from work has been good for me, giving me time to think about what's important. That shallow, insidious jealousy that I used to feel for my family, looking at them like they'd robbed me of my life—I no longer feel that anymore. In fact, I'm desperate to keep my life intact, to solidify it so it can't ever escape me. What I'm feeling here, with Owen, it's just the remains, the debris of that resentment..

'We better get going. We're going to cook Daddy a lovely meal, aren't we, Josh?'

Owen nods. 'Of course, have a wonderful evening and thanks for keeping us company today.' Then he whispers, 'I usually hate these things.'

'Me too,' I whisper back.

I walk away with Josh in tow, aware that Owen is watching me leave.

I strap Josh into his car seat and set off, noticing Owen in my rear-view mirror walking in the opposite direction. We can be friends, he and I, but that's where it stops. I love Harry, and Megan's wrong: I *am* happy.

Just as I turn onto Redland Road, I'm catapulted forward. There's a loud crunch and a screech of tyres as we start to spin; Josh shrieking behind me. My elbow snaps, something hard hits my cheek, and all I can taste is metal. For a moment, I think I'm flying, my hair loose and whipping my face. I close my eyes as a sharp pain tears through me.

When I try to open my eyes, all I see are large white dots and a bright, pale blue tinged with a grey filter. I'm dazed, blinking. I try to revive myself, realising where I am, a small croak from the backseat stirring me. I start scrabbling at the seat belt, but it's stuck.

'Josh,' I croak, my throat hoarse and dry. 'Are you okay?'

He doesn't respond. I twist, desperately trying to see him, but the stabbing pain in my elbow winds me.

Someone's knocking on my window. It's Owen. He's trying to open the door, but it's stuck, and glancing down I see the metal has caved in and is digging into my sides.

'Josh,' I shout, 'get Josh.'

He nods, disappearing out of view. I hear the back door open and Owen's calming voice, 'It's going to be okay, Josh. Are you hurt anywhere? Put your arms around my neck; there's a good boy.'

I start to squirm, my joints feeling slightly more intact, my neck loosening as I turn to see Owen carrying Josh around the car towards me. Another man is pulling on the car door, and it finally gives way. There's a low thud and it falls open. I think he'll help me, but Owen hands the man Josh and reaches forward. 'Are you okay?' he says, his hands running up and down my neck, along my arms, through my hair. He's checking for injuries, for blood, for signs that I'm not okay.

'I feel a bit dizzy... My elbow hurts.' I flinch as he touches it softly.

'We've called an ambulance,' he reassures me. 'Josh seems fine.'

'What happened?' I ask, as he helps me from the car.

'Someone went into the side of you, then drove off.'

Josh looks tiny sitting in the man's arms. 'Josh.' I reach forward with my good arm and stroke his cheek. 'Thank you,' I whisper to the man.

'I'll take him,' Owen says, and the man transfers Josh to his arms. Josh is quiet; he buries his head into Owen's neck and sobs, rubbing grey face paint onto Owen's white T-shirt.

'Are you all right?' the man asks.

I nod. 'I think so.'

'The police and ambulance will be here soon. I saw what happened,' he says, 'So I can give my statement.'

'Did you get the number plate?' I ask, cupping my elbow and turning back towards the car. It felt worse than the damage looks; there's a gaping dent on the driver's-side door, but the car is otherwise unmarked.

'No,' he says, 'I didn't, but it was like the car just didn't see you. In fact ...' he pauses '... it's almost like it sped up at the crossroads when you rounded the corner.'

'In a rush to get somewhere?' Owen says, stroking the back of Josh's head.

'What type of car was it?' I ask.

'Blue, small, it looked damaged when it drove off.'

The ambulance arrives first, and they look at Josh, then give him a little lollipop for being so brave. I show them my elbow but they aren't sure whether it's broken, so decide to take me to the hospital to get it checked and make sure I don't have a concussion. I try to call Harry whilst I'm in the ambulance but he doesn't pick up. I hang up as Owen returns with my things, just as the police arrive.

'Thank you,' I say. 'They want to take me into the hospital to get checked out.'

'I'll come with you,' he says. I can see the man speaking to the police over Owen's shoulder, and the police taking down details of what happened. 'They'll want to speak to you too,' he adds.

I nod. 'I just want to make sure Josh is okay first.'

'Of course. They're going to arrange for someone to pick up the car, and then you can sort it out on your insurance.'

The fogginess behind my eyes has lifted slightly, the beautiful late summer sun cleansing my face. Josh is sat between my legs in the back of the ambulance, sucking his lollipop and watching the police officers. The doors are wide open, but one of the paramedics leans forward to close them. I don't want to disappear into the darkness of the ambulance; I want to enjoy the heat on my face in the hazy sunshine.

Owen climbs in next to me and takes my hand, so naturally. 'I'll meet you there in my car.'

'You don't have to,' I say.

'I'll just worry otherwise,' he replies, looking down at Josh, 'about you both.'

'Where's Lucy?' I ask.

'Her mum picked her up. It's okay.'

'Okay, let's get you strapped in,' one of the paramedics says, as Owen rubs my hand, leaving us in the back of the ambulance. The doors close on his comforting smile.

Owen doesn't arrive at the hospital until half an hour later, with the butterfly paint now washed off his face, though pink glitter still sticks to his hairline and the top of his beard. They ask me to go for X-rays and I leave Josh with him; he has already been seen by a doctor, and has two more lollipops, one for him and one for Baker. He seems to like Owen, and Josh doesn't warm to many adults or— thinking about it—many children. He doesn't cry or stare after me when I walk away with one of the nurses; instead, he grins at Owen, and recounts one of his bedtime stories about dragons.

I try calling Harry again, and send him messages telling him not to worry, that we're at the hospital now getting a check-up, that everything is okay. The pain in my arm has eased slightly when I come out of X-rays and into the doctor's examination room. They're convinced it isn't broken or fractured, just badly bruised, and they expect it to swell up and hurt for a week or so. I blush slightly that it hurt so much at the time, but I've never broken anything, I've never experienced that pain.

The car accident hasn't shaken me like I thought it would, but there's an uneasiness that whoever hit my car is still out there somewhere. *It's almost like it sped up at the crossroads when you rounded the corner.*

Owen and Josh are still sitting in reception when I come out with my arm in a sling. Owen's face drops as he nudges Josh, who rushes to my side.

'Mummy, are you okay?' he whispers into my thigh, his little hands clutching my dress.

'Of course I am, sweetie, I'm absolutely fine.' I look up at Owen. 'Thank you for watching him.'

'Don't be silly, we had fun, didn't we, Josh?' I see now that Owen is holding Baker. Josh won't even let Harry or me near him; he resource-guards it like a feral dog. Owen hands it over and Josh snatches it from him, maybe unable to comprehend why he let someone else hold his beloved toy. Josh's face paint has melted a bit in the heat, and the pink cheeks are now grey, the white teeth smeared down his lips.

'I gave him some apple juice; I hope that's okay.'

'Of course, thank you again.'

'Is everything okay with the arm?' He nods towards the sling.

'Yes, just some light bruising, nothing to worry about.'

He smiles. 'Is Harry coming to get you?'

I check my phone again, but he hasn't seen my messages. He doesn't know.

'Apparently not, he's probably in meetings. He doesn't look at his phone much during the day. We'll get an Uber, no problem.'

'I'll take you home,' he says.

'No, honestly, you've helped enough.'

'I want to,' he says, seriously, his eyes locking on mine. I nod, following him, Josh still clutching my dress.

The car journey is silent, apart from the low hum of the radio. Josh falls asleep in the back; it's been a long day, what with the heat, the sugar, the accident. I look out of the window at the distant fields framed by colourful houses.

'Hopefully the police will get in touch soon and they'll find whoever did this,' he says, as he pulls up outside my house. Harry's car isn't on the driveway. No one is home.

Owen opens the door for me and helps me into the house, fussing over me, telling me repeatedly that it's no trouble. He lifts Josh, who is still sleeping, from the car, and carries him into the lounge, laying him on the sofa to nap for a while. I feel tired watching him. I want to curl up and nap alongside him.

I close the lounge door, feeling Owen standing behind me.

'I better get going,' he says, self-consciously. He's in my home, the home I share with Harry. He starts up the hallway.

'Do you want a drink? It's hot out.' I ask. There's an urgency about it, a desperation. I don't want him to leave.

'That would be nice,' he says, closing the front door. He follows me up the hallway. He's so close, his breath on my neck; there's a need for it, for him. Where is Harry? When Owen is here.

I take a glass from the cupboard and fill it with water in complete silence. Owen hovers next to me, words caught in his throat. I can feel him looking around the kitchen, trying to defuse the situation, but the tension is mounting, and as I turn his lips are already on mine. I kiss him back, and it's passionate, not how I expected; I thought it would be gentle and calm, like him. I thought it would be a kiss I would forget, a mistake before I'd even made it, but it isn't. It's real. It's living. It's going to lead to more. His hands are through my hair again and it reminds me of the way he looked at me after the crash, his gentle hands feeling me for injuries, the concern for me. He begins to drop them. They glide down my body to my hips and he holds me; he doesn't grab me, doesn't bring me to him, just holds me, and it makes me want him more.

My phone rings on the kitchen counter and Josh wakes up and starts to cry. We part, but we're suspended for a moment, before Josh screams for me.

I look at Owen, but his eyes are closed.

'I'm sorry,' he whispers, his hands dropping away from me. He turns quickly and leaves, closing the front door. My phone rings again, vibrating against the tiles. It's Harry.

'Hello,' I quiver.

He gasps. 'Lea, I'm at the hospital, they said you've been discharged.'

'I'm at home,' I whisper.

'I'm on my way. I'm so sorry,' he says, breathlessly. 'I've been in meetings all day, and I can't believe I missed this. Is Josh okay? Are you okay?'

'Yes.' I clear my throat. 'We're fine, just a bit shaken up.' I make my way down the hallway and open the lounge door. Josh is whimpering on the sofa, folded in a blanket, the rest of the face paint pressed into a dusty pink cushion. 'It's Daddy,' I say, putting the phone to his ear. I don't hear what Harry says, but Josh stops crying, says 'yes' and I take the phone back.

'I'll be home soon,' he says. 'I love you, Lea.'

He hangs up and I comfort Josh. 'How are you feeling?' I ask, but he squirms away. It's like he's heard Harry's voice and now I'm insignificant. His dad's on the way home to tell him how brave he is. The night will be about Josh, but Owen, he made it about me. He made me feel like we were a unit. I don't regret kissing him. I regret that he left so suddenly and that we were interrupted.

I wish he was coming home instead of Harry.

The thought sticks to my heart and I can't scrape it off; it just seeps deeper into my veins.

Should I tell Harry? Ten minutes later I hear his car pull up on the driveway, the slam of the door, the hurried rush of footsteps and a key in the lock. Josh has dozed off again, but he wakes at this.

'Daddy,' he says, springing to life, pawing at the side of the sofa to get down.

Harry appears in the lounge doorway. Josh rushes to him and he scoops him up. He doesn't say anything, just holds him, carrying him over to me. He sets Josh on his feet and holds his hand up to my sling.

'Lea.' He starts to cry, loud, uncontrollable tears that startle Josh. He has never seen his dad cry. He has never seen his mum cry. Does he understand adult tears? Do I?

'I'm okay; it's all right,' I say, reassuringly.

'I wasn't there,' he sobs. He falls to his knees and I step back, shocked. Josh drops to his knees too and edges closer to his dad. 'I wasn't there,' Harry repeats.

I squat next to him, trying to find him through the waves of tears. 'You're here now,' I say.

'I love you so much, Lea, if something happened to you, if—' He stops himself. 'I am so sorry. I don't deserve you; I never have.'

'Stop it, Harry, you're scaring Josh.'

'I'm sorry,' he pleads.

'It doesn't matter, me and Josh are fine. It doesn't matter,' I repeat.

He reaches forward and kisses me gently on the lips. We look at each other, our eyes loaded with over five years of love, resentment, boredom, forgiveness, secrets, and now tears. I've laid down a roadmap with Harry. I kiss him back. His salty tears touch my lips, his wet eyelashes skim my forehead. We move away from each other, turning to Josh, who is watching us intently. Harry sniffs, twisting away from me.

'I heard you were brave today,' he says to Josh.

'He was,' I agree.

'Of course you were. You're your mother's son.' He looks at me and smiles.

The police came the next day. Harry wanted to sit with me whilst I gave my statement, but I didn't want him to find out about Owen. I haven't told him about what happened, about Owen helping us, about the kiss.

I said it was a random man in the street, which isn't a lie,

I suppose, but I don't want him to know that I spent the day with Owen, that I left Josh with him in the hospital, that he drove us home, and he held me in our kitchen.

A few weeks have gone by, and the police haven't found the car that hit me. Harry has been getting increasingly agitated by it. I told him to drop it, and he eventually did, but I could tell he still think about it sometimes. I could hear him on the phone in the garden asking the police if they'd found anyone yet.

I haven't seen Owen since that day. He hasn't picked Lucy up from school, and I don't have his number. I wanted to see him so desperately in the days afterwards, but like my arm, I slowly started to heal, and I realised that what happened between Owen and me was a huge mistake, one that I can never let Harry find out about.

Still, a part of me hoped I'd see him at the school gates, that I'd look up from my Kindle and he'd be standing there smiling at me, and maybe we could be friends, because I miss seeing him. Maybe I could set him up with Megan; I think they'd get along. She'd find him funny and sweet— too sweet, she'd say at first—but then she never goes for nice guys, neither of us do.

I try to put Owen out of my mind by focusing again on planning the wedding, finalising the invitations, and I even found this wonderful holiday home in the Peak District, a little cottage with a log burner, country walks on the doorstep. We could go anywhere, Harry said, Mexico? Hawaii? Italy? I shook my head. I just wanted something simple, a honeymoon as a family somewhere with happy memories, somewhere we could visit on anniversaries and talk about our wedding and the days afterwards. Harry understood at first, but recently he's been pushing a honeymoon abroad.

I show him the cottage, just down the road from Bakewell and not far from the Monsal Trail, where we can go for winter walks and cosy drinks afterwards. He warms to the idea. I think he wants to see me happy. He's started noticing my distance, too. Or maybe it's not mine but ours? I've never seen him act like he did after the accident: he wasn't just attentive; he became obsessive, wanted to know where I was going, what I was doing, every day. I wondered if it was because he knew what had happened between Owen and me, if he'd spoken to the police without me knowing and they told him about his fiancée's statement and the man that helped her, the man that felt her for injuries, that accompanied her to the hospital, that dropped her home and kissed her in the kitchen.

'Who are you texting?' Harry asks, coming into the lounge, where I'm sprawled across the sofa. Josh is in bed, and I'm nursing a glass of red wine and watching an old *MasterChef* episode.

'Tracey. She owns the cottage in the Peak District. She's asked if we have any requirements. Do we?'

He shakes his head. Sinking into the sofa and picking up my feet, he places them on his lap and strokes my shin, watching the TV but lost in thought.

'Do you want to see pictures?'

'Of what?' he asks, in a daze.

'Of the cottage?'

He sighs, smiling at me, squeezing my foot. 'It'll be a surprise.'

'Don't you want to pick our honeymoon together?'

'Of course, I'm sorry, just tired,' he says, angling himself towards the laptop propped on a pillow on my lap.

I shrug, closing the laptop. 'That's okay, don't worry about it.'

'Lea, I am sorry.' He takes the wine glass from my hand and takes a big sip. 'Let me get you a top-up.'

'Have you thought about your stag do?' I ask, as he gets up.

'I haven't, no. I'll ask Oscar,' he replies.

'Did you ask him to be your best man then?'

'I did. Is that a problem?'

'No problem,' I say.

He rubs his face, muttering something, then decides to say it again, louder for my benefit. 'I thought you were okay with Oscar now? He apologised, didn't he? Both he and Felicity did. It was all just a misunderstanding, you know that.'

I shrug. 'I guess. Is there any news on that ex-employee, by the way?'

'Who?' he asks, frowning.

'The ex-employee, the one suing the company?'

'Oh, yes, they decided to drop it.'

'Oh, you could have said,' I say, following him to the kitchen. I lean on the counter as he pours two glasses of wine. 'Has this happened before?'

'Someone suing the company?' He shrugs. 'There have been threats, sure. It never gets to court though; it's usually just angry employees who think they were dismissed without good cause. We can always prove there was.'

'And that's what this was?'

'Yes,' he says, handing me the glass. 'I told you that.'

I raise it to my lips; he clearly wants to change the subject. 'Megan's organising my hen do. I think she's arranged for us to stay in the Cotswolds for the weekend, a little pub crawl, homemade cocktails, sounds quite relaxing. I was thinking my mum could take Josh for the weekend, give you some time alone.'

'I'll be fine,' he says. 'You've invited Felicity?'

I shake my head. 'Why would I? She's not my friend.'

'Lea, come on, she didn't mean to upset you,' he says, dismissing me.

'No, she's not my friend,' I repeat. 'And it's my hen do. I don't want her there.'

'You have to invite her,' he states. 'Oscar will be upset if you don't.'

'I'm not playing office politics with you,' I say, walking back into the lounge.

He follows me, his voice raised as he says, 'I'm afraid you are.'

It's so chilling the way he says it, like there's some unspoken contract between us and he's pointing to a clause. I suppose there will be soon, and as his wife, does he expect me to fulfil these obligations? I cast a wide eye back on the last five years, the dinner parties, the events, the schmoozing, the loving partner, always by his side no matter what.

I'm already playing his game, already dancing to his tune: I'm a stay-at-home housewife, cleaning, cooking, picking up Josh from school. Is this what he always wanted? I take a long sip of wine and stare at him as I lower myself back on the sofa.

'No,' I say, and that is final.

Chapter Seventeen

present

I wake up with my cheek pressed against the cold, rough floorboards. Spit and dribble line my numb lips and an intense heat itches my bloodshot eyes. I try to move but my body aches, my limbs heavy and my joints swollen and stiff.

Josh is still screaming. It's the screams that wake me, sharp and desperate like he's gasping for air. I push myself up, the items I took from Tracey's scattered around me, banknotes littering the floor. I'm next to the closed lounge door; she's sat behind there, gagged and tired, probably hungry and dehydrated.

I didn't expect to wake up. I thought the darkness had swallowed me whole and my first thought is my last thought. Of you, Harry.

I have to keep going for you.

I pull myself up, shaking from the cold. I'm still wearing

a soaked coat, the sleeves damp on my wrists. I yank it off, but it sticks to my wound and I cry out. Immediately, Tracey groans behind the door, a muffled, wordless cry.

I shrug off the coat and pull on one of Tracey's warm jumpers. The wool should feel comforting, but instead it irritates my damp skin, fibres tickling the dried blood that has seeped through the bandages. I stagger to the kitchen and swallow water straight from the tap, using a hand to run it over my face and lips, diluted blood dripping into the sink. It makes me feel slightly better, but I'm scared. What if I don't make it?

I make my way upstairs to check on Josh, who quietens as my footsteps approach, I'm coming for you, Josh, don't worry. I unlock the bedroom door and peer in. He's pulled the duvet covers off the bed and arranged them in a pile on the floor in the corner of the room. He's almost lost between them. It reminds me of that scene in *ET*, when he's disguised among the stuffed animals. I shudder.

'I'm sorry, Josh, I lost track of the time. Are you okay?'

He nods. 'I thought you weren't coming back.'

'I'm here, let's get you some water and a bath, how does that sound?'

He rises from the folds of sheets and pillows, dragging Baker with him, his feet scuffing the floorboards as he does. He's tired too, exhausted, we both are. I hope that Owen books us somewhere warm, somewhere safe in the sun, where Josh and I can sit on a veranda and sip iced tea and listen to the crashing waves in the distance.

He follows me downstairs, and we both sit for a while in silence at the kitchen table, lost in our own thoughts.

I'm so scared, Harry, and you're not here to tell me it will be okay. The snow has stopped now, only a few stray flakes fluttering in the quiet wind from weighted branches. I don't know how long I was asleep for, but it's getting dark. We can't go anywhere tonight.

I need to check on Tracey. I carry a glass of water down the hallway, telling Josh to stay put and I'll be back to make dinner soon. I don't know if I can manage dinner. I wish we were in Bristol and we'd order pizza and watch crap TV. We'd have no worries.

I pry open the door and Tracey is lying on the floor, her eyes wide open in horror as I enter. I place the water on the table, stooping over her, barely able to stand myself.

'Remember,' I say, taking the cushion cover out of her mouth. 'Don't scare Josh.'

She gasps, looking me up and down, like she's more concerned about me than herself, but she should be, shouldn't she? I'm her ticket out of here; I'm the only thing standing between her and freedom; she *should* worry about me.

'I have a cut,' I say, lowering myself onto the sofa opposite her. 'It's bad, really bad. I took some medicine from your kitchen, but I don't know'—I shrug—'it might be infected.' I clutch my arm, noticing a blotchy red rash climbing up my fingers.

'Bully…' she whispers.

She leans forward slightly, her matted hair framing her round face.

I ignore her. 'We aren't going anywhere tonight. You were right, the snow is too deep, the car wouldn't budge.'

'I need the toilet,' she says bluntly.

'I can't let you,' I reply. 'You'll run.'

She laughs at this, a bitter laugh. 'I'm not going anywhere.' She's not crying anymore; she's defeated.

'I'm so sorry, but I have to protect Josh, you understand? You would do that for your children.'

She nods. 'I understand.' To my surprise she smiles at me, a weak, sympathetic smile. 'What is it you're running from, Lea?'

I lean forward, and I think of you, Harry.

'The Devil,' I whisper. If I untied her, she'd be able to overpower me. I'm too weak to stop her. I glance at the knife; would I really use it? I could hold it to her neck as she lowered herself onto the toilet. I've done it before, when I tied her up, but I had more strength then. I was running on adrenaline, but now I'm exhausted. Maybe I would use it, if it meant survival.

'Okay, I'll take you to the toilet, but your hands stay tied, I'll just cut the rope around your feet, and if you run,' I say, picking up the knife, 'I won't hesitate.'

I grab the knife and start cutting through the rope I'd wrapped around her ankles. She smells odd up close, like she's already wet herself. I glance at her jeans and they look damp. How long have we been here? Should I let her wash? I could lock her in the toilet? Barricade the door so she couldn't get out? Yes, that seems more manageable than this, and then when I'm gone, they'll find her in the bathroom, clean, watered, I'll even put a couple of days' supply of food in there.

The pain in my arm returns. All the adrenaline I summoned slowly dissipates and warmth spreads through my body, like arms twisting and coiling around my limbs, a monster inside me reaching through my throat. I bend over, and I'm sick. I scrunch my eyes together, but cold moisture pries them back open and salty sweat laces my cracked lips, as I throw myself back up, gasping for air.

'Wait here,' I say, stumbling out of the door, using the walls to balance myself. 'I need to do something.' I leave the knife on a table in the hallway and with a shaking arm I fill a glass with water and take long gulps with tablets, tasting sick and bile at the back of my throat.

I pick up the knife on the way back to the lounge at the front of the house.

The front door is open and the security light is on.

'*Tracey?*' I call, running into the open lounge.

She isn't there, just a pile of frayed rope.

'Fuck.'

I run towards the door, clutching the knife. The snow has thinned slightly, but darkness has settled and I can't see ahead.

'Tracey, please,' I call. I stop still, straining to hear her footsteps. Is she hiding? I turn back towards the house. Did she even leave? There's a crunch in the distance, a cry for help. I tear towards it down the path, past the water fountain and towards Tracey's guesthouse.

On the path I see a shadow up ahead, illuminated by the lights left on in the bedroom of Tracey's home. My legs burn; my chest heaves; my arm has gone limp. But I'm still holding the knife in the other hand. I'm still prepared to survive.

The sound of a car door being open and slammed shut. No engine. A clawing at the wooden front door. A shriek.

Bully.

I'm almost there. I'm holding the knife out at arm's length, fighting through the darkness, using it to propel me forward. An outline stands still at the side gate, looking down at a large mound on the floor.

I had to do it. I had to get in the house.

She's so close now. Does she hear me? I hover behind a tree, watching her bend down to stroke her dog, her best friend, her only ally in all of this. It feels unbelievably cruel.

She screams.

She doesn't care that I can hear her. She's lost everything.

I leave my spot behind the tree and walk up to her slowly, but as she turns, she's holding something, another shape in the blue moonlight. She swings it towards me, screeching like she has nothing to lose.

Chapter Eighteen

four months earlier

I drop Josh at school, hovering by the front gate, thinking about spending the day out of the house meeting Megan for coffee and planning the hen do. I'm looking forward to getting away for the weekend, just me and the girls holed up in a cottage with bottles of wine, boardgames, and films.

As I watch Josh disappear into school with the teacher, I can't help but look forward to time away from him too. He's been different since the accident, aloof and ambivalent towards me, more than normal. Always screaming for Harry and making a fuss when I come instead. He asked me this morning why Daddy couldn't drop and pick him, and I had to tell him *again* that Harry was working. I think Josh blames me for the accident. He didn't at first, but after

Harry came home, I became the baddie, the parent that couldn't keep him safe.

Could Harry have spoken to him? If he wasn't allowed to sit in on my statement, did he ask Josh what happened? I asked Josh not to tell him—I didn't want him to have to dredge it up, I didn't think that was fair—but he might have anyway. He could have told Harry about Owen.

'Hello.'

I twist on my heels, already knowing it's Owen standing behind me, his soft voice barely a whisper.

'Hi,' I say, thinking I'd be happy to see him, but I'm angry. He goes to speak, but I storm past him towards the car.

'Please,' he calls after me. 'I'm sorry I freaked out.' He leans forward as I open the car door and pushes it shut. The boldness startles me.

'Get off my car,' I say.

'I'm sorry I left,' he pleads, leaning towards me.

I step away, looking around; people can see. 'You didn't just leave; you've ghosted me for a month.' I shake my head. 'It doesn't matter, it was a stupid mistake. Get off my car. I'm leaving now and I don't want to speak to you ever again.' I thought we could be friends. I almost laugh; I thought I could set him up with my best friend, but now he's in front of me, the kiss has come flooding back, my desire to be near him, to hear what he has to say, but I can't. The last month has been sobering.

'I'm getting married,' I say.

He nods, like he's thought about this. 'That's why I left,

because I didn't want to stop that, I didn't want to break up your family.'

'Then why are you here?'

He's so close to me now, his lips just a whisper from mine. Is this lust? It must be. I'm marrying Harry. I repeat it like a mantra as we stand in silence staring at each other, the intensity of the energy between us palpable. I swat at it, trying to unstick myself from him. He lets me open the car door and climb in. I close the door and sit there for a moment, with Owen on the other side. He walks slowly around the car, opens the passenger door, climbs in next to me, and we sit together for minutes, until it becomes too much, and he leans over and kisses me deeply. Pulling away, he cups my head in his hands.

'I really like you, Lea,' he says. 'I think I'm falling for you.'

I lean back, the moment gone. I shake my head. No, not love, that's not what I want. I love Harry.

'Get out,' I scream.

'Please,' he whispers.

I want him to kiss me again, but it's changed now, and I can't go further, I can't get what I need from him.

'Get the fuck out,' I say, coldly.

He opens the door and hesitates before he climbs out, then turns back to me. 'I want you, Lea.' It's the way he says it; his gentle, soft voice sounds determined now.

'Never speak to me again, do you hear me?'

He shuts the door and I watch him walk away, my cheeks warm from his touch.

That night I put Josh to bed before Harry gets home, and when he does, I wait upstairs for him in bed.

We make love, but it's dispassionate and clumsy, not what I need from him. When he falls asleep, I lie awake staring at the ceiling, still feeling Owen's gaze, the touch of his hand, his lips on mine. I thought I knew myself better. I didn't think I'd ever get caught up in something like this. If I'm falling out of love with Harry, then I have to fall somewhere, don't I? I will myself to go to sleep because I don't want to be alone with my thoughts. They are too dangerous, too alien to me.

They are too real.

Chapter Nineteen

present

Do you know what I loved most about you, Harry? It was how little you spoke; you were all actions instead of words. You'd leave arguments before they even began. You'd kiss me instead of telling me you loved me. You'd not come home if you were mad at me. I got more from your actions that I ever did from your words, but they could not save you—save us—in the end.

When I found out who you really were, I surprised you, didn't I? That's why we're here, because your favourite thing about me was that, as you said, 'You're always full of surprises.' You underestimated me, Harry, made me your puppet, satisfied me when I needed satisfying, but you went too far, and so did I. We should never have gotten married; that day should have never been allowed to happen. I guess if we spoke, if we used words, it wouldn't have. Because our worst trait, our shared deplorable quality, is that we're liars, to each other and to ourselves.

I look down at Tracey's dead body, blood smeared over her caved-in face.

I've never seen anything like it before. The peculiarity makes it easier to digest. Like it isn't real. Like I'm staring at a painting, and you'll tap me on the shoulder, Harry. We'll be in a gallery and you'll say, 'That is disturbing, but almost beautiful.' I'll agree; it is both of those things.

I regret this mess; it'll only slow us down, and as the moonlight pries through swollen clouds, I debate whether to try and do something about it, or whether, as with you and me, Harry, the inevitable will happen.

I trudge back to the main house, imagining Josh peering out of the window waiting for me.

I decided to leave the shovel –it took all my strength to lift it in the first place, the last bit of adrenaline I had, but now my energy is depleted. As I walk, there's a sickening feeling building in my stomach, a realisation dawning on me as I see the cottage lights in the distance.

The snow has slowed, but it isn't settling. It won't bury Tracey and Bully; instead they'll freeze, black ice climbing over them like ivy, pulling them into the undergrowth. I'm caked in melted snow, mud, and blood, but I'll let Josh see me like this, because I need to scare him; he needs to feel the urgency and desperation I feel. Does it work like that with children? Do they understand consequences of actions? When we leave on a flight and I sit next to him on the plane, holding his small hand as we take off, will he then know we aren't going home again?

I didn't want to kill Tracey. My heart almost broke when she said she could help me, but she can't. She doesn't know what's coming for us, like she didn't know what was coming for her. I desperately hope her sons aren't the ones who find her. No one should have to see that. To my surprise, I start to cry, tears that blend in with the sleet, pooling icy water at my feet as I glance at the snow melting from the statue on the fountain, its serene features glistening an ocean blue beneath the stars.

I would have loved to be here with you, Harry, walking in the moonlight, getting cosy by the fire, making love with the window open, the icy chill licking our sweaty bodies. I miss every part of you.

'I'm sorry,' I cry, when I know it's you who should be sorry.

I open the door and Josh is already standing expectantly in the hallway.

'Where have you been?' he asks, staring at my trousers, at my blood-stained face. He starts to cry.

'We need to get ready. We're leaving as soon as it's light,' I say.

'Where?' he sobs.

'Away from here, it's not safe anymore.'

'The bad people?' he wails.

'Yes, they're coming.'

'No,' he sobs.

'We have to leave, pack up our stuff, get all of this,' I say, gesturing to the items scattered on the hallway floor. '*Now*,' I scream at him. He flinches. 'I'm going to get the car, a new car, and we're going to load it with stuff, and then we're going to drive and we're going to get on a plane and go somewhere safe they can never get us.'

'Where?' he screeches, dropping to the floor, Baker lying next to him like Tracey and Bully.

'Away,' I cry.

'Daddy!'

'He isn't coming, Josh!' I say, taking a step towards him. 'He used us. He never loved us. We were never anything to him.'

He is completely still on the hallway floor, curled up on the rug with Baker. I walk over to him and he doesn't even try and edge away. He lets me bend down and run a bloodied hand over his delicate, pale features, smearing his skin with blood.

Together we will escape this.

Chapter Twenty

three months earlier

Megan said a few nights away would do me good, an opportunity to clear my head. I didn't tell her about Owen; it didn't feel necessary. He said he liked me, really liked me, but I couldn't allow it to go further than that when I've come so far with Harry. She knew something was up though, but I didn't want to tell her things anymore, not since that night in the pub when she questioned my happiness, questioned whether I should even get married. Now we're heading to the Cotswolds for my hen do, Megan's driving me and we're meeting our childhood friends, April and Kate, there. Felicity is also coming. After weeks of arguments with Harry, I relented so as not to cause a rift between him and Oscar; I wonder if she said yes for the same reason.

The cottage we're staying at for the weekend is in Castle Combe, only forty-five minutes away, just outside Bath and dubbed one of the prettiest villages in the Cotswolds. In the early years of our relationship, Harry and I would drive out to pubs in the Cotswolds and sit outside along the road, watching cars and people pass by, Harry nursing a red wine and me with a gin and tonic, Josh, only young then, either tucked in the pram next to us or left at my mum's for the day. We haven't done anything like that for years, just the three of us watching the world go by.

As we turn into the village, Megan spots the pub on the corner, where we could go for dinner. Winding down the window, she takes a deep breath. 'Lovely to get out of the city for a bit.'

I nod, agreeing, starting to ease into the weekend. We pull up at the cottage, a beautiful stone double-fronted house with a large front garden, decked out with tables and chairs. I smile. 'We should grab a bottle and wait for everyone else out here.'

We unload the car, which is full of bottles of wine, spirits, and mixers as well as boardgames and cooler bags of food. 'I probably bought too much,' Megan says, heaving the bags onto the kitchen counter. The cottage is smaller than it looks on the outside: a kitchen diner, a lounge, and upstairs three bedrooms and a bathroom. 'We'll share, obviously. Felicity can have her own room.' She pokes her tongue out. 'Seeing as she's such a little diva.' Megan throws open the patio doors and snorts. 'Well, would you look at that view.' It's stunning: the raised decking is lined with flowerpots bursting with reds and blues, dropping off into a wide, open lawn, and beyond views of verdant green fields and engorged oak trees. 'You could get married here,' Megan says, waving an arm. 'Not quite a castle, though.' She winks.

We take a bottle of rosé outside and have several glasses as we wait for the rest of the party to arrive. April and Kate turn up first, music blaring as they round the corner in April's powder-blue Fiat 500. Megan jumps up with her glass, waving hysterically as they call our names out of the window. I haven't seen them both for so long. They live in a shared flat in London, and although they ask me to visit, I've always said no, because of Josh, Harry, my job, life. Eventually they stopped asking.

They both look so young as they climb out of the car in low-slung denim jeans and colourful baggy T-shirts, matching woolly beanies and sparkling white trainers.

'Lea!' Kate says, her thick curls brushing my face as she pulls me in. 'It's been too long.'

April hangs back, a lot cooler and less tactile than Kate. She smiles into the sun. 'You guys started early.'

'Well, our best mate is getting married, so why the hell not?' Megan says, as Kate hugs her too.

'Is the other one here yet?' April asks, taking a sip of wine from my glass.

'Not yet,' I say.

'Exactly how old is she?' April says.

'Age doesn't matter,' Kate quips.

April shrugs. 'I guess not, as long as she can keep up with us.'

'Well, cocktails and boardgames don't require much keeping up, do they?' I laugh.

'Oh fuck that, Lea, we're going out,' April says, taking my hand.

I shake my head. 'No, definitely not.'

'Oh come on, Lea, when was the last time we saw you? We're all together for the first time in years, that means something. We're going big.'

'Tomorrow night,' Megan agrees, 'we'll get a taxi into Bath. It'll be fun.'

'Aren't we too old for that?' I say, instantly regretting it. Because I'm only twenty-six, I should be going to parties, and bars, and staying up too late, and feeling shit the next day. Will it be worse when I'm married? Will I never do anything like this ever again? 'Okay, tomorrow night.'

'Amazing, tonight we can do boardgames if we really must,' April says.

We hear a car pull up outside on the gravel and turn to see Felicity's silver Mercedes. She sits in the car for a moment as we stare at her, a part of me hoping she'll start the car again and drive off. But she emerges, her boot heels wedged into the gravel as she struggles to find her balance as she gets out of the car. She's wearing a long leopard-print dress and thick black glasses the size of her face.

'Hello, girls,' she says through painted red lips and then she says something I don't expect. Pushing out a hip, she smirks. 'Are we getting fucked up or what?'

My friends love Felicity.

They spend the evening laughing at her stories and squeal with delight when she makes everyone espresso martinis and gets out a bag of weed. Shaking it with her manicured fingers, she says, 'Let's go lie on the lawn, look at the stars, and forget our worries.'

I shake my head. 'No, I don't think so. I think I'll just go to bed.' I watch them grab blankets from the lounge and bedrooms, and take them outside into the October frost. Megan follows me inside, making sure I'm okay, and I smile, promising her I am. I just want to get to bed, enjoy some time alone, and she understands, or at least pretends to.

I look out of the bedroom window; their giggles carry in the wind. I can just make out their outlines lying on the grass in the dark, the back porchlight shining on their feet. I suddenly feel very alone, and I yank the curtains closed. I climb into bed, listening to laughter and excitement. My head swims with the thought of growing up, of my life, of not being as fun as I used to be. I throw back the covers and go downstairs in my pyjamas, walking out onto the decking barefoot, letting the cold, damp grass tickle my toes.

They scream with joy when I join them, Megan reaching over and tucking her head into the crook of my arm. We lie like that, smoking, drinking, screaming into the night, until Megan calls it, rising and plucking us up one by one. We stagger inside, drunk, and tired and alive.

I turn to close the patio doors, but something moves, something beyond the lawn. A shadow amongst the trees.

I wake up, feeling a bit groggy. I leave Megan in bed and pad downstairs to make coffee. Felicity is already sitting at the kitchen table, her hair up in a towel, wearing a silk robe, a fresh, steaming cafetière next to her. She's flicking through a lifestyle magazine but tosses it to the side when she sees me.

'Morning you, coffee?' I nod, sitting down opposite her. 'Last night was fun, wasn't it? Your friends are a blast.' She pours me a black coffee and pushes the sugar towards me. 'I needed this.' She says it like the weekend is for her. Taking a smug sip of coffee, she beams at me. 'How are you feeling?'

'Good.'

'And the wedding plans? Is it all coming together?'

'Yes, it's basically all done.'

She nods, thoughtfully. 'You know, my friend thought she saw you by Redland school. I said it was entirely possible.' She smiles. 'I know your son goes there.' She pauses with the mug by her lips, then lowers it. 'But she said you were with a man, that'—she lowers her voice—'that you got into a car together.' She raises her eyebrows and shakes her head. 'I said that couldn't have been you.' She's already looking at me to explain myself.

Someone saw Owen and me; did they see us kiss? Did they hear our conversation? I didn't know Felicity had friends with children at Josh's school, but Bristol is small, I shouldn't have been so stupid.

'He's just a friend. He helped me that day of the accident.'

She nods. 'That's nice.' She purses her lips and leans over, touching my hand with hers gently. 'Be careful, Lea,' she says, just as Kate walks in.

I try desperately to remember if I saw anyone, what exactly Owen and I said to each other, but the kiss? That's the worst thing and she knows, of course she does; Felicity knows everything. I wish she wasn't here to remind me that I'm a terrible person, that she's better than me, that she knows what's going on in my life more than anyone else. The way she says it, the way it rolls off her tongue, she's enjoying it.

I excuse myself and go for a shower, trying to wash it all away, but it sticks to me, ebbs into every part of me. Would she tell Harry, or just hold it against me and bring it up from time to time?

We go for a walk through the rolling fields and stop for lunch at a pub. Megan comments on how quiet I am today, but I brush it off, just saying I'm tired and how it'd been a century since I'd done weed or drank like that. When we get back, we start getting ready for our night out, April insisting I wear one of her tight, sparkly dresses. I feel silly when I put it on; it digs into my armpits and presses on my chest. She's a lot smaller than me. But when I come out the bathroom, Kate and April are sat on the end of my bed saying how perfect I look.

I don't want to be there, and I try to drink the feeling away. Harry has sent me a couple of pictures of Josh today, but when I look at them, I just feel sick, at what I've done to my family, and that Felicity knows.

We climb into the taxi. April has a little flask full of gin that she passes round as we make the journey into Bath. I look across the taxi at Felicity, whose dark eyes rest on mine. She smiles, a knowing smile that prods the guilt back into the foreground. This was supposed to be my weekend, I think as Megan leans over and kisses me on the cheek. This is my time, but yet again, Felicity has made it about her. Something stirs in me, something nasty.

When we arrive at the club, we're already drunk. I stagger out of the taxi, looping my arm through Megan's as we follow April, who's leading the way up the cobbled street to a low archway. We spill into the club, our heels clicking down the stairs that lead to an underground bar, music vibrating against the walls, the low thrum of voices, and the smell of sticky cocktails.

'Shots for the future Mrs Lewis!' April cries as we follow her to the bar through the dense crowd. I push into sweaty bodies, some dancing into me, others immovable. When we reach the bar, April is already twisting around to face us, clutching shots of tequila, slices of lime resting on top. I swallow mine quickly, the smokiness clutching my throat as the sharpness of the lime cuts through. My legs start tingling as Kate slides her arm around my shoulders.

When was the last time I was this drunk? I start to dance on the spot, in the middle of a crowd of people my age. I sing, throwing my head into the air and raising an arm. I close my eyes, relishing the absurdity of it, the strange sensation of stepping out of my routine, like I've walked into another life. I want to stay here for ever, dancing underneath the flashing lights.

We find a tall table away from the music and Felicity buys another round of drinks. She slips in and out of the crowd like a natural, giving a flicker of a smile to a group of guys who are checking her out. They whisper something to her as she walks past clutching a bottle of champagne, and she leans in coyly, throwing them a flirty look and pouting as she whispers something back.

She places the champagne on the table and laughs. 'I don't know how you lot do it; boys your age are relentless.'

April laughs. 'We don't really.'

Kate nods, reaching for the champagne. 'I haven't been on a date in years. It all got very tedious. When I do settle down, she'll be one lucky lady.'

'What about you, Megan?' Felicity asks. 'Anyone special?'

She shrugs. 'Not really.'

'Really?' Felicity urges.

'Like April says, I don't date.'

'God, if I were you guys, I'd be dating all the time, letting men take me out for fancy dinners every other week. I used to have so much fun before I settled down with Oscar.'

'Well, like you say,' Megan smirks, 'they're all boys, and like us they aren't interested in dating.'

'Even better,' Felicity says, handing me a glass of

champagne. 'I'd like to say they will all grow up, but we know they don't. Right, Lea?'

'Right,' I say, taking a sip.

'Hopefully Oscar doesn't have his mid-life crisis soon, trade me in for one of you girls. Remind me to keep tabs on you all at the wedding. He'd like you,' she says to April. 'You have that spirit that men want to snap in half. You're infuriating to women and irresistible to men.'

'I don't think so,' April says, frowning.

Felicity starts to slur. 'Yes, it's what Harry saw in Lea.' She looks at me intensely. 'But you'll get to my age soon, and places like this will make you realise how much you have to lose. Right, Lea?'

Everyone falls silent. 'I'm going to the bathroom,' I say, leaving them standing at the table staring at one another, not sure what to say, not sure what it means ... but I know what she means. I close the toilet door, snuffing out the noise of the club, leaving just the sound of heels clipping on tiles and drunken laughter. I breathe slowly, taking a second for myself, unsure whether Felicity has had enough to drink to say something. Would she tell them about Owen?

My temples pulse with the amount of alcohol I've consumed; my lips are numb, my head heavy and hazy, my tongue dry and leathery. I reach for the toilet roll but miss, and my hand slides along the bathroom stall door. I blink, but my eyes don't move. I blink, and I can't open them at all. I loll forward, hitting my head, and I think someone asks if I'm okay.

I open my eyes and I'm in the gallery toilets on the night of my engagement party.

The toilet door creaks open, the music floods in and stamps out as the door closes. There's a click of heels across the tiles. Has Felicity followed me? I don't want to speak to her, I can't. The footsteps stop outside the cubicle and for a moment there is silence as I hold my breath, but whoever is the other side of the door doesn't say a word. I catch burgundy stilettos, just visible beneath the door, pointing straight at me. Then they leave, and confusion replaces the anger I just felt.

'I don't feel well,' I say to the woman behind the door.

'You should really go home then,' Felicity says back.

My head spins until it feels like it'll fall off and I crash onto the bathroom floor. The door opens against me, and manicured nails pull me up. 'You should really be more careful, Lea. You have enemies.'

'I do?' I ask.

'Yes, you think it's all coincidence. The ex-employee who sued Harry's company. Harry locking his office door to stop you sniffing around. The car accident. The shadow at the bottom of the garden. Something or someone is coming for you, Lea, and all you can do is run.'

'No,' I cry. 'Harry loves me.'

She strokes my hair gently, grazing my forehead. 'He won't love you when he knows what you've done. But it's only a matter of time anyway until he trades you in for someone younger, someone better.'

'He wouldn't.'

'You don't belong here, Lea.' She bends down and whispers, 'Run.'

I try to scramble to my feet, but I lose my footing and stumble from the cubicle.

Before I pass out, I look up and on the mirror, in bright red lipstick, are the words:

Run, Lea, before he kills you.

Chapter Twenty-One

present

By morning most the snow has melted, but a thin layer of ice has formed over the driveway. I hold Josh's hand, a backpack and two bags slung over my shoulders. I'm sweating despite the chill. The fear of being so close to getting away, of having so much more to lose.

The early morning sun is lost behind swarms of angry clouds as we hold on to one another, trying to find our footing across the ice as the sky starts to spit. Water drips from the face of the statue, disappearing down her cheeks and cascading off her chin like she's crying silent tears. Everything is quiet. The trees sigh, shrugging off snowy remnants as slush starts to form on the banks. The light patter of water in a gutter is the only sound that accompanies us down the narrow path towards Tracey's car.

My arm, the one Josh holds, feels like playdough, like plastic, like Josh could walk a few steps ahead, turn and break it off and it would fall and melt into the snow.

'It's just at the end of the road,' I say, as he slows.

I've spent the night reassuring him, but the words were only for my benefit, as I let Josh sleep on the sofa, while I stared at the frayed rope where Tracey sat hours ago. She didn't have to run. She could have hidden. She just needed to be patient and I would have let her go, wouldn't I?

'I'm not sure anymore,' I say to Josh, as we near Tracey's house, but he isn't listening.

His fears are an extra weight for me to carry. That's what being a mother is, isn't it? Feeling everything he feels? But I need him to feel my worries too, and as we see the red car in the distance, I realise he'll find out soon.

I've cleared my car, taken everything I need from it, though I imagine we'll get new things wherever we're going. I allowed myself to dream last night, just for an hour whilst we waited for the morning, for the snow to melt, and to hear the churn of grit in the distance. I dreamt of me and Josh in a villa in Spain—an enchanting terracotta house, with flowers climbing up the side and a little patio with a swimming pool—of evenings in the local bar, me reading with a glass of wine and Josh running around the cool streets with his new friends. On the weekends we'd go to the beach, maybe we'd go out on a boat and bob soundlessly on the water, just the rhythm of the current and nothing else for miles. It would never be cold.

I grip Josh's hands as we approach the car. 'Look

straight ahead,' I whisper, but he doesn't. His eyes have wandered to the two bodies at the side of the house, the upturned boots and splayed arms, dried blood snaking the white snow, a darker crimson circling Tracey's head like a halo, and next to her, matted brown fur. 'Keep walking, Josh,' I say, as he loosens the grip on my arm. He doesn't scream, doesn't cry, doesn't make a sound; he just watches them, like they're playing sleeping tigers, that game he plays at school, and they'll suddenly jump up and chase him.

I let him look a moment longer whilst I pack the car. He'll forget about this soon; it'll be a distant memory, just a bad dream.

'I need you to get in the car, Josh. We have to leave.'

He turns towards me. 'Where?' he asks.

'We're getting on a plane. You love planes.'

'Yes,' he says hesitantly, glancing back at the bodies. He shakes his head, like he's ridding himself of the sight of it.

I help him into the car, letting him sit up front next to me. I reach over and sweep back his hair from his head. So much like you, Harry.

I start the car and it kicks into life, edging off the driveway. The tyres ease over the ice and soon we're on the road.

I'd do anything to protect him, but the bad people, they're coming for me, not him. He could still have a normal life, a future without me in it. All of this could so easily be scrubbed away; it would just take me giving him up for that to happen. I've thought about it a lot overnight, how much we've been through, how I so desperately wanted to get him to safety that I've killed for him.

But it was never about him; it was always about me. We'll be in Liverpool by lunchtime, and that dream of Josh and me sitting somewhere warm all comes crashing down.

'I love you, Harry,' I say.

'Daddy,' Josh whispers.

'Yes, Daddy.'

'Is he going to be on the plane?'

I bite my lip, reaching over to pat Baker on the head, trying to force a smile through the tears. 'No, he won't be.'

Josh is the last piece of you remaining. To part with that would break me. But I always thought I was keeping him safe, when the best thing would be to let him go. I've come so far, done so much I'm not proud of.

'Why are you crying?' Josh asks, but I can't answer that.

I swat at the radio, hoping to listen to music, to take my mind off what's coming.

It crackles, there's a short buzz, and then, clear as anything, a woman with a calm, direct voice says, 'Harry Lewis passed away in the early hours of the morning, while there is still no news on his wife's whereabouts.'

I scream, stabbing at the radio, my forearm burning. I lose control of the wheel and slam on the brakes, but we still begin to spin, the tyres screeching then locking. And we fly.

I close my eyes and think of you, Harry, hoping that maybe soon we'll be together as a family.

Chapter Twenty-Two

two months earlier

The rest of my hen do was a blur. Megan found me passed out in the toilet, a girl standing over me trying to wake me up. They almost called an ambulance, but I stirred, telling them not to make a fuss, slurring as they managed to walk me out of the club and put me in a taxi. I don't remember any of it, just the taste of bitter lime and burnt aniseed.

When I woke up, Megan was lying next to me, watching me intently. She asked if I was okay and then stroked my hair telling me I'd just had too much to drink, that was all.

I shook my head, telling her something else had happened, it was more than the drink, but I could tell she didn't believe me. I sat up in the bed and gulped water, waiting for the fog to clear, and when it did, I asked where Felicity was, but she'd already left.

The drive home was agony. I curled up on the back seat and repeated that I'd been drugged, that it was Felicity, but Megan counted on both hands the amount I'd drunk, shaking her head, telling me that I wasn't used to it.

When I got home, Harry was already aware of the weekend we'd had before I'd even told him. Oscar called; Felicity had arrived home early, said she had to leave me in bed unwell from the drink. He was so disappointed, worried even, that I'd behaved like that in just a few nights away. He called me irresponsible, said I'd put myself in danger, and for what? I protested that it wasn't the drink, that something had happened, but he didn't seem to think so. *Felicity had seen the entire thing.*

It seemed futile to argue with him, and as I lay in bed and he fetched me cups of tea and slices of toast to try and make me feel better, he said, finally, 'I don't think Megan is a good friend.'

It didn't surprise me when he said it. I know he'd always felt it. He'd made a few comments once or twice, similar to how he'd spoken about Carly. *She's very immature,* he'd say.

'I know you've been friends with those girls for a long time, but you never seem to like yourself much when you spend time with them.'

He wasn't wrong. That group of friends provided something my life with Harry couldn't, but Megan? She's my closest friend, everything I have outside of my family. But the seed was planted, and when I didn't hear from

Megan for weeks afterwards, I started to wonder if he was right.

My life has become increasingly isolated. I tried to pinpoint when it first started, but it happened gradually: losing my job, pulling away from my friends, falling out of touch with Megan. My world has become small and when I turn over in bed at night now and watch Harry sleeping, I can't help but feel he's the person who's taken everything from me and left me with nothing, but him.

After my hen do he said I should take a break from painting and focus on the wedding. We seemed to go for more dinners with his clients, like he was pulling me more into his world and further from my own. Two weeks ago, we went to dinner at Oscar and Felicity's house and she cooed over me, telling me she was sorry she'd had to leave early and she hoped I was feeling better, making comments throughout the night about how I couldn't hold my drink. She'd glance at me across the table before slipping it into conversation, but she went too far when she said, 'Men were all over Lea, it's a good thing we took her home when we did.'

Harry waited until we were in the car on the way home before he said, 'I didn't know you were talking to other men.'

'I wasn't,' I whispered.

'That's not how it sounded to me. In fact, Felicity told Oscar that you were flirting with a group of guys, and I decided to let it go—you were drunk, after all—but I don't want my wife behaving like that.'

I got angry then. 'I didn't behave like anything. My drink was spiked, I told you this.'

In the week afterwards, Harry ignored me completely. I even wondered briefly if he'd call off the wedding, saying he didn't want to go through with it, that he didn't want a wife that behaved like I did.

But a few days ago, he took my head in his hands and kissed me on the lips and asked if I was okay. He tried to tell me I wasn't myself, but it wasn't the truth. Then I looked at him one morning over coffee and said, 'I think someone's messing with me.' But the words didn't leave my mouth, I just thought them, and he rose from the table and kissed me on the cheek and left for work and I was left alone with my thoughts all day.

I wanted to reach out to Owen at those times I felt lonely. But that's all it was: loneliness. I felt myself becoming a bored housewife before I was even a wife. Getting up, taking Josh to school, cleaning the house, painting in the back garden, watering the plants, picking Josh up, cooking dinner, waiting for Harry to come home.

Always waiting for Harry to come home.

Then he'd disappear into his study and I'd lie on the sofa with a bottle of wine and watch crap TV.

As I stand now in the kitchen, stirring a pot of chilli and wishing something would wake me up, Harry appears in the doorway.

'Can I speak to you?' he whispers, eyeing Josh at the kitchen table, who is deep into a game on his console.

I nod, following him along our hallway until he's

convinced Josh can't hear us. He leans into me and I smile, not sensing the tension in his jaw until it's too late.

'Who's Owen?' he whispers.

I pull away, but he's already seized my wrists and pulled me back.

'There was a man in this house, and I have the right to know who it was.'

I shake my head. 'You have it wrong. He helped us, the day of the crash, that's it.'

He nods disappointedly and lets go of my wrists. Licking his lips, he sighs, 'Don't lie to me, Lea.'

'I'm not,' I say, glancing back towards the kitchen to make sure Josh can't hear us. 'He took us home. He's just a dad of one of the other children. That's all there is to it, I promise.'

Harry points towards the ceiling and circles his finger slowly. 'I see everything,' he says, before he walks away back down the hallway towards the kitchen, his tone lightening as he embraces Josh and says merrily, 'What are we playing then?'

A game, I think. We're playing a game. And I'm losing.

I finally message Megan. She agrees to go for a walk with me across the Downs and as I see her coming across the path, I think back to better times, when Megan and I would go running here and then pick blackberries, heading back to mine afterwards to make a pie. All my happy memories are before Josh came, before Harry.

'Hey,' Megan says, as she lowers herself onto the bench next to me. 'I'm glad you sent a message. I'm too stubborn, I'm sorry.'

'Don't be.'

'No, I just felt awkward after that weekend and I don't know why, or maybe I do. But if you say you were spiked, then you were. I just don't think it was Felicity.'

'Why?' I ask.

Megan shrugs. 'Just a hunch, I guess. I know you don't like her, but she wouldn't do that.' She turns to me, swiping her fringe from her concerned eyes. 'I have something to tell you.' I look at her, but she glances away. 'I saw Carly a few months ago.'

'My old boss Carly?'

Megan nods. 'I was in a coffee shop in town and she came in. She recognised me immediately and tried to slip away without being seen, but I caught up with her with every intention of giving her a piece of my mind about firing you, but'—Megan stands up and waits for me to join her. We start walking along a pathway between fields—'she held her hands up and apologised before I could get a word in. She looked really terrible. It's not how I expected the conversation to go.'

'She looked terrible?'

'Yeah, she said she didn't even work at the gallery anymore, that she'd also been fired when the gallery lost money from the artists suing for damages. I snorted, told her that you were the sacrifice so she could keep her job, but she shook her head. She said it wasn't like that.' Megan sighed. 'I'm sorry I didn't say anything sooner, but I just didn't believe her. Now, I'm not so sure.'

'What happened?'

Megan yanks my hand and pulls me off the path and through a clearing in the trees. 'She said that she had to fire you; she was made to because of what happened at your engagement party.'

'*Made* to?'

Megan nods. 'By Harry.'

I pause, but Megan keeps walking. She keeps speaking, but I can't hear her. 'Lea,' she calls. 'I tried to get her to speak to me, but she pulled away, saying she didn't want to get into it again, but I don't know, she looked frightened.'

'I don't understand.'

'I just thought you should know. I wasn't going to say anything, but you getting fired, it wasn't your fault, it wasn't like that.'

'What do I do now?'

Megan shrugs. 'You could ask him to tell you the truth.'

I look at her and bite my lip. 'Maybe it's just a misunderstanding.'

'I find that hard to believe,' Megan says, rolling her eyes. 'How are things with Harry?'

'They're good,' I lie.

'And the wedding? Only two months to go, right?'

It's the way she says it. There's doubt in her voice; she's looking for me to tell her I'm not sure about the wedding.

She's known for a while—I know she has—and I haven't had to say a thing. But I can't say it out loud, because then it's real. I do love Harry; my life is with him. He found out about Owen and he didn't want that to be the end of us. He's been good to me, and he's the father of my son. What am I without Harry? I don't have any money, a job, a way to support Josh. I can't walk away when I'm completely reliant on him.

Then a new and more disturbing thought presents himself. Is this what he wanted? To make it so I couldn't ever leave him? I think about the surprise engagement, the question 'why now?' Then everything that's happened in the last year is like a grip tightening around me. I didn't want to get married for security; I wanted to get married because I love Harry, but the secrets we have scare me. And now this.

'I'll ask him,' I say, 'I'll know if he's lying.'

'And if he is?' Megan probes.

'I don't know, I haven't thought that far.'

'The whole thing stinks to me,' Megan says.

'But why would Harry ask Carly to fire me? It makes no sense.'

'Maybe she knew something… Maybe,' Megan says, turning back towards path, 'he didn't like you working there.'

'What do you mean?'

Megan shakes her head. 'Forget it.' She takes my hand and pulls me in, holding me in the middle of the pathway. 'I better go,' she says, releasing me. 'Let me know if you want any help with the wedding,' she says with a sad smile.

'I will.'

I watch her walk away back down the pathway towards Clifton, but I turn and find a bench to sit on to collect my thoughts. Why would Harry do that? Why would he not want me working there?

Because of what happened at your engagement party.

When I get home Harry and Josh aren't there. I check my phone and there's a clipped message from Harry saying he's taken Josh to swimming class, adding at the end, *Had I forgotten?* I pad slowly upstairs to change into something comfier, stopping outside Harry's office door on the way to the bedroom.

He still keeps it locked despite me knowing what's in there, and he keeps the key on him now, just in case.

What would I find now if I went in there? More secrets, more lies he thinks he thinks he can explain. I think back to last time, finding the solicitor's card, Harry having to leave town due to a disgruntled employee. Harry had always wanted me to quit, hadn't he? He wanted me to be a full-time mum, to stay at home and be there with our son, and I'd always said no, but what if no wasn't good enough for him anymore? The thought makes me sick.

I change clothes and walk out into the garden, sitting on the swinging bench with a large blanket to keep me warm in the November chill. I bring up the name of the lawyer, the one written on that business card I found in Harry's office all those months ago. I can't trust Harry to give me the truth.

'Travis Hopkins?'

'Hi,' I stammer, 'I was calling because—' I pause.

'Hello?'

'Sorry, I was calling because I'm Harry's fiancée.'

'Lea?' he whispers. I can hear a door squeak open and close and the sound of voices quieten as the footsteps pick up. 'Why are you calling me?'

'I … want to know what Harry needs from you.'

'Needs from me?' he asks, confused. 'I can't discuss my client.'

'No, I know, I just—' I pull the blanket in tighter, not knowing what I expected him to say.

'Lea, let me stop you right there. Is Harry with you?'

'No,' I whisper.

'Does he know you're calling me?'

'No.'

'I'd keep it that way, if I were you.'

I nod. 'Okay.'

'Can I give you some advice?

'Yes.'

'Don't marry him,' he says flatly, before hanging up.

I let the phone fall to my side just as the back door opens and Josh runs along the patio towards me, his hair damp from swimming, his cheeks red from the cold air. 'What you doing out here, Mummy?'

Harry appears in the door looking confused and irritated. 'Come in, it's cold.'

I take Josh's hand and he leads me along the patio path and into the house. I try and act normal even though I can feel my pulse in my throat. Josh lets go, running up the hall towards the lounge. I stare at Harry, but he won't look at me. *Don't marry him.*

'Why are you not speaking to me about Owen?' I ask and he stops, looking at me slowly.

'What is there to speak about?' he says.

'I kissed him.'

Harry nods. 'But you won't do that again.' He walks, but stops, turning. 'You know what, Lea, you're an incredibly selfish person. You wanted to get married; we're getting married. You wanted to live in a house in Redland; well, here we are. You wanted to be an artist like your mum; now you can be. You have everything and you seem intent on blowing it all up. Why is that?'

I can't speak, I just think about Harry's finger circling the space between us and his words *I see everything*.

'I liked my job,' I whisper.

'Is that what this is all about? That thing with Owen is because you're bored? Do you hear yourself?'

'How do you know who he is?'

Harry frowns, then his face relaxes. 'I don't blame you; I blame him,' he says. 'You weren't to know. You were vulnerable and I wasn't here. I blame myself as well.'

'I wasn't to know what?' I ask.

He shrugs. 'It doesn't matter.' He walks away to join

Josh in the lounge, and I can hear them both scream with excitement as Harry ruffles his hair and picks up the second controller. I walk after them, trying to drown the voice in my head telling me to run.

When Harry falls asleep that night, I slide out of bed and walk slowly and quietly downstairs, aware of the floorboards creaking slightly under my feet. I skim the banister with my hand and use it to take the weight off the staircase as I descend to the hallway. One foot at a time I make my way into the kitchen, clutching an empty glass to offer an excuse if Harry wakes up.

I pull myself along the kitchen counter and feel around the top of the cabinets, searching, desperately, until I find it, tucked at the back in the corner, covered in cobwebs and dead flies.

It's a camera.

It's small and round, pointing down at the kitchen. And it's flashing red.

What does that mean? Is he still watching me? Is he upstairs looking at my face in the camera on his phone right now?

I hear a creak from the bedroom. A slat moves slightly and then there's the drumbeat of feet on the ground. I stuff the camera back where I found it, waiting for Harry to appear, but he doesn't. The noise subsides and I'm left standing alone in the darkness.

I slide off the counter and look around the kitchen, into every corner, every hidden spot I can think of. How many more cameras are there? Are they in every room of the house?

I pick up the empty glass and fill it with cold water, my hand shaking as I take a sip.

Why is Harry watching me?

Chapter Twenty-Three

present

'Hello, are you okay?' There's a violent knock by my jaw, glass vibrating like someone's hit me.

'Harry,' I groan, struggling to open my eyes.

I suddenly fall to the side, my arm loosening. It flops to my thigh. My fingers feel nothing but my leg twitches from the touch.

There's another loud, sharp knock which slips down my jaw and causes a piercing pain in my neck.

'I saw your car spin off,' says a low, dulled voice and when I finally open my eyes and peer into the light coming through the car window I see that an elderly man is standing there, wearing a woolly beanie and a coat zipped up to his eyes, deep crow's feet stretching across to wispy grey hairs. 'Are you okay?' he repeats.

I nod in confusion. I am okay. 'Josh?' I whisper, and he nods.

'He's okay.' He points to the passenger seat.. 'Do you want me to get him out?'

I lean forward, shaking my head, but the pain remains. I wind down the window and the man leans in. 'You hit the stone verge. The snow broke the impact, but there's a lot of black ice. You need to be careful.'

I twist to my side and see Josh staring at me, completely unharmed, unfazed. I remember the accident in Bristol all those months ago, when he was in the back seat and I was so worried about him. I reach over. 'Are you hurt?'

He shakes his head. I run a hand down my face, trying to find something that's causing this pain, but it's been there all along. My arm is numb, as though detached, and the pain has reached my neck, pinching my jaw.

'Let me get out of the car, see if there's any damage,' I say, as the man stands back, giving me room to wriggle free.

The car is halfway up the verge, inches from the stone wall, but he's right, the snow stopped us from hitting it. The front of the car has caved in slightly, a smashed headlight and fragments of broken glass lying glistening in the snow. Grey ice vines up the tyres, muddy snow caking the front bonnet.

I don't have much time.

I turn to the man to thank him for stopping, but he's already staring at me, his head bent to the side as he considers me carefully. I glance away.

'Thanks for your help, but we're fine,' I say, climbing back into the car, but he doesn't move. He just watches me.

'Are you from around here?' he says. 'I can tail you back home in case you get into any trouble.'

'We're fine,' I repeat. 'We don't live far.'

'I thought you looked familiar,' he says, taking a step closer.

I try starting the car, but it growls back, the motor whirring and spitting angrily before there's a sharp snap from under the bonnet.

'Oh,' he says. 'Could be the battery.'

'No,' I cry, trying to start it over and over again, but it's the same wheezing and hissing before smoke appears.

'That's not good,' he comments. 'I can give you a lift back. You said you don't live far?'

I need him to leave; I need this car to start; I'm running out of time.

'I'm running out of *time*,' I scream.

'Do you need to be somewhere?' he asks. 'I really don't mind taking you.' I look past him, at his small van parked up on the side of the road opposite. We got this far, haven't we? 'Whereabouts do you live?' I could overpower him; there's a knife in the back, just in case. I could threaten him, take what we need, but it's getting harder now. Someone would see him; he'd give them the number plate; and I'd be tracked down in less than an hour. It would be impossible.

Do we have any other choice?

'Yes, let me just get my stuff,' I say, getting out of the car again, and walking around to the boot. I pretend to collect our bags, but I rummage through the backpack, feeling to the bottom for the knife wrapped in one of Tracey's cardigans. I grip the handle, the blade catching against the fabric as I pull it free.

There's a dull vibration in my coat pocket. I reach in. It's Tracey's phone. I thought I'd left it behind. How could I be so stupid?

I take it out, ready to drop and bury it in the snow, but I recognise the number.

'Owen?'

'Thank God, where are you?'

'I'm on my way, but the roads, they're icy and—'

'They're coming.'

'What?'

'I can't help you anymore. They're coming. I'm so sorry, it's over.'

'No…'

'Someone must have seen you.' I look over the open boot to where the man was standing, but he's not there, he's crouched by the car speaking in a hushed voice to Josh. I can't hear what he's saying, but I slam the boot shut, making him jump.

'Get away from him,' I scream as he falls backwards onto the ice, shock spreading across his face. 'What are you doing?' I say, hearing Owen's distant voice crying my name. The man struggles to stand as I walk towards him with the knife. 'Did you tell them where I am?' I say, lowering the knife to his face. My arm tingles, bile rising in my throat, my chest so tight I can barely breathe.

'No,' he cries, scrambling to his feet. He backs away towards the car, as I bring the phone to my ear.

'Are you there? You can't go to Liverpool. I did everything I could,' Owen pleads.

I start to cry as the man throws open his door, eyes wide, looking shaken and scared, and begins to drive away, skidding on the ice in panic and disappearing into the mist.

'Where do we go?' I ask.

'I think it's over,' he says.

'I'll die, Owen. They'll kill me.'

'I have to go. I love you,' he says. 'Just, wait there, don't do anything.'

'What about Josh? Who will keep him safe?'

'I'll make sure he's okay,' Owen whispers.

'Please, they can't take him from me; he's all I have left.'

I hang up, dropping the phone on the snow and rushing back to the car. I try to start the engine again, but it won't work.

'Fuck!' I cry, kicking out. My arm catches the dash; my wound splits open; and blood starts trickling down my wrist.

Josh starts whimpering, a sharp, cowering cry as he tries to push himself away from the blood. I think I might pass out, my head lolling back and forth as sick dribbles from my mouth, pooling on the floor by my feet, sticking to the pedals. My foot slides away and I hit my head on the wheel.

'Get out of the car,' I scream. 'Now, we have to get out; we have to *go*.'

'I'm scared,' Josh whispers, covering his face with two

gloved hands. 'I don't want to go anywhere. I just want to go home.'

'We can't go home. We have to keep moving. *Get out of the car.*'

'I don't want to. I won't do it,' he screams, his face turning red as he balls his hands into fists and punches his cheeks, sobbing into his clenched fingers.

'Do you want to see Daddy?' I ask.

He stops crying, lowering his hands. His eyes widen and he gawps at me.

It's the first time the possibility of you has crossed his mind. He saw you lying there. I tried to shield him from you. But there's no denying he saw you.

'Just get of out the car and we'll go.'

He doesn't move.

'*Now,*' I scream, but I can't move myself.

It's over.

The bad people are coming.

Chapter Twenty-Four

one month earlier

Harry left for his stag do this morning. Oscar hired a villa in Italy and planned for them to fly first class to Milan for a week of wine tasting.

I wasn't looking forward to it being me and Josh for the week, but I needed the time away from Harry. The wedding is only a month away and the guilt about what happened with me and Owen outweighed anything Harry had done. I decided not to ask about Carly. I wanted a fresh start and I thought maybe the wedding could be that for us.

As I move around our home I'm always aware of the cameras. I found at least one in every room downstairs. The thought that Harry had seen me looking for them and chosen to ignore it filled with me a different kind of dread; that he didn't care that I knew he was watching.

I thought about trying to turn the cameras off when he went away, but what good would that do? A little time completely to myself out of his watch. I twirl the engagement ring around my finger.

I would never have that ever again.

The only place where Harry can't see me is in my painting studio at the end of the garden, and every morning after dropping Josh at school I slink off to the shed with a pot of tea and a packet of biscuits and don't emerge until it's time to pick Josh up again. Sometimes I don't paint at all; I just sit on my wooden stool with a blanket and the electric heating, reading books, or looking out through the window, just passing the time.

After dropping Josh off this morning, I flick the kettle on and glance up at the camera in the kitchen corner. It's so clearly visible now, I don't know how I didn't see it before. I wince, thinking about Owen and me kissing in the kitchen, the way he held me, his fingers running through my hair, his hands on my hips. I pull open a kitchen cupboard and let my head drop, releasing a deep breath when I know I'm out of view of the camera.

The doorbell rings and I look down the hallway. I don't want anyone to be here. I want to make my tea, to take myself to the bottom of the garden and forget about it all. It rings again, urgently. There's a shadow behind the frosted glass, so close I can see the outline of their slim shoulders and short brown hair. Megan.

'Hi,' I say, opening the door, but her face is stony, her

eyes are slanted and sad, but her lips fixed in a tight grimace.

'You couldn't have said that to my face?' she says, stepping closer, and pressing a hand to the door.

'Said what?' I say, as she pushes on it, placing one foot inside the door, but she retreats, shaking her head.

'I shouldn't have come,' she says.

'What are you talking about?' I ask.

'I got your message?'

'Message?'

'The one where you call me a bitch, where you accuse me of kissing Harry years ago at some stupid party I don't even remember. You really think I'd do that to you?'

'No, of course not. I didn't send that.'

'Yes, you did, and I was going to reply to you, but you deserve to explain this to my face,' she sighs. 'How could you think I'd do that?' She starts to cry, biting her lip, then she looks at me and there's a flash of guilt in her eyes.

'I didn't send that message,' I repeat, slowly.

She shrugs. 'I have to go,' she says removing her hand from the door. I call after her but she pulls her coat hood up and steps out into the rain and I can't help but look directly into the camera above our doorbell.

I turn and pace back to my phone in the kitchen, steam from the kettle masking it with a light film. I swipe the moisture and scroll down to the messages between Megan and me, but there's nothing there. I text her asking 'what message?' I wait all afternoon for her to reply as I sip tea down the bottom of the garden, but she doesn't respond. The only message to come through is from Harry. 'Landed safely, miss and love you.'

Later, when I'm in bed, I close my eyes and try and remember what party Megan must have meant, and why she thinks I accused her. I turn onto my side and open my eyes, staring at my phone on the bedside table. I scrunch my face, kicking back the covers, feeling hot despite the December frost.

There's something bothering me about it, and it's not that I never sent that message; it's that I had a thought, only briefly, that something had happened between Megan and Harry years ago. It was when Josh was a new-born and Mum had been staying at the house with us to help with childcare. Harry had a work event, nothing unusual. A party in an underground bar in Clifton for one of his clients. I wanted to go, but I'd left Mum with Josh so many times in the last few months that I felt guilty, so I stayed in and we watched a movie and Josh screamed the whole way through it.

But he finally settled when Harry got home, and Harry, drunk, staggered over to his crib and cooed that he was such a good boy. I cried silently in the darkness, as he lay on our bed.

'I saw Megan tonight,' he said. 'She was at the party.' His voice tailed off as he fell asleep. 'She was alone, so I kept her company.'

'That's nice of you,' I whispered.

And with that, he fell asleep. I might not have thought anything of it, but when I saw Megan a few days later she was tense, awkward, and when I brought up the party, she looked at me in horror and said, 'I went home early, so I don't know.'

'Don't know what?' I asked.

She started to cry. 'I don't know why I'm like this.'

She wouldn't talk about it after that, but a look passed between her and Harry the next time she came to the house, a look I couldn't forget for a while, until too much time passed and whatever I'd felt faded away.

I don't know what wakes me. The light from my phone. The creak of the stairs. The sound of a door closing below me. I'm lying in bed, the covers still pushed back, my skin bare, the way I'm used to sleeping.

I'm clammy; the heat has spread up my throat and sweat clings to my forehead. Am I sick? Imagining this? I feel Harry's side of the bed, cold and empty like how he left it. I check my phone, but nothing. I climb out of bed, pull my dressing gown off the chair, wrap it around my aching limbs, and lower myself onto the end of the bed. The back door slides open. I sit upright.

'Josh?' I call, rising. I throw open the bedroom door and start to run down the hallway, pushing on Josh's open bedroom door, but he's sound asleep, his nightlight casting a warm glow on his small face.

A gust of wind, a plant pot falling over, the windchimes wrestling uneasily in the night.

I slowly make my way downstairs, a foot at a time, my arms held up defensively. When I'm halfway down the stairs, I pause, trying to make out any sounds still lingering in the house. Is someone there? Should I call out?

I take another step and watch as an elongated shadow cast up the hallway slips out of view. I turn, throwing myself back up the stairs, bursting into Josh's room. He jumps and then turns away sleepily, but I pull him out of bed and hold him against me, rushing down the hallway towards the bathroom. I let Josh go and he falls to the floor, sobbing with confusion. He rubs his eyes under the fluorescent bathroom light and mumbles something I can't make out.

I don't have my phone on me, but I pat around trying to find it anyway. I need to call the police. I need to tell them someone is in the house. Josh sobs into my thigh and we both sit like that until the sun starts to pry through the frosted bathroom window. Until it's safe to open the door. Until the house is completely silent.

The police arrived later that morning to check for any signs of a break-in, but they left unconvinced that anyone had been in the house at all. When asked if I'd seen anyone, I shook my head, then nodded, I had. I'd seen a shadow of a person, I'd heard them leave. I called Harry when the police left, but he didn't pick up and I decided not to worry him, so I sent a message telling him everything was fine.

If you saw the house, everything did look fine. There wasn't a thing out of place. As I sit alone in my painting studio, staring at the back of the house, I wonder if I imagined the whole thing.

I wasn't feeling well last night, I had a fever, I was restless and maybe slightly confused, I could have hallucinated. My mind playing tricks on me.

I wander back to the house just before it's time to pick Josh up from school, but something crosses my mind. I look up at the corner of the kitchen, just above the cabinets where the camera sits. I walk slowly around the house, looking at each camera, wondering if Harry is looking back. I can't access them myself, but I could ask Harry, I could tell him there was someone in the house.

But I don't call Harry, I call someone else.

———

The next day I step out into the dark, frosty morning and walk over the road to the small oval park that divides the street. I see Owen in the distance, sitting on one of the benches in the far corner. He watches me approach, his gloved hands crossed and resting in his lap.

'Thanks for coming,' I say. He doesn't respond. His shoulders rise and fall slightly, and he smiles ruefully. 'I need help.'

He nods. 'I gathered.'

I point towards my house. 'There are cameras in my home. I need to know how to access them.'

To my surprise, he laughs. 'Why did you call me?'

'Harry's away,' I say, 'and, well, I didn't have anyone else to call.'

'Can't it wait until he's back?' he says, standing to meet me.

'No, it can't.' I suck my cheeks in. 'I think someone was in my house a few nights ago.'

He looks at me for the first time, a sheen of concern glazing his brown eyes. 'In your house?'

I nod. 'There are cameras in every room of the house. I just didn't think at the time.'

He fiddles with the sleeves of his coat awkwardly, avoiding looking at me again. 'Why do you have cameras in your house?'

I shrug. 'Security,' I whisper, but I can see he doesn't buy it. I'm not sure I do, either. He sighs. 'I just need your help, please.'

'You couldn't figure it out for yourself?' he says, the words biting, but he softens, his face relaxing. He doesn't want to be here, but he's wondering if I asked him for different reasons, and maybe I did. 'Do you want me to show you?' he says.

'You can't come to the house,' I whisper.

He nods, throwing back his head. He points. 'I just need to be close enough to get on the Wi-Fi and then I can connect it for you. What make are the cameras?'

'I don't know.'

He smiles. 'Okay, well, let's see, you'll need to download an app. Give me your phone.'

I follow him towards the house, and he stops as he gets

to the front driveway, pausing by a large oak tree. He flicks through my phone and I wait patiently until he holds it up, facing me.

'There you go,' he says, handing it back. 'You should be able to see recordings of the last week. It records motion so anytime someone is in a room, it starts recording.'

I look up at him and something passes between us. It's not lust anymore; it's a deep concern about what Harry saw. Should I tell him that Harry knows? Would that make things better or worse?

'Are you okay?' he asks, but he doesn't move nearer, doesn't want to hold me. I can feel whatever tension there was between us fall away.

'I'm fine,' I say. My breath hovers in the space between us.

'Did you call the police?' he asks.

I nod. 'Thank you for this.'

'You get married next month?'

I blush. 'Yes.'

'I hope you're happy, Lea.' He sucks in his lips. 'But please don't call me again.' He doesn't say it to be rude; he says it because this is hurting him.

'I won't,' I promise, and I mean it.

I watch him leave, and it's not until he rounds the corner that I start up the driveway, glancing at the camera doorbell as I slide the key in the lock.

I head straight outside into the garden clutching my phone, but it's not until I close the door of my studio and settle on my chair that I pull up the app and start to carefully and slowly go through the footage from the last week, curiosity eating into me: if Harry's been watching me, who's been watching Harry?

I wonder if Harry knows I've downloaded the app, if he gets an alert that someone's accessed the cameras, but do I care? It's my house too.

I scan back to two nights ago, to the time I saw the shadow slide across the hallway floor. What time was it? 4am? I hadn't checked, I'd just pulled Josh from his bed and into the bathroom and waited there until sunlight pried through the frosted glass.

I went to the beginning of the night and slowly scanned the footage, starting in the kitchen, then the lounge, the hallway, but nothing. Nothing all night. Maybe it was my imagination, the shadow could have been from a tree or an animal outside. Then I notice something, a room I hadn't known there was a camera in: our bedroom.

There I am, asleep with the covers thrown back, naked on the bed, exposed and vulnerable. The blinds and curtains are open, the way I like to sleep, the natural light waking me up in the morning. I went to bed late that night, almost midnight; it wasn't like me, but I wasn't feeling well. I wasn't myself. I start from there, scrolling through the timestamps, my eyes darting around the room to try and catch any slight movement, when—

Someone steps out of the shadows, just one leg sliding forward until they're standing at the end of my bed, completely still.

I think I've paused the video, but I can see my chest rise

and fall with each breath. I can't see the figure's face; they are dressed all in black, facing away from the camera.

They don't move, just watch me. For ten minutes they stand there, at the end of my bed, until they walk slowly towards me, an arm reaching out from a long cloak, like Death extending a bony hand towards me.

But then it falls again, and instead they pick up my phone from the bedside table with a gloved hand. The screen lights up, and I stir, so they place it back down carefully, quietly. They step closer to me, until their whole body covers mine, a cupped hand lowering towards my lips like it'll smother me. Then it retracts quickly into its body, twisting away from me like an animal stalking prey. It retreats. The hunt is over. It slinks back into the shadows, but I can't find it on any other camera. I can't see who it is.

Someone was in my room. Standing above my bed. Watching me sleep.

I try calling Harry, but he doesn't pick up, so I call Megan. I tell her that someone had been in my home, that someone had sent that message to her. Now I remember, it wasn't the light on my phone that had woken me in the darkness. It was the feeling that someone was there.

She tells me to call the police, and I do. They ask me to send over the video, and I start to cry, confusion plaguing my thoughts. Who would do this? I go back to the video, but when I do, it isn't there. None of it is. The footage from the last week has disappeared.

I claw at my phone, refreshing it, restarting the app. Nothing.

I storm back to the house and keep reloading it, but it's no use. the video has gone.

I don't know how that could happen, but I wasn't the one that set it up. I wasn't the person in control. Someone deleted this. Someone knew I'd seen it.

I look up at the kitchen camera. The red light flickers back.

Chapter Twenty-Five

present

We leave the car on the side of the road, and I help Josh over a low brick wall. He clings to me, turning back occasionally as we start to cross the field. The bottoms of our trousers become soaked in the melting ice, and my toes start to turn numb from the bitter cold.

When I look back, the car has disappeared behind the low hedge, the front caved in slightly from the crash. There's nowhere left for us to go, and I'm scared the man we saw will come back with police officers, telling them what he'd seen. My face is probably all over the news, your lost wife, but I won't be lost for much longer.

There's only the comfort that the world has found out who you really are, Harry, and what you put me through.

In the distance, the field meets a narrow path, which

snakes through clusters of rock and vines up a tall ledge. I don't know where it leads, but I remember climbing a route like this with you once, how beautiful the view had been as we stood at the top, and how you leant over and kissed me and told me you'd always love me.

'Where are we going?' Josh pleads as I yank at his arm.

'We have to keep moving,' I call to him. The wind starts to pick up, rattling my ears as we ascend the icy path.

I feel a gentle tug and turn to see Josh, stopped still at the edge of the path, tears running down his red cheeks.

'No,' he whispers. I let go of his arm and it falls to his side. He puffs out his chest and screeches, '*Help!*'

No one is around to help us, Josh. But he doesn't understand. My arm throbs and I'm sweating despite the icy wind. I don't know how much longer we have, but all I can do is keep moving. I lunge and grab Josh with the last shred of strength I have, and pull him into me.

'Help isn't coming,' I say as he punches my waist defiantly. 'Stop it,' I scream back, but he wriggles free.

I glance towards the main road, but no one is coming, no one can hear us. I look up at the trail. It's a place I wanted to visit with you, Harry. A long, winding path and a short climb to a flat ridge at the top where one view is nothing but marsh and heathland for miles and the other is of the rolling green hills, now tarnished with grey ice.

I don't know what will happen when we reach the top, but I can see from here the flat stone ridge jutting out. There doesn't seem to be anywhere to go but up. My eyes follow the drop from the view onto the rocks below.

'Come on,' I say, pulling Josh again. He has stopped hitting me, his breathing heavy, fighting the wind as he tries to throw his weight into my thigh. I want him to give up, to know that we're in this together, that there is no one else in the world left for him apart from me.

All the noise in my head suddenly falls silent and I can only hear the whistle of the wind. I allow myself to think back to the day you and I got married, how there had been so many warning signs leading up to that day. How my only family had asked me if I really wanted to go through with it. But I was blind. I thought I was in love.

You took that love, Harry, and twisted it into something indescribable, and I've spent the last five years living in fear of us, and the last few days living in fear of what we might have become if I'd stayed.

Owen was right about you, about us. If only I'd listened, then the pain might not have been so bad. When I found out who you were and what you were hiding, I wasn't surprised; I was relieved, because it meant I wasn't mad, I was right. But that satisfaction quickly faded and was replaced by a need for you that I couldn't reason with.

The day of the wedding was long, and slow, like being dragged through all the worst parts of our relationship. It got more torturous as the day went on and when I thought all the smiling was done, the night fell on the day, and the worst of it reared its ugly head.

That's when the last five years quickly unravelled, when it all built up to that one moment neither of us could control. It was our undoing.

I stare at the ridge up ahead, visible between a layer of mist.

I've come too far.

Chapter Twenty-Six

the day of the wedding

I'm standing in front of a long wooden mirror. My mum is smoothing out the bottom of my dress and Megan is picking dried petals from my bouquet. I should feel like the luckiest girl in the world, but I can't even bear to look at myself.

My dress is satin, strapless and straight. It is plain and simple, maybe not what I imagined growing up, but I don't think any wedding is how anyone imagines. I didn't think I'd have a child by now; I thought I'd still be dating, that marriage would come late for me, and everything else would follow. I thought I'd be an artist, like Mum, pictures hanging in a gallery, adorning the walls of people's homes.

This life feels like it never quite fit me, and Harry knew that from the beginning. I sometimes wonder if he got me pregnant on purpose. He hadn't seemed surprised, just happy. It's hard to trust my memories, the bad and the good. Now when I think about sitting in that flat with Harry on one of our first dates, I remember him begging me to stay with him, topping up my wine too much so it would be dangerous to drive home. I never questioned any of it, because it was all too convenient and comfortable, and then five years went by and I'm standing in front of a mirror, in a castle, in my wedding dress, trying to remember why I ever wanted to get married.

'Are you okay?' Mum whispers. She stands up and runs her rough hands over my bare shoulders. I nod as she picks up the veil from the dressing table. She slides it on top of my tight bun and I look up, catching her reflection before I see my own. I look pale today. The white dress washes me out, and Megan is already standing there with pink blusher in hand like she thinks it does too.

'Just a dab more?' she asks. Maybe anyone else would be offended. She should be telling me I look perfect; we should be laughing, clinking champagne glasses, and cooing about how beautiful I look and how wonderful the day will be, but the mood is sombre. Mum moves quietly around, tidying the honeymoon suite. Megan sips champagne without looking at me. April and Kate are sitting outside on the spiral staircase laughing at something, their laughter carrying through the cold stone walls, the only noise in the room.

'I'll go get the girls for a photo,' Megan says, smiling meekly at me before leaving.

'You sure you're okay?' Mum says immediately.

'Everything with Megan sorted? I know you had that little spat a month back.'

'It was nothing, just a misunderstanding.'

She shrugs. 'Yes, I remember. You'd gotten yourself into a right pickle that day thinking you'd seen someone in the house.'

'But I hadn't,' I whisper.

'No, of course not. I've just been worried about you. That message you left saying someone broke in… You were hysterical. It wasn't like you at all.'

'I was wrong,' I say. I was wrong; the footage disappeared. It was never recovered, and life sort of swept it away when Harry came home early from the stag do to tell me I was imagining things, that I was just stressed.

'That's what I mean. Maybe just the stress of the wedding is getting to you,' she says, almost like she can hear my thoughts. Or Harry told her to say that. I can imagine him calling Mum after he made me a bed on the sofa and brought me a tea, closing the lounge door gently and picking up the phone to Mum, whispering. She's fine, she's just a bit stressed from the wedding, thought we had a break-in, but it was nothing.

'You look stunning,' she says, taking my hand in hers. She hesitates, before leaning forward and tucking a stray hair behind my ear. 'I just want to make sure'—she pauses again—'that you're sure.'

All the doubt I've been feeling washes over me and I feel sick and exhausted. I don't know how so much changed in a year, but the uncertainty was always there, wasn't it?

From the night we got engaged and we sat down in the restaurant, and I saw those women laughing across the street. How free they looked. I stare back at my mum and she knows she's hit a nerve, that she shouldn't have said what she did, and that I'll react defensively—I can see it all playing out in front of me—but this is my wedding day, so I nod, slowly, and she releases a tight smile, just as Megan and the girls burst into the room, giggling in their dusty pink bridesmaids' dresses.

'Oh Lea, you look amazing,' Kate says, beaming.

'Pictures?' April adds, clasping her phone.

I blink back tears, smiling as Mum takes the phone from April and holds it up. They flock towards me and we pose, a false smile plastered on our faces.

'Are you ready? We should go down now,' Megan says.

'Yes, two seconds.'

'I'm going to tell them we're on the way. Why don't you come with me?' Mum says to Kate and April, before she smiles at me, and they duck under the arched doorway. I gather my flowers and take one last look in the mirror, seeing Megan hovering behind me.

'I'm glad we got a chance to speak,' she says. 'I just wanted to say sorry because, well, I haven't been alone with you since that day I came to yours.' She starts to shift awkwardly from foot to foot, her heels clipping on the stone floor. 'I couldn't bear that you'd think I could ever do a thing like that to you. I would never—' She bites her lip, holding back tears.

'I know, I don't think you could,' I say.

'But—' She rushes forward and cups my hands, tears now running down her face, leaving a pale line down her rosy cheeks. 'What if—' She starts breathing rapidly, her nails digging into my fingers. 'What if there was some truth to it, would that change things?' I search her features, but I don't know what she's trying to say. 'What if you were right, but—' She shakes her head. 'Not me, but … if Harry'—she looks relieved after she says his name—'if he was capable of something like that?'

'Like what?' I say.

'That message you sent.' She shakes her head. 'Or didn't send.'

'I never saw it,' I whisper.

She looks horrified, like it hasn't crossed her mind. Does she think I'm lying, that I did send it? I think back to her standing in my doorway. What she'd said… *The one where you call me a bitch, where you accuse me of kissing Harry years ago at some stupid party I don't even remember, you really think I'd do that to you?*

'What are you trying to say?' I ask.

She licks her lips and loosens her grip on my hands. 'What if I saw Harry do something? What if I saw him kiss someone else?'

I can feel my heart in my throat. I swallow but choke instead, unable to breathe through the weight of what she's claiming. I pull away from her, turning my back, clutching my veil, ready to pull it from my hair, but I stop. I remember Owen's lips on mine, that I was just as bad, that Harry and I are caught up in this fucked-up game and

I'm trapped. I let my hand fall to the side. 'We'll be late,' I say.

'What?' Megan says, breathlessly.

'We need to go, or I'll be late.'

She nods, emphatically. 'Of course.' She wipes away her tears.

'Are you okay?' I ask.

She laughs, spluttering, 'Are you?'

'Yes.'

I gather my dress and Megan straightens my veil. 'Are you ready?' she whispers, but the words carry more weight after what she's told me. Why did she never tell me? Why did she let it go so far?

'Why now?' I say, clutching the door handle.

She sniffs. 'I'm sorry,' she says, like it's obvious. She's saying it in case I change my mind; she's saying it before it's too late. I could pull my hand away from the door and yank the veil from my head. I could tell her that I'm not getting married. But it's already too late.

I pull my shoulders back and thrust open the door, seeing Mum at the bottom of the stairs, waiting expectantly.

It was too late the moment Harry walked into my life.

As we stand in front of each other and say our vows, Harry's lips are moving but I can't hear him. I feel like I'm watching a film in slow motion, begging the main character to just walk away, leave and run before they say 'I do', but the words fall freely and I can't hesitate in case people notice, but I want to pause; I want one last moment to think this through.

Harry slides the ring onto my finger and kisses me, but his lips feel strange on mine; his smell is different; his hands slip through my own; but they are not the hands I've grown to know. He looks into my eyes and I force a smile, grinning so his lips touch my teeth. To anyone observing, we are the happiest couple. Our son runs up to us and throws his hands around Harry's shoulders as he bends down and scoops him up.

I glance towards the crowd. Everyone is clapping, apart from Megan, and next to her my mum notices, but she's preoccupied with her own reasons for not being entirely happy for us. I feel mad at them, that they let it go this far, but I've done so much to cement this life of mine. How could they know how desperately I wanted to upend it? How could they know how little I trust my new husband? What my life will now be?

The reception is a blur of people congratulating me, taking my hands in theirs and kissing my cheek gently or bringing me into a warm embrace. I gaze around at the life I always wanted, a beautiful wedding in an old stone castle. Harry leans in and calls me a princess and together we walk onto the dance floor and our song comes on. I press my cheek against his shoulder and he whispers that he loves me.

Over my shoulder, I see Megan standing at the front of the crowd, holding Josh's hand and doing her best to smile at me.

I won't be friends with her after this—I can't be, because every time I look at her face I'll hear those words, *What if he did kiss someone…* I'll always know what she kept from me for all these years and thought to tell me on the day of my wedding.

My world is getting smaller and as Harry pushes back my hair, glancing down at me with a wide smile, short hairs on his chin rub against my forehead as he steps back and takes a bow.

The song is over, but the night isn't.

Later, Felicity comes up to me and pecks my cheek, telling me how happy she is to finally welcome me to the wives' club, and my stomach sinks, the champagne caught in my throat, my lips dry and fat.

The wives' club.

She says it like it's an honour, like I should be grateful, but there's so much that's happened in the last year that's pushed everything to the surface, that I don't know how I managed to get through all those days of pretending to be a wife, of pretending to like Harry's friends, of staying home all day alone, of waiting for him to arrive home.

When we climb the spiral staircase to the honeymoon suite, Harry is a few steps ahead. He's holding my hand loosely, and I could easily pull it free and turn and run, but it's as if he senses what I'm thinking and his fingers coil around mine and he starts to pull a little harder. Now his jaw is tense and it's seeing him crack, seeing the first signs of him falter, that makes me pull away.

'What's wrong?' I whisper, slowing.

'You tell me, Lea. You haven't been yourself all day,' he says.

'This was a mistake,' I say, louder than I intend to. I balance myself on the cold wall and take a deep breath, letting my neck fall and my head drop from the weight of it all.

But Harry doesn't seem surprised, why would he? Instead he leans forward and whispers. 'Let's go inside.'

But I don't want to. 'You're a liar,' I say.

'Please, Lea, can we go inside?'

I shake my head. 'I can't ignore this anymore.'

'If you come in, I can explain everything.'

I reluctantly follow him as he pushes open the heavy wooden door. The honeymoon suite has been cleaned. Fresh rose petals line the floor and bed, and a bottle of chilled champagne sits on the dressing table next to a plate of dusted-pink truffles. Harry ignores it all and slumps onto the edge of the bed, swiping at the petals, which crumple and fall to the floor.

'I feel like I don't know you,' I whisper.

'Of course you do, Lea,' he says, reaching forward, trying to grab my hand, but I swat him away.

'Did you kiss someone … at a party a few years ago?'

He frowns. 'What?'

'Why do you really need a lawyer?'

'What are you talking about, Lea?'

'Did you delete the footage from the cameras?' I take a step forward, pointing a finger. 'Why do we even have cameras?' I rip the veil from my hair and throw it on the floor. 'Tell me what's going on.'

Harry loosens his tie and rubs his thumb and forefinger over both eyes. He looks up at me. 'I'm so sorry, Lea.'

I go to speak, but there's a knock. 'It's me,' Mum calls.

I pause, before opening the front door. Mum has an apologetic smile on her face and she glances down at Josh, who's red-faced and blubbering, snot running down his nose and covering his mouth. 'Mummy,' he sobs, looping his arms around my legs, rubbing snot on my wedding dress.

'He wouldn't calm down; he really wanted to come and stay with you tonight. I'm sorry,' she says.

'That's okay,' I say, quietly, taking Josh's hand.

'Are you okay?' Mum whispers.

I nod. 'We were going to bed anyway, it's been a long day.'

Mum smiles. 'I did try, but it's just all the excitement, he's just overtired.'

'Shall we set you up on the sofa, Josh?'

He nods into my waist and slowly lets go. 'Night, Mum,' I say, closing the door, but she leans forward and places a hand to stop me.

'Tell me, Lea, if you're not okay.'

I nod. 'I'm fine.'

She lets go and I close the door, watching her disappear.

'Shall we get you to bed?' I say to Josh, leading him through the hallway to the small lounge off the main bedroom.

'Josh?' Harry calls.

'Mum brought him up. He wouldn't settle; I'm going to put him in the lounge.'

'I want Daddy to put me to bed,' Josh says, wriggling out of my grip.

Harry looks frustrated, but he tries to muster a smile as he takes Josh's hand and leads him into the lounge. I go into the bedroom and look around at the dried petals, desperately wanting to erase the day.

When Harry comes back, all the anger has risen in my stomach and starts to fizz under my chest.

'There's something you don't know about me, Lea,' Harry says suddenly, twisting his wedding band on his finger as he walks slowly towards me. I spin around, gripping the side table and edging away from him. He lowers himself back onto the bed.

'But I did all those things to protect you.'

My heart presses against my chest. 'You kissed someone?' He nods. 'And the cameras? There was someone in the house, wasn't there?'

'Yes,' he whispers.

'I'm taking Josh and we're leaving, and I swear, if you try and stop us, I will—'

'What will you do?' Harry snaps.

'I'm not scared of you,' I shout.

Harry stands slowly. His arms fall to the side, his lips pressed tightly together, his fist clenched.

But he isn't looking at me. His eyes skim my shoulder. He's watching the door.

'You *should* be scared of him,' a voice says.

When I look around, I see a woman standing in the open doorway.

She's wearing a large black duffel coat. Her blonde hair is scraped back revealing small, tired eyes, and wrinkles are etched into her cheeks.

The room is silent for a moment as I lock eyes with the woman. She smiles at me like we're friends, not strangers.

'*Get back*,' Harry shouts, pushing my waist with his outstretched hand. I stagger behind him, falling onto the edge of the bed.

The woman takes a step forward. She's twisted her head towards Harry, but she's scanning the room, muttering under her breath. 'I didn't think you'd actually go through with it,' she says. 'Have you learned nothing, Harry?'

'Who is this?' I say, breathlessly.

'Leave,' Harry commands, but the woman shakes her head, tutting as she takes another step forward.

'You didn't tell her about me, Harry?' she whispers. She turns to me and grins. There's so much similarity in our features, but she's older, about Harry's age.

'Who is this, Harry?' I repeat, fear warping my voice as I glance towards the closed lounge door. Why does it feel like we're in danger? The woman notices me do this and smiles.

'Is Josh in there?' she says quietly, but there's surprise in her voice. She wasn't expecting that.

She unzips her coat and Harry takes a step towards her, but she lunges forward first and flashes me a look of disdain. Harry holds up his arms held up defensively as he throws his weight at her.

I cry out in confusion as the woman falls back, clutching her face with one hand. She inhales sharply and growls, a deep otherworldly snarl that rises up through her body. She bends over and charges, baring her teeth as she screeches, her body knocking into Harry, who falls backwards, screaming in agony.

There's a burst of warmth—a paintbrush flicker—and when I look down, I see my white wedding dress has spots of blood trailing over my shoulder and skimming my arm.

I slowly twist my head to see the thick line drawn across the white bedsheets.

I turn back in horror. The woman is clutching her arm, blood seeping through her furled fingers and running off the black coat onto the cream carpet.

She's standing over Harry's body.

She blows the hair off her face and licks her lips. Then she rises slowly, not even acknowledging Harry as he starts to scream, reaching for me with one hand, the other grasping his stomach as he writhes on the floor.

There's a creak, and in the corner of my eye, I see Josh appear, poking his head round the door. He watches me intently, but his eyes fall on Harry. He knows something is wrong.

The woman hasn't noticed Josh yet. She composes herself, her eyes widening from the pain. She's grasping a knife, now covered in blood.

She steps over Harry's body as he coughs and splutters.

She didn't come here for him though. She came here for me.

She raises the knife and it all happens so quickly I don't have time to react. I see uncertainty in her movements as she struggles towards me.

I close my eyes, waiting for the blow, but I don't feel anything. I open them slowly to see the woman has twisted away from me, her foot inches from Harry's face.

She's looking at Josh.

'Hello there,' she says quietly. 'It's okay; you don't need to be afraid.'

Josh pushes the door open and trots towards Harry, but the woman stands in front of him. I glance back at Harry and see he's face down, blood seeping from his chest. He's completely still.

'We don't want you to see that,' the woman says, lowering herself to the floor to pick up my phone from beside Harry's blazer, peeling the veil off the floor as she does. 'Let's go get you a nice hot chocolate. It's been a bit of a day, hasn't it?' Her cheeks rise into a full smile, but spittle breaks through her clenched teeth as she flinches at the pain in her arm.

She turns her head towards me, but doesn't look at me. I just see her lips move.

'Bye, Lea,' she says.

Chapter Twenty-Seven

present

There are red lights flashing in the distance, the bad people, but they aren't bad, are they? I am. Their power illuminates the snowy verge like they're going through a tunnel and I am the brick wall at the end. It's dark, even though it's daytime, but that's how it always feels to me right now, that I'm just stumbling around in the darkness, trying to find something to cling on to.

That's when I found Josh.

I didn't want to hurt you, Harry, but look how much you hurt me.

I am your wife, and we are still married.

I never signed those papers, no matter how much you asked me to. No matter how much money you offered me, I wouldn't go away. You treated me like I was a nasty thorn in your side, and her—*Lea*—like she was the rose that you admired. You looked at her like you never looked at me.

I watched her, you know, for years, but when I saw you clumsily propose at our spot, the place we would go for walks no matter the weather and stand arm in arm looking over the valley at the suspension bridge and the passing cars below, I realised that I was just practice, until you thought you could get it right.

I used to be beautiful when I was younger. I had a dazzling smile and creamy blonde curls that shaped my blue eyes. I looked a lot like her, but my hair started turning grey, my skin loosened, my cheeks growing fuller than you would like. I knew we were coming to a violent end, but like a volcano, a heat has been burning under my skin for years, and it was all I could do to contain it—until I saw you, in our spot, with her.

I met you, Harry, when we were in our teens. You were my first love, my only love. I stood by you when we were poor and we had little money, both of us doing what we could to survive. I didn't go to university. I had dreams of being a singer and I didn't know how that would help me, so instead I sang in grimy bars and clubs, the occasional wedding here and there, and you told me you were proud of me. We lived in a little flat in central Bristol and I supported us as you started your business, as you went to make something of yourself, but singing didn't make enough money, did it? So I waited tables, washed dirty plates, spent the last of my inheritance money on getting your business off the ground.

It was tough, but we were together. You'd come home at the end of the day, exhausted, and you'd loosen your tie and tell me you loved me and we'd lie on the bed side by side, reminding each other it would all be worth it one day.

'Where are we going?' Josh asks.

'I don't know,' I reply. 'We just have to keep climbing.'

The police cars pull up at the bottom of the incline.

I wish the lights would stop, but they don't, even when they get out of the cars and close the doors. The flashing beacons are all I can see. Someone's voice carries through the mist, telling me to come back, but it just makes me push harder.

Why does no one understand that? Even you, Harry, you were supposed to know me better than anyone, but the more you pushed, the more I clung to you, the more I tried to be everything and anything you wanted me to be.

When your business did take off, it all happened quickly. You got a business partner—Oscar—and he and his wife would come round to our poky flat and have meals at our small table. They were a lot like us, starting out, ready for what was next. We all put in the years, did the time, stood by our partners, and worked hard to make this happen. I remember taking a bottle of champagne and a picnic basket to the Downs, just us four, and we toasted a new era.

It was all so hopeful.

We moved out of the small flat and into a grand apartment overlooking the wharf. It had a balcony with hanging baskets and a kitchen with an island. It was cream and white, but I couldn't wait to paint it beautiful, bright colours. You carried me into the hallway and cupped my hands and said things would be different now, that I could go back to singing, that we could be the couple we'd always wanted to be.

I think that was the moment it all started to fall apart. The couple we'd always wanted to be? But we were already there. What was more perfect than curling up in each other's arms each night, or plucking cardboard pizza from the freezer and sitting around the TV watching old sitcoms, or taking long walks through Bristol hand in hand? You were everything. I never wanted to be anything more than that. But you did.

You started coming home later; we both started getting older; and then one night you didn't come home at all. I sat waiting for you, I called all your friends, but no one knew where you were. So I started phoning hospitals, and that's when I got a call from Felicity, telling me not to be so naïve.

I thought you'd die before doing that to me, but I was the one that died in that moment.

When you eventually came home smelling of someone else.

Their lips had been on yours, their fingers threaded through yours, but worst of all, you had looked them in the eyes; you had made a connection; and you had severed ours. What were all those years for now? They're tainted and toxic. I can't look back fondly anymore, but I couldn't see ahead either; my only option was trying to salvage the present.

But you grew more confident. You suddenly didn't like

old sitcoms or want to get junk food and sit cross-legged on our rug with warm ales and smiles plastered across our stupid faces. You wanted to go to fancy bars and restaurants, wanted to hang out with people I thought were painfully dull. You wanted to squeeze yourself into all these tight spaces where there wasn't room for me too.

I didn't like the dresses, the canapes, the politeness of silly dinners, or your looks across the crowd, the disappointment that I didn't fit into your new life.

So, one night you came home reeking of her, and I'd cooked us a nice meal, even watching a video on how to make lamb shank. I dressed up in a pretty pencil dress and wore heels and did my hair and coated my face. In the mirror I looked so unlike myself. I'd always worn baggy clothes, dungarees and black T-shirts with bands on them. But I was wearing a tight red dress and my curls were tight too and I thought I looked like Marilyn Monroe. I twirled, delighted, thinking, possibly, I could make this work.

But when you got home, you were sad, and during dessert, I asked whether you thought it was time we tried for a baby and you threw your spoon down and said you couldn't do it anymore, that you were leaving me.

Had I been surprised? Not really. But I wasn't going down easily. Not without a fight.

She took what was rightfully mine.

But as I watched her closely throughout the years, I realised how trapped she was in that life, how controlling you'd become, because I'd disappointed you.

I was old and tired, and I couldn't be moulded into this

new perfect life, but her? She was everything. Slim and pretty, blonde, but not so blonde that she looked cliché. She had a wide smile and full lips, and I remember seeing her for the first time when I was watching outside our apartment one night. It was a week after you asked me to move out and she was already moving in. I thought she was trespassing, but you lured her into a trap.

I've seen that over the years, that while she looked and played the part, she was never quite there, never quite where you wanted her to be, and I can imagine how much that must have frustrated you.

You wanted a wife, not a partner. She was too ambitious for that, artistic blood in her veins. You fool, Harry, you were never going to hold her down, but you tried anyway.

She got pregnant quickly, didn't she? That hurt. It stung so badly that I couldn't eat or sleep. All I could do was follow her and soak it all up, wanting so desperately to walk forward and into her shoes and not be a shadow anymore. But I watched as her stomach swelled and it was all I could do not to step in front of her and warn her about you, that she too would be replaced someday because she didn't fit your mould.

You asked me for a divorce, and I told you, marriage is for life, Harry, and that's when Oscar started calling, then Felicity, all begging me to let it go, but why should I? Why does another woman get to step into the life we created because I was the one that didn't change? You did. How about the fact that you didn't fit my life anymore? Did you ever stop to consider that sacrifice? That I stopped singing and started cleaning? That I gave up what made me happy, to make you happy? It was torment, our whole relationship. Because I experienced the good of it for so long, it made losing you so much more unbearable.

'*Stop*,' a man's voice yells. He says it with authority, but I ignore him and continue up the hill, towards the ledge, gripping Josh.

Josh starts to cry, but I can't imagine she would have been able to stop him if she were here. She wasn't good with him, because she didn't want him, that was the problem. Whereas I was willing to try and make myself your ideal wife, she was not going willingly.

But you loved her, I could see that.

Just how far does love stretch though, Harry?

We reach the top. I clutch a jagged rock and it digs into my palms as I pull us both up. There's a path leading up to the stone ledge and that's the path we'll follow. The police officers are getting closer. They're faster than we are, and Josh is holding me back. I love him anyway, though he has your face and eyes, Harry, but I don't see much of her in him. She was always so awkward around him, and if I ever saw her again, I'd tell her that her son didn't ask for her once, he just called for his dad.

I regret what he saw. Taking him was never part of the plan, but when I turned around and saw him standing in the doorway to the lounge, rubbing his eyes sleepily and asking what was wrong, I panicked. He saw you slumped over, blood seeping into the cracks in the stone floor, and she was grasping your head, crying, begging you to be okay. I was still holding the knife when you died, Harry, unsure what to do with it next. Should I kill her too? Or set her free?

I decided on the latter.

I'd been so close to her delicate features, but I'd heard her say she was leaving anyway. I did her a favour. I rid the world of you. But more than that, I took Josh. I made it so she could go back to whatever life she had before you came into it and ruined it for her.

I won't tell another soul about what your new wife did, Harry. Because she did nothing, she didn't try and stop me, she just watched her son being dragged away by the woman who killed her husband.

That's why it became so important I keep him from her, but that plan slowly expired, because there's nowhere to run anymore.

Josh and I stand on the middle of the ledge. I take a step forward and tell him it's okay. Together we watch as the fields drop in and out of the mist, dappled white and green, smatterings of grey strung along the outline of the horizon.

I close my eyes.

'Emma, please, release the boy, take a step back.'

Josh has stopped crying, his breath heavy next to me. I take another step forward until the tip of my boot rocks on the edge and I stumble slightly. Josh screams, holding onto me.

I'll love him the way she never could, Harry.

We raise our arms. There's the stamping of feet on rock, the wind in my hair, the force rushing through my fingertips.

We are flying.

Chapter Twenty-Eight

six months later

I open my eyes and I'm staring at a cloudless blue sky.

I frown, wishing there were clouds, even just a few, the threat of rain, so we might go home. We've been here for a while, and I love watching Josh play with his friends but I'm also afraid.

I'm hoping one day I won't feel this way. That I'll wake up and everything will feel normal, but I fear Josh and I will never be normal again.

We moved out of the house in Redland. That was the first thing we did, me and Josh. We've moved into Mum's poky Bedminster house while we look for somewhere else to live. Mum says we can stay as long as we want, but Josh and I need our own space as we try to rebuild our family.

The three of us have cups of tea and watch reality TV and Josh is always painfully quiet at home, but he is never upset. I'm still learning, though, still getting to know him slowly again, still trying to rebuild that trust between us.

I like closing my eyes and listening to his cries of joy as he runs around Clifton Downs playing rounders with his friends. I was worried he would withdraw and isolate himself at school and with his friends, but he wanted to go back to school, even though other parents whispered to one another as I dropped him off and he came home one day and said very plainly, 'Jack asked if my dad was dead.'

It was rhetorical; he was just informing me, like it was something he worked on at school or some praise the teacher had given him, delivered like a note. He's spoken to multiple therapists, and they've all said that he's doing well. But doing well doesn't mean that he is okay.

He has never spoken about what happened in the days that he was taken from me.

I've asked once or twice, but the therapist said that's what they were working towards. I wish they'd get there faster. Not knowing is what keeps me up at night, and she would never tell the police the truth. The media speculated anyway, like they always do, and investigative reporters and TV producers started circling like sharks wanting to turn Josh's trauma into a TV series or podcast. If anything like that ever did get made, I'll be stupid enough to digest it, just in case they know something I don't.

What do I know? They found him on top of a cliff in the Peak District. He was cold and hungry and he'd walked for miles through the snow and ice to reach a stone ledge.

She had jumped, but it didn't kill her, it only fractured

her jaw and broke one of her legs. The news covered her story a lot, the progress she was making in hospital, because they were all keen for an interview, but as far as I know, she's never said a word.

Her arm had become infected from where the knife caught her in the struggle with Harry, and I'd seen her on the news a few times, her arm in a sling, her face blotchy and stained with tears, but her eyes unreadable, vacant, unapologetic. Then she'd stare right into the camera, like she was looking at me.

It wasn't until a few weeks later that the police told me about Emma's brother. Owen. How he had been instrumental in helping her force herself into my life. That he was trying to help her leave the country with Josh. That he'd even planned to come to the house and pretend to console me, just to get Josh's passport.

But I'm scared, sometimes, that as the trial date looms nearer there's a possibility she might get away with it all despite everything. My lawyer has been frank with me that she plans to say it's self-defence and that her arm injury caused her to have hallucinations, that she doesn't even remember what she did to Harry, or the days that followed.

I watch Josh across the field. It's his turn to bat and he steps up to the line they've drawn. The kids are screeching with happiness, egging him on as the ball flies towards him, but he misses, and tries again. The other parents are sitting near me, in the shade, trying not to look my way and leaning in to each other to whisper, occasionally clapping when it's their child's turn.

It's easier, when the weather's warm and the days are long, to distract myself from the events of the last year, and I guess, all the years before that.

Because it started at the beginning. I was always being watched, being followed. Now it's hard to shake off the feeling that someone is watching me. My skin still itches and the hairs on the back of my neck stand on end like a warning that someone is waiting in the shadows.

I went back over the last year or so, ever since Harry and I got engaged, trying to piece together all the lies. What if he'd just told me? Would things have played out differently? Would I have been able to save us?

I try not to think about Harry, but as the cold creeps in and the darkness settles, in bed, alone at night, that's when I'm not in control of my thoughts anymore.

I'm conflicted. Some nights it's like my heart has been ripped from my chest and all I can do is wish for the morning until I can focus on Josh, and finally feel like I can breathe again. Other times it's a searing anger, one that's so stifling that I choke from the heat of it, wanting to have never met him.

Then rarely, on days like today, it's quiet—a passive yet enduring acknowledgment that I never knew him, but I loved him, all the same.

Today it's six months since Josh was returned to me and, as he waves, a hand shooting up towards the light blue sky, waving enthusiastically even though he's missed the shot again, I wave back, hopeful for our future.

Carly contacted me a month after, when I was a sleepless

mound on Mum's sofa, only managing to eat a few biscuits every day. Everyone thought I was mourning, but it was the guilt that haunted me—it still does.

Carly turned up at Mum's, holding her hands up defensively and begging me to hear her out. We sat in the little courtyard garden and we didn't say anything to each other for the longest time, until she whispered quietly, 'I'm sorry.'

It wasn't what I wanted to hear, but I couldn't blame her for that. I didn't reply, though I did think, 'It's not your fault, Carly.' I didn't realise how many parts of my life Emma had invaded; I was starting to become numb to the revelations.

Carly leant forward and pressed a hand onto the table like she was steadying herself. 'I got a call from Harry early on the morning after your engagement party.' I wince when she says his name, but she doesn't notice. 'I was so surprised when he rang. He told me you weren't yourself, that he was worried you were going to do something very reckless. I was so worried about what he meant, but he said he couldn't find you, that you'd gone off after a bad argument with him and he thought you were going into the office. He told me you did that sometimes when you'd had a bad fight. I guess I didn't question it, because you did rush off that evening looking flustered and upset, and you hadn't been yourself, Lea, you just hadn't. So I got dressed and I left early, expecting to find you curled up on the sofa in the break room, but you weren't there, so I checked the gallery, and that's when I found it. I called Harry straightaway, because I didn't know what to do and he confirmed it, said you'd come home and your hands were stained red.'

I sighed, partly angry at Harry for taking so many measures to keep her away from me, but angry at myself for not questioning any of it. Why had Harry not told me about Emma? Was he ashamed? Had too much time elapsed? Was he scared he'd lose me if he told me? As each day passed, did that become more of a possibility to him? I would have left him, I admit to myself.

'I didn't want to fire you,' she continued. 'But I thought it was best that you took some time to yourself. I thought you were unwell, but Harry told me that you were stressed and exhausted and I asked you if were okay, and you hesitated... Why did you do that?' She shook her head. 'I'm sorry, I thought I was doing what was best for you. I didn't think you had defaced the paintings, but Harry'—she paused— 'I guess it doesn't matter what Harry said.'

I didn't respond to her, and we just sat in silence until she pointed towards Mum's art studio and asked, 'Can I have a look?'

I nodded, watching as she opened the door and peered in. Most of my paintings were propped against the wall, covered in sheets, but she spotted the easel in the corner, the back of the canvas facing us. 'Working on something? Or is it your mum's?'

'It's mine,' I said. 'You can take a look if you want.'

She trod carefully across the studio, avoiding the

paintings lying face-down on the floor, the ones I'm waiting to throw away—one day.

When she got to the painting, her mouth dropped open slightly, her breath caught in her throat as she took a step back. 'Oh, Lea,' she said, looking up at me. 'This was so personal. I shouldn't have looked. I'm so sorry, I just was hoping you'd found your way back to art, that's all.'

'Well, as you can see, I have.'

She nodded.

'It's helping me work through it,' I said, shrugging.

'You're very talented,' she said sadly, holding a hand up to the picture, her fingertips almost touching it. 'You should submit it to a gallery—when and if you're ready,' she added.

'Do you think it's good enough?' I asked.

She smiled. 'Yes.'

Now tonight's the night of my art exhibition.

I finished the pieces I'd been working on and called the collection 'The Darkest Days of Winter'. It reminded of an old Italian fable, 'The Days of the Blackbird', in which a white bird mocked and taunted the winter months by waiting out the cold, but on emerging victorious, winter delivered the harshest and coldest three days of the season, and the white bird sought refuge in a chimney, turning it a deep black.

I submitted the collection to a local gallery where Carly was now working, and they wanted to deck out the entire studio in my pieces and to have a huge launch event. I declined, saying I didn't want to be involved in all that, but they could do what they wanted with the pieces, as long as the money went to Tracey's family.

I think about her too sometimes, how scared and alone she must have felt. How her family weren't able to sell the property because of the grisly murder that took place. How her happy family home became a tainted and tragic place. I drove up there once. To all the places Josh had been. They let me into the house and I walked slowly around as we all tried to piece together what happened there.

Then I walked down to the guesthouse, and I stood outside staring at the empty windows and lifeless garden until the police told me it was time to go. I had to pull myself away from that place, but it turned my heart black, to know such hate lived in the world, and it could work its way there and infect someone else's life so permanently.

I became consumed by the cottage, and I told Tracey's sons that I would buy it from them once the money for the house in Redland came through. And that one sold quickly, because it didn't have the same stain as Bramble Cottage. I'd only ever spoken to two of her sons on the phone, but they didn't think it was strange that I wanted to buy the cottage. They didn't question it at all. I guess they know I have unfinished business there. I just don't know what it is. I was surprised they didn't want to salvage the happy memories, but I was told the youngest son found her, and that was a memory they could never erase. It would always win over everything else.

'Mum,' Josh cries as he comes running towards me. The game of rounders is over and the group starts to part, disbanding in different directions towards their parents. My face feels cleansed by the afternoon heat, but I've enjoyed the time to work out my feelings, to sit in silence and process everything. I would usually retreat to the art studio in Mum's garden and work on my collection, but it feels important to address things, every now and then. And today is an important day.

'What's for dinner?' Josh asks as we walk towards the car.

'What would you like?'

'Pizza.' He smiles up at me.

'Pizza it is.'

There's something hopeful about today, but I can still never quite shake it, that I was being watched for so long without knowing … that it feels, sometimes, like there's still someone there.

———

When I arrive at the gallery, Carly greets me at the door and flaps her hand. 'We won't make a big deal of it, just mill around with the other guests, okay? I'll come find you in a bit?'

I nod, glad that she doesn't want to introduce me. I didn't ask Mum to come tonight. I wanted to be alone, to see my work on the walls and stare at it for a moment. Before walking away. It's bittersweet to finally see my art hanging on a wall of a studio, and to know where all the inspiration came from, that those dark places in me are darker than ever.

It's busy, a good turnout for an opening, and at the front there's a sign saying, 'All proceeds will be donated to the victims of the Bramble Cottage murders, Tracey Smith's four sons.'

I told them about the gallery opening and sent them pictures of the artwork. They seemed moved by the idea of an exhibition being held in Tracey's honour, but they weren't ready—not yet—to be in a room with people tipping their heads to the side and stroking their arms asking if they were okay. I laughed quietly at that: how many people must have loved her; whereas people avoid me. I guess there's always a lingering question about what really happened in that room the night she took Josh, the night Harry died.

Harry's old friends barely spoke to me afterwards, only at Harry's funeral, where they all muttered how sorry they were, but they didn't consider me a friend anymore. All the legal aspects of Oscar and Harry's business were dealt with by a lawyer. I approved the letters my solicitor sent and saw Oscar's replies—he seemed irritated by them—his solicitor saying that 'his client doesn't believe the terms are fair.'

There's nothing fair about this, about losing who I thought was my husband, to live with the conflict of that love and hate. To know it was all about to fall apart before she even arrived.

Felicity took my hand at the funeral and held it in hers for a moment, but she didn't say anything, not a word. She knew about Emma, about Harry's wife, and she knew there was nothing she could say to me to make that better.

I walk slowly through the gallery. I'm handed a glass of champagne, which I take, but don't drink; I just clutch it like a prop as I smile sheepishly at guests, hoping they won't know who I am.

The artwork is a series of paintings starting with the promise of spring, beautiful pink blossom arching over sparkling streams. As you walk through, the seasons slowly change, the leaves drop from trees, the blue sky parts making way for angry clouds. The colour drains from each one, dripping down the painting and onto the walls, different colours icing the frames—yellows to blues to browns to nothing. The paintings become void of colour, monochrome images of winter, vicious greys tearing through bright whites. At the end of the hallway there's a statue of a faceless woman standing atop a fountain with a blackbird resting on the tip of her outstretched hand, a dense streak of black arching over its silvery feathers as it cries into the darkest day of winter.

When I approach it, I can barely look. I feel a hand on my shoulder, but I start to cry, turning away, rushing back down the hallway to the exit, champagne sloshing over my glass as I clumsily place it on an empty tray, desperately trying not to look up, not to let anyone see me.

I burst out into the quiet evening, gasping for air. There are footsteps behind me.

'Sorry,' I mutter, turning, expecting to see Carly.

But it's not her.

It's Owen.

'Lea,' he whispers.

I take a step back, but he keeps edging closer, an outstretched hand almost brushing against me.

'Get away,' I cry, but my back hits the metal railing that separates the canal and the pathway. There's nowhere to go.

'Please,' he says.

'You can't be here. You're not allowed to be.'

'I'm going, I just—' He pauses, taking a step back. 'Please.'

'I thought you were in prison,' I say.

He shakes his head. He looks terrible, so much smaller and greyer than I remember him. I feel sick just thinking about him touching me, about what it meant to him, about why he was doing it.

'I'm out on bail. My trial isn't for another couple of months,' he sighs, pushing his hands into his coat pocket. 'I could get into a lot of trouble for being here,' he says, 'but I wanted to come and explain myself.'

'The police told me everything. She sent you to mess with me. You can save yourself the time,' I say.

He nods, solemnly. 'I just wanted to say I'm sorry. She did ask me to follow you and befriend you, but I knew it was wrong. I knew she needed help, but she made me believe it was Harry holding up the divorce. I didn't know how deep it ran until the day of the crash.' He takes a step forward. 'Please believe me.'

I shake my head. 'She's your sister; of course you knew. The police told me you knew, that you were trying to get her out of the country, both her and Josh. There is nothing I have to say to you.'

He takes his hand out of his pocket, holding something. I flinch, but he whispers. 'It's okay, it's just a letter.'

When I open my eyes, he's holding a slim white envelope which he gestures for me to take.

'What is that? Is it from you?'

He shakes his head.

It's from her.

'I would get into so much trouble for this, but she begged me to bring it to you. She just wanted to make you feel better.' He motions again for me to take it but I stay fixed to the metal barrier, my hands gripped tightly around the rail. 'Please take it.'

'I don't want it. She doesn't have anything to say to me.'

'Doesn't she?' he says, almost irritated now. 'I know what she did was wrong, and she'll pay the price for that, we both will, but she said it was important and I believe her.'

'No, it's not.'

'She said it's about that night, the night she took Josh.' I don't reply, I swallow back tears and fear as he slowly bends down and places the envelope on the cobbled floor by my feet. 'It's up to you,' he says. 'But I said I'd get it to you, if it's the one thing I do right for her, because I'm her older brother, and I couldn't keep her safe.' He bites his lip, his face contorted into a desperate, pained half-smile as he takes one step closer to me. 'I'm so sorry,' he whispers.

I watch him turn and leave, disappearing into the

darkness of the night, wondering how he knew where to find me. I exhale, tears running down my cheeks as I pick the letter up from the cold stone street. I'll take it to the police. They can use it as evidence.

It has my name scrawled across the front.

Lea.

It's like the name is so familiar to her, it looks natural, a messy kind of understanding in the way she's written it, like she's worn the name too.

I pace back to the railing and gaze out at the black water, the lights from the pubs and riverboats casting a bright, promising sheen across the surface. I turn the envelope over in my hands. What could she have to say that I don't already know?

But it's about that night—the night she took Josh.

A letter to Lea

My dearest Lea,

I'm not sure where to start. Maybe the beginning? But that seems so long ago now, doesn't it? I don't know how much you know about me, or what happened after I left you, but I used to be you. Harry and I got married young. We were each other's first love, but not each other's last.

I thought I owed you an explanation, because I was never given one. I was expected to disappear into the background and let you take centre stage, but I never really went away. I guess I wanted to say that you aren't crazy. I heard you, the night of your wedding, I was standing behind the door listening to it all play out and I didn't know if I'd go ahead with it, but you needed me, and I needed you.

I saw the desperation and pain on your face. You wanted it all to go away. You were trapped, and I freed you.

Owen tells me that Josh still calls you Mum, that you and Josh have become closer.

I'm glad if I helped in some small way to make that all possible. There are probably questions you have that I'd happily answer if you ever wanted to visit me. It would be nice to talk to someone that understands.

Your wedding was a sham. I am still married to Harry. Death couldn't even part us. I've been watching you over the years, waiting for you to turn into me, and I believe the time was coming, until he realised who you really were and how he could never make you fit. He got you young, but he never gave you enough credit, Lea.

I started watching you as soon as I knew who you were. But that turned into following you, and then, when you got engaged, it morphed into something else entirely. I was angry at you, Lea, for falling for him. You reminded me so much of myself, it was like looking in a mirror. You seemed quite reserved at first, never giving yourself to him fully. I guess that's how we differed: I gave him my whole self and so when he left, there was nothing.

I know he didn't tell you about me, because he was ashamed. I'd become quite old and worn. I became a part of his life he wanted to erase. But you can't erase a marriage, no matter how hard he tried. And he did try.

I will say this about Harry, though. He loved you, in a way he never loved me, because he became a different person, and we weren't compatible anymore. He only ever did things to protect you and maybe that's what made me snap, that you wouldn't bend to him and he was going to try and make you anyway.

Killing him was the only thing that freed us both, because I couldn't bear for you to end up like me. You might think I disliked you, but I never did and I never could. I told Harry the day after you got engaged how wrong it was to trick you. He always wanted to marry you, Lea, but he couldn't, because of me. So he was just going to go ahead with it anyway?

I wasn't going to let that happen. I was doing you a favour by staying married to him. I was keeping you safe. But the more I watched, the more I saw.

I hadn't been in contact with Harry for a while, but when he slid that ring onto your finger, that's when I came out of the shadows. I made things really difficult for him. He even hired a lawyer to try and warn me off. He tried putting a restraining order on me. He tried to divorce me over and over again, but none of it worked. He had to know that I wasn't going anywhere, and when I couldn't get to him, there was only one last place to turn, and that was to you, Lea.

I took your keycard from your purse the night of the engagement party. I was the one that threw paint at all the ugly works of art and later planted the card back on your pillow. I'd had an awful fight with Harry that night. He'd seen me across the street staring at you through the window as you laughed and smiled in that beautiful green dress, your face lit up as you scanned the room for him. But he wasn't there. He'd seen me, and he was coming. I told him I'd make a scene, that I'd walk in there and you'd turn slowly towards me as I screamed that I was his wife.

Instead he ushered me into a taxi and we drove along the road that runs along the gorge. We were silent, and I thought he might lean over and kiss me and tell me he was sorry, but it was his silence that became our undoing. I imagine it became yours as well. Instead, he took me home, told me to stay away from you, and that if I ever came near you again, he'd kill me.

I was so angry, so I went back, with your keycard in hand, and I stood in the middle of the brilliant white gallery and I danced and spun down the hall, paint flying in all directions. It was really beautiful. A work of art in itself.

I got out my phone afterwards and took a picture, sending it to Harry as a warning I was not done. He must have been worried about you working at the gallery after that. I hadn't given back the keycard, and I didn't plan on it until I was satisfied. I heard you lost your job, but I'm sure Harry orchestrated that. Maybe it was control, or maybe he was scared that I'd get to you one night when you were alone, clearing up after an event, or working late in that poky upstairs office. He was right.

But I could always get to you, Lea. There were other ways.

What Harry didn't realise is that I still had his old laptop, a hand me down he lovingly gave to me. The one with his passwords on it. Well, not everything, of course, he changed his email login and Amazon account, I assume he shared those with you. But he left a few things for me.

You've been on some lovely holidays over the years, stayed in some gorgeous places on Airbnb, and so did Harry and I when we were together.

I almost felt like I was there with you. But it was when you started talking to Tracey, when you showed interest in her sweet little Bramble Cottage in the Peak District for your honeymoon.

That's when I really started paying attention.

Owen was a mistake. I sent him to find out about you. I didn't expect him to fall in love. It made me even more curious about you, this woman that men couldn't resist. I didn't expect you to give Owen the time of day, but you did, you liked the attention. I watched as you spoke by the front gate and afterwards I'd call Owen and he'd tell me everything.

Well, not everything.

Some things he wanted to stay between you and him, and they always will, I suppose.

Then, one day, it was the day of the school fair, and I watched as you and Owen strode out of the gates, his face covered in paint, your children smiling at one another. You were blushing, and you'd worn this revealing dress that wasn't appropriate for a school fair. I was so angry you were using Josh as a prop to get attention from another man, whilst Harry was doing his best to support you. I wouldn't have done that to him.

I watched as you got in your car and drove slowly down the road towards the life that should have always been mine. I turned down one of the roads opposite and circled around. I did it without thinking. I started my car and slammed my foot onto the gas until I heard the crunch of metal and felt the impact on my neck. I was sorry immediately afterwards, but I couldn't risk you seeing my face, so I drove off, hoping that you and Josh were okay. I called Owen and sobbed down the phone to him once I'd parked up a few streets away. I wanted to make sure Josh was okay. I was angry at myself for doing that to an innocent child.

But it just drove Owen further towards you. I know he went to the hospital with you and took you home afterwards. He called me that evening saying he couldn't do this anymore. It had gone too far. I whispered, 'You love her', and he didn't deny it; he just hung up.

Owen and I had a rough childhood. Our parents died in a car crash when we were both very little and all we had was each other. You can never turn your back on that, no matter what I did to him, and what he did to me. Falling for you? It was almost my breaking point.

The last thing Owen said to me was that your wedding was going ahead. I couldn't have that.

I followed you to the that little cottage in the Cotswolds and watched you and your friends roll about the garden, drunk and happy. Felicity was there, which surprised me, because you didn't seem to like her. I never liked her either. Maybe we could have bonded over that, Lea?

Felicity was the woman Harry wanted us to be. I knew her at the beginning, before she was all manicured and ridiculous, when she didn't fawn over expensive wine and pretty dresses. I knew her when she was plain and small, but she grew with the role of Oscar's wife, revelled in the success and slowly started to become their 'gal', and all three of them turned on me.

I watched you closely that weekend and smiled as you rolled your eyes at Felicity. Yes, she is a royal pig. Maybe I should have gutted her too.

I went to that cottage with every intention of telling you who I was, but I saw how much she got in your head, and I knew that Harry would never let you believe that I existed. I felt so painfully desperate in that moment. So, I followed you to the nightclub and I put something in your drink when you weren't looking, and—don't you remember?—I was the other side of the toilet stall and I whispered to you to run and not marry him, but you were out of your mind. I'd gone too far.

I heard the click of heels, and Felicity and your friend Megan came running in, so concerned about you, and I sat in the next stall and heard it all play out. She relished it, you know. Felicity, she enjoyed your suffering.

But Megan, she seemed different from the girl I saw Harry with years ago. She had been with him; she had watched him lean over and kiss another woman at that party. She seemed awfully devoted to you. I'm surprised she never said anything. Cowardly, is she?

It was the first time I'd followed Harry in a while and he didn't see me coming until it was too late. He spotted me through the crowd and I smiled and waved. He didn't know I knew about you. He was talking to this woman, and then he panicked. He leaned in and kissed her right in front of me, and when I followed him to his car afterwards, he turned suddenly and grasped me by the throat and pushed me back and said, 'Can't you see I've moved on, Emma? Leave me the fuck alone.' He spat it at me like I was nothing to him.

'Moved on with who?' I asked.

'With whoever the fuck I want to,' he said, walking away. I followed him until he got into a taxi.

I tapped on the glass and smiled sweetly at him. 'I know that woman's not Lea.'

He couldn't stand it when I said your name. He threw open the taxi door and asked me to repeat myself, but I didn't need to.

I always wondered if he kissed that woman to throw me off the scent of you, because he didn't realise how intimately I knew his life, or if he really did kiss other women when he was with you. I guess we'll never know, will we?

It's another thing you'll have to live with, like you'll always live with the fact that you didn't stop me the night of your wedding. That you watched me walk out the door leading Josh by the hand as he screamed for you.

He realised in that moment that he could never rely on you again.

He can rely on me, though, Lea, and I miss him dearly.

Don't worry. Like I said, I won't tell a soul. It's enough of a weight for you to carry by yourself.

I so hope that you've found some happiness in your new life. I hear you're a painter now. That your pretty art lines the white walls I once coated red. That you got a lot of money out of what happened to Harry and Josh. That you go out dancing at weekends with your friends. That you have the life you always wanted.

Just know that it was all because of me.

Love,

Harry's wife,

Emma

Read on for an extract from *The Girl Upstairs*...

How well do you know your neighbour?
Would you trust them with your life?

Chapter 1

I heard Emily before I met her. The harsh smack of heels against cheap wooden floorboards. The gentle buzz of a phone followed by a surge of high-pitched notes, sometimes angry, sometimes excited, rarely sad. The sadness came through the slim pipes in the bathroom, the soft gurgles that slipped down the plumbing and escaped through my extractor fan. The incessant music thrumming through the ceiling, invading my space. Emily has terrible taste, mostly new tracks, screeching pop singers holding long, high notes, the same beat in every song.

I knew Emily before I met her. Italian food on Mondays, meatballs rich and smothered in tomato sauce. Tuesdays, something eggy. Wednesdays, something meaty. Thursdays and Fridays, mostly wine. A takeaway on Saturdays, usually Chinese, the sticky leftover noodles escaping through the shared food waste bin like silky worms breaking through soil. Sometimes I could smell the food

301

and other times I knew from a discarded receipt in our communal hallway.

On Sunday the shake of bottles being emptied into the recycling bin outside from her weekly wine shop. A crate of six, always. They sound lovely from the tasting notes I found clinging to the letter box. A Malbec, blackberry and vanilla notes with a finish of chocolate and nutmeg, soft and warm.

I've been in London for over ten years now and I haven't found a quiet place. I live in Angel, Islington. The nice part, with the grand white townhouses, the ones advertised as being on tree-lined streets. I can't see any trees, just blunt shavings in the ground, weeds rising and arching over the stubs like gravestones. I'm on the ground floor of a two-storey house and Emily is above me. She moved in over six months ago and I thought she might leave, as people do here. People Emily's age, early twenties, they come and go like the seasons and it's spring now. Time for new life. Time for Emily to leave.

How do you afford to live there? It slips off everyone's tongue so easily. Why is everyone so concerned – so intrusive? I'm in marketing, I say, and I can see the forced smile at the broad term, the mouth widening and the gentle nod. Meeting new people has become tiresome, so now I prefer to stay inside with my books. Things that can't judge, objects without expression. Thirty-five, living alone, in marketing. I stare out onto the street as the rain sluices through my open windows and down raspberry-coloured curtains, like fingers through hair. The black streetlamp glows faintly in the ghostly evening haze, a cat is whisked into a bush and cars fight through the wall of rain. There is always noise.

I pick up a cup of coffee from the table wedged into the bay window and take a sip. I let the bitterness tear through my mouth, down my throat and into the warmth of my belly. It grumbles. I'll cook dinner soon, a lasagne tonight. Mondays are Italian night after all.

Work was long today, monotonous, and I think how much I don't care. Do people know? They must. I exist at work, quietly and unimposingly, but that's threatening, isn't it? It threatens the nature of those who swap stories on what they cooked for dinner, the film they saw at the weekend, the latest true-crime documentary. I work at a design agency, in the copywriting department. I close my eyes. A stepping stone, I always used to say, but there is nowhere left to step. The specks of rain ricochet onto my face and I smile. An ambulance roars in the distance and a man's coarse voice rises in the street outside. I take a deep breath and taste nothing but the expelled fumes from a passing car; I open my eyes and lean forward to close the window.

I see Emily walking up the street, her slight frame shielded by a large umbrella, her incongruous red wellies flicking dirt into her path. She has her tanned legs exposed in a short denim dress, a charming brown coat skims her figure and long brown hair emerges, clutching her face like a web. I sink back behind the curtain. The familiar jingle of Emily's heavy keychain and the rattle of the key. A sharp slam of the door and a fuss to get her wet wellies off. She'll leave them in our shared hallway, as she always does when it rains. I've laid paper out for her before, but she misses, leaving them inches from the edge. I choose not to think it's deliberate, but I know people like her, entitled and uncompromising.

She trudges up the stairs and I risk a peek around the corner of my door. The red wellies lie on their side, mud mixing into the shabby carpet and flicked up the small table we use for our post. I put my door on the latch and tread carefully into the hallway, stand up the wellies and place them on a spread newspaper. Emily won't know, she won't care. I glance at the post on the table; she didn't take hers up. I can see a letter in a slim white envelope with her name and address scrawled in curly handwriting. Not important to her, nothing is. I take the letter, walk up the staircase quietly and place it on her tattered doormat where she won't be able to miss it.

I stoop carefully back into my flat and close the door. I walk across the small lounge and into the kitchen area. I bend down and pluck a lasagne from the freezer and turn the oven on. Emily flicks on her TV and the noise drones down as if escaping her. She is heavy-footed, and I can hear her move from room to room, the various sounds that she is home. The snap of the fridge door, the flush of the toilet, the phone calls. Noises designed to cover her loneliness. Well, it won't work, I say aloud. She won't hear me.

The smell of tomato and basil sifts through the ceiling and settles on my taste buds. She plonks down in front of the TV and the sofa shifts forward, the TV turned up. She's placed her phone on the floor and I can hear the dense vibrations directly above me, taunting me. I look up and catch myself in the lounge mirror, my face scrunched and deep frown lines clawing my forehead, my pale complexion a host to dark purple circles under my eyes. My sandy blonde hair is knotted into two plaits resting on bony shoulders. I sob, but I can't hear myself above the deep static tones of Emily's television; as with her, noise is more important right now and I let the tears drift away and place my lasagne in the oven.

I slip my phone out of my bag and see the familiar missed calls, my mum and my sister. They'll be worried. I text the group family chat saying I'm fine. My mum sends a hug emoji back, followed by:

Shall we call later?

I wince at the thought and type back,

No I've got some work to do, maybe tomorrow.

She won't take it personally, but she'll worry. I look up. I need for her not to come here. It will break me if she does, noise I don't need, can't fit in right now. I type again,

We'll video chat, it'll be nice.

I look around again. I won't video chat with her here – it can't be here.

Chapter 1

Emily gets up and moves to the kitchen, I hear the movement of cutlery, plates clattering in the sink, the pots edged up to the kitchen tiles. I wonder if she is messy. I think of the wellies in the hallway and smirk; of course she is.

I grab my new version of a Joe Hill novel, the spine sharp and fresh, the front cover smooth and unmarked. There are no memories in this, I think, and I revel in that for a moment.

My timer chimes to get the lasagne out of the oven, just as Emily strides over to the TV and switches it off. Her phone is vibrating aggressively and then it stops. Her voice, shrill and keen, laughs, laughs again. I wish I knew what was so funny. The high voice, the giggles, the long, drawn-out sentences can only mean she's talking to a guy. I've heard men up there. I'm never sure if it's the same man, or different men that flit in and out of her life. I've heard Emily before, the creaking of the bed as it rocks back and forth. I've turned my music on then, so loud, to let her know that I hear her, that I hear everything. She'll never stop though, because she's twisted in it, selfishly enjoying the feel of a man. I gulp, looking down at the wet lasagne as I slide it onto a plate. I push it away, no longer hungry.

Emily ends her call and shuffles to the bathroom. I hear her piss sink in the toilet bowl and then the flurry of water down the pipes. Maybe she's getting ready, maybe the man from the phone will be around soon and she needs to prepare. The shower starts and dinner is forgotten. I smile, remembering when I used to forget dinner, the excitement of the evening too overwhelming, too thrilling to bother. Now, it is a regime, a signifier of time.

I slump on the leather chair and coil the blanket around me. I pull in the Joe Hill book and cradle my chin between my knees. A man is yelling over the road into his phone and motorbikes full of food deliveries pace the streets as water sloshes to the side of the pavement. I curl further into the blanket as the night descends and the streets grow more vicious. I bury myself in the chapters of my book, occasionally glancing between the cracks in my curtain, watching shapes move past, each more threatening than the last.

———

The sound of music revives me, sending my book toppling from my lap onto the floor. I lean up and glance at the book sprawled across the rug at my feet and can smell the lasagne going stale on the kitchen counter. My head thumps to the music. Emily. The sound of laughter, hers, and a man's low, enticing voice. I can make out the words to the song. I mime them as I clutch my head, 'I'm a sucker for you.'

I curl my fists into small balls and fight back the tears. Without thinking, I fly towards the door and flick it on the latch. I storm up the stairs and come face to face with Emily's front door, Flat 2, the 2 crooked and rusty. I bang on the door, hard. I feel the weight of the movement vibrate through my clutched fist.

The voices stop, I hear movement off the sofa and Emily whisper, 'I don't know, shall I answer it?' I slam my fist into the door again. *Yes, you should answer it.* The door opens slowly and Emily's small face peers around. She sees me and a flash of recognition and concern crosses her features. She furrows her eyebrows and opens the door wider.

'It's my neighbour,' she says, looking at me.

I hear a body shift in the background. Emily looks up at me, her brown eyes glistening and confused. There's a harshness to her features; she's frustrated at my presence, bored almost.

'It's your music,' I say finally.

Her expression doesn't shift. She doesn't go to defend herself. It's like she's heard it a million times – other neighbours, her parents, other people.

'I'll turn it down,' she says, already shutting the door.

'Okay, thanks,' I say quietly, but the door is already closed on me and I can hear Emily stride across the room, irritation circling her words, 'Turn the music off. Let's go to the bedroom.'

I'm left alone in the hallway, all my anger evaporated and all that's left is a longing to speak more, to say something. To scream into Emily's closed door. Instead I pad downstairs and stare at her red wellies. I yell, thrashing towards them, and I kick as hard as I can, but they just flop to the floor. How they were when she left them.

Chapter 2

I've just finished work, but instead of heading back home, I walk out of Angel tube station and turn the other way. I push through the crowds towards the small green patch separating the rows of townhouses with colourful doors and expensive cars parked outside. The sky is grey and bleak, reflecting the stale faces of those that fly past me. Since I moved to London, I never quite adjusted to the rudeness, the selfishness, the 'me' mentality. I'm from a small seaside town called Hove, where the morning dog walkers greet everyone with a grin and a small wave. Every bartender knows your name, your drink order and your favourite baguette. The air tastes thin and sweet, like damp bark and sea salt. You can walk a metre without intrusion, but now as I evade oncoming Londoners, the air is heavy and tastes thick like diluted tar.

I push into a crowded coffee shop, the noise plaguing me as I find any available seat. The windows are steamed up and the incessant chattering from other tables echoes through the shop. A lady wipes my table, but ignores me. I lay my coat across the chair and walk to the till; someone dives in front of me and doesn't look back. I order a black coffee and hold my card out, recoiling at the cost. I carry the coffee back to my table and look around. I can feel eyes on me and I try to swat them away like pesky flies, but they continue to look.

I retrieve my phone from my small backpack and video call my mum, pushing back wisps of my hair behind my ear. I force a smile. I plug in my headset and do my best to look together, pulling the coffee closer to the edge of the table in focus.

My mum's pixelated face appears on screen and so does mine. I catch myself and smile more, wider, until I don't recognise myself. My mum is waving into the camera, her white teeth shooting across the screen and her soft red hair falling elegantly to each side.

'Mum,' I cheer.

'Suzie.' She grins back and fidgets to the side. 'Your dad is just pouring me a glass of wine.' She jumps up and swivels the camera onto my dad, who stands waving in the background. His thick grey eyebrows high on his forehead and red lips stretched wide.

'Hi, Dad.'

'All right, love, how's it going?'

My mum leaves him in the background and walks out of the room.

'Are you not going to let me reply to Dad?' I say, half laughing.

'No,' she giggles, waving her hand. She grins more. 'Where are you?' she says.

'I'm just in a coffee shop, having a quick coffee before I head out for dinner.'

My mum looks surprised. 'Who are you going for dinner with?'

'Just some London friends,' I reply, my face fixed in a permanent smile.

'That's nice. It's good to do things like that, even if you don't want to.' Her lips quiver.

I nod. 'I think we're going to The Breakfast Club – you know, that place we went with you and Dad.'

Tuesday, something eggy.

'Oh, that's nice. How's work?' she continues.

'Fine, slow at the moment, but fine.'

She nods slowly.

'You're looking thin,' she says finally.

I lean back and take a long sip from my mug, letting the powdery coffee rest on my tongue, wishing I had prepared. I let the chatter of the coffee shop consume me and I turn slightly to the crowd, looking at them differently now; they are my ticket.

'Sorry, Mum, it's busy in here.'

She ignores me. 'Shall Dad and I come up soon? Or do you want to come home for a bit?' she says, rushed.

I feel my eyes glistening, the familiar warmth in my

Chapter 2

chest and the words caught and distraught in the roof of my mouth.

'We can make up your old room and look after you for a bit? Lunch down the pub and coastal walks, doesn't that sound nice?'

'I am home,' I say quietly and so hesitantly that even I don't believe it.

'I want to look after you.'

Anger floods me and I fight back the tears. I feel so hot, frustrated and anxious. My chest is tight and I can feel the heat in my cheeks rising.

'I can look after myself.'

'Don't push us away,' my mum says, her expression passive.

'Mum, I have to go.'

She doesn't fight me; a weak smile slips across her face and she brushes back her long hair.

'Call your sister, let her know you're okay.'

'Yeah.' I hold up my hand and wave. My mum waves back; her long fingers, limp and pale, scrunch in front of me.

'Bye,' I say, my hand already on the red *hang-up* button.

I place the phone on the table, the screen face-down. I take a deep breath and push away the remainder of my coffee. I let the tears slide down my face and cool the warmth in my cheeks. I swipe at stray hairs circling my face and gather my belongings.

When I moved to London, my cousin had told me that 'everyone in London is invisible', but as I turn I see the unapologetic faces staring at my blotchy face. I drop my bag and the contents spill onto the shop floor. No one moves to help, they just watch. I don't feel invisible at all.

The stuffy street air clings to me as I move through the small strip of green towards my flat. My shoulder bangs against other commuters as we move fiercely in our own direction, all driven by a different purpose. I glimpse the familiar yellow glow of my local off-licence in the distance, with its large fruit and veg stand jutting out onto the pavement and the group of local kids piled on bikes, eyes searching for a distraction. I think how horrible it would be to grow up in London, nowhere to explore, no trees to climb or woods to get lost in. I think about sweet ice-cream cones down the beach in Hove, lemon sorbet sliding down my chin as a child and my mum zipping up my white puffer coat as we waddled with our deck chairs to the beach. My sister Clara always a step ahead, bounding in silver jelly sandals towards the sea, her sun-kissed hair flowing innocently in the gentle breeze.

Home, I think. I pass the kids on the bikes and enter the shop, shielding my face from the guy behind the counter. He knows my name, but I don't know his and I think, I'm part of the problem. I grab a couple of microwave meals and a pack of chocolate biscuits. I press my hand over the freezer and stare at the tubs of lemon sorbet, my mind lost in a distant memory.

'Suzie.'

The shopkeeper is standing beside me, giving me a flash of white teeth. A small basket clings to his outstretched hand.

'For your things,' he says, shaking it.

I let my purchases clatter into the basket and take it from his hand, smiling as I do. I mutter thanks and bow my head away towards the toiletries. I can feel him hovering behind me, questions edging towards the tip of his tongue. Instead he clears his throat and moves away, back behind the counter. Good, because I couldn't answer him.

I pay for my things and take the thin blue plastic carrier bag from him, never once making eye contact. I leave the shop and see the kids cycling away towards the canal, shouting into the evening air, one or two arms raised into the sky, as if they were waiting for night to fall.

I check my phone and see a message from my mum telling me to have fun tonight. I scan the rest of my messages and see all the group chats I've left recently, the friends that have slowly fallen away. Maybe I should go back to Hove, but as I round the corner and see my flat perched there, I know I could never make the journey; it would be too painful to leave. I quickly text Clara saying we should catch up soon, and think about her in her small terraced house in Brighton, cuddled up to my niece and nephew, her husband, Ian, crashing through the door and bundling his family into his large, strong arms.

When I enter my flat, I see Emily's letter right back where I found it, sitting on the communal table. She doesn't want to deal with the responsibility of whatever's in it, I think, entering my flat. I pick at the pack of biscuits as I read and slurp flat Diet Coke from a mug from the comfort of my leather chair. I hear Emily bustle through the front door, plastic bags brushing against the wall as she makes her way upstairs. Company tonight?

Emily walks into her flat and suddenly my evening is over and hers begins. The TV soars into action, the kettle flicks on and howls in her kitchen. She's wearing heels today; thick chunky soles smack onto her floor and she doesn't take them off. She's on the phone, but she's not flirty today, she's angry. Her voice is raised and fast, I can't make out the words, but her tone is curt and wooden. Short sentences are barked out like orders. Maybe someone cancelled on her? The man from yesterday? The phone hits the floor and I jump, sending my mug tipping to the ground, and black bubbles slosh onto my piles of books. I unfurl myself and collapse to the floor, pulling the books from the small puddle forming.

Emily is crashing across her lounge and towards the bathroom. I leap up and follow her into my bathroom and hear her tears echoing in the room above. 'Fuck,' she says over and over. I hear a tile shift and the sobs quieten. For a moment there is just the gentle whirl of her extractor fan. I stand staring at the ceiling, unsure of what to do. I reach up and let the tips of my fingers trace the pattern on the ceiling and, as if in response, Emily rises, but this time without shoes on, and slams the door of the bathroom behind her. I stand, feeling shut out, like a mother scolding her daughter and being told it's none of her business and to leave. I wrap my arms around my ribcage and start to cry.

Pop music floods the flat and I wipe my tears away and go into the lounge. I hear every word explode into my home, the harsh beat raining onto me. I don't think before racing to the kitchen cupboard and pulling out a broom. I place myself directly under the worst of the noise, where the sofa is, where I know she's sitting, wallowing in it. Holding up the broom, I smack it as hard as I can over and over until I see a small dent appear in the ceiling. The TV halts and the music softens. I throw the broom to the floor in triumph.

For a moment the only noise is the soft drumming from the music, until I hear Emily's bare feet against the floorboards trampling towards her front door. The sudden charge of her feet on the staircase in the hallway and the hollow rap of her fist on my front door. I freeze, embarrassed, and look around. I try to mask my flat, throwing sheets and throws in every direction, but it just makes it worse. I creep towards the door and this time it's my turn to peel open the door and peer around. Emily's face is stained with mascara; she is bright red and her dark auburn-brown hair sits in a high bun like a bird's nest atop her head.

'Just a sec,' I whisper, before glancing back. I open the door a little further and edge my body into the gap in the door between Emily and my home.

'Was that a broom?' she says callously.

Chapter 2

'Yes, I—' The anger has fizzled and has been replaced by shame. I go to speak, but Emily is there first.

'This is my home,' she says, a statement I can't contend.

'I know, but the music is so loud. Can you turn it down?'

'This is my home,' she repeats, petulantly.

'This is also mine,' I whisper.

'I am not making too much noise.' Another statement, not a question, no argument or debate to be had. 'My speaker is tiny, tiny,' she says, holding up slim fingers to demonstrate the size of a small square box. She holds her palm out and points at it.

'I don't'—I hesitate—'think it matters about the size of the speaker.'

Emily leans back onto her heels and tries to look behind me.

'You shouldn't live in a flat if you don't like noise,' she says finally.

I can't argue with her; she has me pinned. I start smiling and break into a laugh, remembering other similar conversations. Emily stares bewildered and then she looks me up and down, and a new emotion laps over her features – pity.

'I'll try and keep it down,' she says, before turning and walking away upstairs.

I rest in the doorway and my smile fades to a frown. I look at Emily's unread letter bunched on the communal table in the hallway. I reach forward and grab it viciously. Pity this, I think, slamming the door. I throw the letter on my floor, but I don't feel victorious, just self-conscious and ashamed.

I scoop my laptop up from the kitchen counter and pick up the letter. Emily Williams. I open the laptop and scramble back on the chair. I type in 'Emily Williams, London' and *search*. I don't have Facebook or Instagram, I never saw the point, and it might make this more difficult, but I'm good at research, I'll find her. I frantically search through results pages and images trying to find Emily's face. An Instagram account appears on the first search page and when I click on it, I'm faced with rows and rows of pictures of her. I click on the first one of Emily in a pale pink jumpsuit clutching a slim glass. The caption reads 'The Fence with work chums', posted recently. I go back to her main account and pore over each image. Emily blowing on a hot chocolate in a cosy café. Emily pawing at her scarf as she giggles, against the backdrop of what looks like Hampstead Heath. Then older ones from the summer – Emily playfully chewing a straw and clutching an iced coffee. Emily staring down at a large fishbowl cocktail, her hair in loose waves cascading down her delicate face. Emily rolling her eyes at the camera as she sits cross-legged in a park. I scroll down the page, consuming every image of her, until a pop-up asks me to sign in. I exit the page and feel my stomach tighten. How much she wants to be seen, to be heard. *Well, I hear you, Emily.* I have LinkedIn though. I swat the Emily Williams profiles and scan the page. I pause to think why I'm doing this and let the thought simmer quietly – because I want to know what she's doing here.

Because I need to know how she affords to live here by herself. Because I must know if she'll leave soon.

My finger slides across the touchpad and Emily's small face comes into view, her long golden-brown hair in a neat ponytail, trailing down her small frame. She's in a grey dress and a creased black blazer, and red lipstick lines her pouting mouth. Deep brown eyes stare back, buried under dark eyebrows. She's more tanned in the picture; she looks stoic, a contrast to her Instagram. Underneath her picture I see her name, Emily Williams, and just the job title 'Sales Executive'.

My phone starts to vibrate, and I scramble to find it tangled in a throw on the floor. I see Clara's name appear on the screen and remember I'm supposed to be at dinner with friends from London. The call screen fades and I pull up her messages, typing,

Just at dinner and drinks with friends, will call you tomorrow, send my love to Ian and the kids.

I stop to think about my sister, sitting on her hideous green sofa she picked out from the DFS sale. Cat sick. That's what Ian had said when she got it home, adding, 'Don't blame it on Bruno,' their old affectionate tabby that Clara had had since she was nineteen. I had laughed and Clara had this stubborn smile on her face, holding her swollen stomach as the delivery men carried it in.

I suddenly long to speak to her and hear her whimsical voice tell me that it's okay to feel sad, that it's normal. I look around my own empty flat and feel the familiar pang of sorrow ooze from my puffy eyes. I clutch the phone and press the sides so hard that the small buttons make dents in the palm of my hand. I settle the phone to the side and say to myself that I'll speak to her tomorrow. Emily's TV blares into the night and I gently close the laptop and sink down under the bundles of covers into the chair. A car horn roars relentlessly outside, a motorbike speeds up only to slow down for the speed bump, and a siren whines a few streets away. I pull the blanket over my head and take a deep breath, praying for the noise to stop.

Chapter 3

The next day, after work, I decide to call the landlord upstairs about Emily. I've got to know him well since I bought the ground-floor flat five years ago. I asked the estate agent on the second viewing, 'Who owns upstairs?' The reply: Mike, a nice guy, sensible, described as a bit older. I remember nodding enthusiastically; it all sounded so perfect. A few days after I'd moved in, I wandered upstairs to introduce myself to Mike and give him my details in case he ever needed them. I hadn't seen him coming or going from the flat and apart from the little movement I heard upstairs, I hadn't heard much from him at all. But Mike didn't open the door when I knocked. Instead a young guy did and when I asked if Mike was home, he told me that was his landlord and fetched me Mike's number. I stood for a while outside Flat 2, confused.

It turned out Mike did own the property, but he let it out after he and his girlfriend needed a bigger place, and over the years I've seen people come and go, some worse than others, but none quite as bad as Emily. When the tenants have been bad, I've called Mike and he's apologised and told me that it's only a six-month lease, they'll be out of my hair soon. Emily has been living in the flat upstairs for just over six months and I waited for the moving boxes that never came.

Mike answers. 'Suzie, everything okay?'

'Hey, Mike, you know…' I let my words trail off.

I can hear him nod, his grey stubble brushing against the collar of his jacket.

'Is this about Emily?' he asks, straight to it.

'I'm afraid so. I'm sorry to call you, but it's just—' I bite my bottom lip and struggle for the words. I can hear Mike shift and the light tread of his feet as he walks. 'Have I caught you at a bad time?' I ask.

'No, don't be silly,' he says briskly. 'What's she been doing?'

'I don't want you to think—' I stutter. 'I know to expect noise.'

I feel like those words have left my lips so many times that they sound odd to me now. Expecting noise, like it's a part of living, as seamless as breathing, as existing. I think spitefully about the people crammed into the city, the daily herd moving for the tube or the bus, and what it's all for. To live. I should expect music between the hours of 8am and 11pm. I should expect that someone should wear the shoes they want around their own flat. I should expect to hear my neighbour.

'It's the music,' I say finally.

'Okay, is it past 11pm?'

I smile, rolling my eyes. 'Yes, most nights.'

'I'll give her a call, sort this out.'

'Is she staying in the flat, do you know?'

Mike is silent for a while before saying, 'She's got a year's tenancy.'

'Oh, okay, I just didn't know as people usually stay for six months.'

'Sorry, Suzie,' he says, but he sounds distant and like apologising is the right thing to do, not because he means it. 'I had to let it out again because the last girl cut the tenancy short. I'm not doing any six month lets anymore. How you holding up?' Mike adds.

I cross my legs across my leather chair and stroke the arms gently as I gaze around my flat.

'Fine,' I lie.

The wind whistles into the phone as if it were mocking me.

'Okay, I better be off,' Mike says and before I can reply, he is gone.

The pungent smell of lemon chicken fills the air and I sit reminiscing about Sunday roasts at home, always pork with apple stuffing. I think about Mum's sly smile at me, when Clara would moan at the repetition; Mum knew it was my favourite. I've always been like that, comforted by familiarity and routine. Meanwhile Clara, so boisterous and flighty, had travelled the world and seen so many places I longed to see. She spent most of her teens and twenties in

France, South America and India. She'd send masses of colourful, beautiful photos and I'd send back sarcastic emojis and pictures of the same pub in Hove, a twinge of jealously poking me, but the weight of home more real and exciting than any photo she sent.

It's funny how we swapped places along the way, and now she's settled in her own home, a house in Brighton, married to a lovely guy and with two beautiful children. Now the jealousy is real because I have none of that and she sends me the pictures I always wanted to send her. I stare at the emptiness of my flat, and can't imagine filling it with anything, but I can't move either. I can't leave.

I check Emily's Instagram account for an update and she has been out a lot, frequenting bars, mainly The Fence, different coloured cocktails perched in her hands as she pouts for the camera. Who's on the other side, taking the picture? People she works with – 'work chums'. Even her Instagram is selfish, adorned with pictures of her, a smile plastered across her face.

Emily shifts upstairs and the oven clangs as she checks on the cooking chicken. I hear her stabbing at a timer and I soak in the soft citrusy juices as they float down. Wednesday, something meaty.

Emily's phone rings. She has it on loud today – maybe she's expecting an important call. She's quick to the phone, expectant. The ringing stops but I can't hear her speaking; whoever is on the other end is doing all the talking. After a few minutes, Emily says yes. I can only just make it out, but it's short and clipped. Yes. The phone call is over.

Chapter 3

The second call I make tonight will be to Clara, but it won't be a video call because I can't look at her right now. Her face is more expressive and her features run deeper than Mum's. I know she'll try and convince me to go back to Hove or to visit her. I know she'll offer to come and stay, and if I waver, if I give her anything, then she'll be in her car and on the way. This will be the hardest test, calling my sister and telling her I'm okay. The person I shared a room with growing up, who I swapped clothes with and went for lazy bike rides with on Sunday mornings. Who I let cut my hair and dye my hair and plait my hair. Who I could tell anything, but I can't say that I'm not okay, I can't do that.

I pick up the phone and call her. I'm already close to tears at the thought of hearing her and I go to hang up after three rings, but then she's there and all the pain brims to the surface like an over-boiled pot.

'Sorry, just clearing up after dinner,' she says.

'Sorry,' I gulp, 'I can call back later.'

'Don't be silly, you're my chance to escape.' I hear her say something to Ian and then blow kisses to her kids, then the sliding of her conservatory door. I can still hear the commotion in the background, the clatter of dishes and cutlery sliding of plates, Ian saying to be quiet and my niece's high-pitched squealing. A different kind of noise, I think.

'How's it going, Zee?'

'Yeah, not bad, how's you?'

'Oh, you know, busy,' she says breathlessly. 'How's smog city?'

'Smoggy.' I laugh.

'I bet. And that neighbour upstairs, is she still giving you hell?'

'Yes, but I called Mike earlier though, so hopefully it'll get better now.'

'You could come stay here, you know? Or with Mum and Dad? Clear your lungs.'

I wince. 'And miss all this? Plus I'm not sure I'd be able to get the time off work.'

I can feel her swat the air. 'Time off work, fuck that, Zee. If you need time, you take it.'

I smile.

'What do I always say?' she adds.

'Hustle or be hustled.' I laugh.

'Exactly.'

We're silent for a moment.

'I need to be here,' I whisper.

'I know,' she says quietly. 'I'm not saying it's unhealthy.'

'I think that's exactly what you're saying,' I say jokingly.

'Well, maybe it is, but I just want you to be happy.'

I bite my lip, digging my front teeth into the dry skin.

'London never made you happy.'

'No, but he did.'

We don't say anything. I know Clara doesn't know what to say next and I want to let her off the hook. She's not sure how to tread and I'm not sure where I want her to go.

'How's Ian and the kids?' I say finally.

I think she's crying, but I can't be sure. Her voice croaks,

'They're good. Ian got a new contract managing the electrics for the Co-op that's going up down the road.'

'That's great news.'

'I miss you,' she says suddenly. The conservatory door slides open and I can hear Ian whisper to her and my sister reply that she's coming.

'You go,' I say

She ignores me. 'I can come stay.'

'No, sounds like you've got a lot on.' I muster a laugh. 'I'll visit soon,' I lie.

'No, you won't,' she says, her upbeat tone laced with cynicism. 'Love you, Zee,' she says.

'You too, Cee.'

I hear her speaking to Ian before she's hung up the phone, and smile thinking of the evening she'll have, tucking the kids into bed and kissing their foreheads. Her and Ian settling down to watch Netflix on their ugly green sofa with a couple of cheap, warm ales. Bruno the cat squashing himself into the dip of the sofa seats between them.

I lay a flat hand over the arm of the leather chair and dream of old evenings spent here. Us curled up under a cream fleece, our personalised tumblers sweet with the smell of Highland whisky and orange peels. The room dark and the TV flickering tirelessly. You are watching intently, and I am lost in thought, my head planted on the groove of your chest, your heartbeat solid and firm.

ONE MORE CHAPTER

YOUR NUMBER ONE STOP

FOR PAGETURNING BOOKS

One More Chapter is an
award-winning global
division of HarperCollins.

Subscribe to our newsletter to get our
latest eBook deals and stay up to date
with all our new releases!

<u>signup.harpercollins.co.uk/</u>
<u>join/signup-omc</u>

Meet the team at
<u>www.onemorechapter.com</u>

Follow us!
 <u>@OneMoreChapter_</u>
<u>@OneMoreChapter</u>
<u>@onemorechapterhc</u>

Do you write unputdownable fiction?
We love to hear from new voices.
Find out how to submit your novel at
<u>www.onemorechapter.com/submissions</u>